RICK PARTLOW

DROP TROOPER BOOK FOURTEEN

COLLATERAL EFFECTS

www.aethonbooks.com

COLLATERAL EFFECTS
©2023 RICK PARTLOW

This book is protected under the copyright laws of the United States of America. No part of this publication may be reproduced, stored in a retrieval system, or transmitted, in any form or by any means, without the prior permission in writing of the publisher, nor be otherwise circulated in any form of binding or cover other than that in which it is published and without a similar condition including this condition being imposed on the subsequent purchaser. Any reproduction or unauthorized use of the material or artwork contained herein is prohibited without the express written permission of the authors.

Aethon Books supports the right to free expression and the value of copyright. The purpose of copyright is to encourage writers and artists to produce the creative works that enrich our culture.

The scanning, uploading, and distribution of this book without permission is a theft of the author's intellectual property. If you would like to use material from the book (other than for review purposes), please contact editor@aethonbooks.com. Thank you for your support of the author's rights.

Aethon Books
www.aethonbooks.com

Print and eBook formatting and design by Steve Beaulieu.

Published by Aethon Books LLC.

Aethon Books is not responsible for websites (or their content) that are not owned by the publisher.

This book is a work of fiction. Names, characters, places, and incidents are the product of the author's imagination or are used fictitiously. Any resemblance to actual events, locales, or persons, living or dead is coincidental.

All rights reserved.

1

Check out the entire series here! (Tap or scan)

[1]

Mysteries teased at the edges of our perception, taunting us with the hint of knowledge we would never have, things we would never see again.

"I wonder how they live," Victoria Sandoval murmured, leaning against my shoulder.

The view out of the observation bubble was less informative than if we'd been watching the holographic projections from the bridge monitors, but neither told us what we wanted to know about the blue marble hanging in the blackness off to the *Orion's* portside. We were under a comfortable one-gravity acceleration so we didn't have to worry about magnetic boots, and we were theoretically at peace with the Nova, which meant we didn't have to close the armored shields over the transparent aluminum of the bubble. All I had to concern myself with was the civilization down there, under the swirling cloud cover.

"I can tell you *some* things just from the sensor readings," Dwight answered the question unbidden, and I rolled my eyes.

"Dwight," I said to the AI, "how many times have I asked you not to interrupt us while we're up here in the observation bubble?"

"My apologies, Captain Alvarez," he said, his avatar appearing in the small comms console beside the hatchway back into the safety of the main hull.

The avatar was generic, a bland-looking younger male in a Commonwealth Space Fleet utility uniform. Originally I'd thought that a strange choice, since he was a creation of the Resscharr who we had come to know as the Predecessors, and *they* were assuredly not human, for all that they'd evolved on Earth. That was before I'd found out that Dwight and all the other sentient AI had been fashioned using the brain patterns of humans. Humans who hadn't survived the process.

"I heard the question," Dwight went on, "and thought you might be curious."

He trailed off, the smile on his avatar's bland face twisted with wry humor. He *knew* we'd have to ask.

"All right," Vicky sighed. "What have you found out?"

The smile turned genuine, as if Dwight was happy to be useful... or maybe just to be appreciated.

"Well, the Nova ships have been very specific about keeping us at what they consider a respectful distance from their home-world during our passage through to the next jumpgate..."

"You can say that again," I muttered, the cluster of swift-moving stars at the corner of my vision reminding me of the squadron of Nova cruisers shadowing us. And yes, we could take them down if we wanted to, but it would cost us damage and time, and by the time we finished them off, hundreds more would be all over us.

"They might have agreed to let us use their gates," Vicky put in, "but that doesn't mean they trust us."

"They might not trust *us*," I pointed out, gesturing at the pale-green glow to starboard, too far away to put a shape to, though I knew it was an elongated cylinder, "but I think they trust Lilandreth."

Did I? That was a good question. I'd let her have command of the Predecessor starship the Nova had gifted to us, but she wasn't over there alone. Dr. Spinner had volunteered to accompany her, maybe because he felt uncomfortable among so many aliens. He was of the Grey, from the humanoid aliens on the world we'd just left, and even though it had been his idea to leave with us, I sensed he still wasn't entirely adjusted to the mannerisms and differing cultural mores of humans. Or the smells. Having shared the *Orion* with a platoon of Tahni for a few months, I knew firsthand how bad alien smells could be.

Beside Spinner, we'd sent a lander and a flight crew over there, as well as a skeleton crew of engineering techs to learn what they could about the ship. Not nearly enough to stop Lilandreth if she got a wild hair up her ass and decided to take off... but then, the Predecessor ship wasn't fully functional because we'd damaged the hell out of it in the fight with the Nova. It had no working weapons, and even before that the ship had been incapable of FTL travel. She could go faster than us to get to the next gate because the Predecessor craft's gravity drive didn't build up inertia from acceleration the way a reaction drive did, but we were all going the same place.

Dwight cleared his throat. Well, he *imitated* clearing his throat, since he had no throat to clear.

"As I was saying," he continued, eyeing us archly. "The Nova have been keeping us well away from their worlds this entire voyage, and there've been no transmissions to intercept since they use laser line-of-sight communications rather than microwave. That makes it difficult to discern anything about their culture other than what we've seen of their military."

"Not like we could understand it anyway," I commented, putting a hand against the surface of the bubble as if I could reach out and touch the earthlike world. "They're talking octopuses, for God's sake."

5

"That's being overly simplistic, Captain," Dwight objected. "They do, indeed, bear *some* resemblance to the cephalopods of your world, but I can assure you that the similarities are only skin-deep. They..."

"On topic, Dwight," Vicky warned him.

"Yes, sorry. The long-range sensors have detected enormous solar collectors in close orbit around the system's primary star —*dozens* of them—and my best guess is that they're powering particle accelerators to generate antimatter."

"That's a lot of antimatter," I said and shaped a silent whistle. "They need *that* much for their fleet?"

The Tahni had used solar-powered antimatter factories to produce fuel for their warships, but that had been a matter of one production plant per system.

"No," Dwight agreed, grinning, "and that's the fascinating part. As best I can tell, they use antimatter for primary power production in their civilian industrial centers as well."

"That's... cool, I suppose," I allowed, shaking my head helplessly, "but why is it so fascinating?"

"Because it means they have a very centralized society."

The voice seemed to come out of nowhere, and I jumped then cursed, recognizing the source as the intercom speakers... and the man behind them.

"Captain Nance," I ground out, staring around, instinctively searching for something to glare at. "Do we have some kind of emergency?" Because otherwise, I didn't say, there was no excuse for the man to be listening into our conversation from the bridge.

"Naw," the *Orion's* captain admitted, not showing any signs of remorse, "but we've been crawling between systems for a week and I'm bored out of my mind, so I was about to ask you if you were still planning on heading to the Predecessor ship tomorrow."

Tomorrow was an inexact term when we were on a starship between planets, but it was easier to say than *after your next sleep cycle*, and everyone knew what it meant.

"Yeah, still planning on it." Though it was a pain in the ass. But I did want to keep an eye on things on the other ship. "What were you saying about the Nova and why them using antimatter means they're more centralized?"

Because as annoying as yet *another* interruption was, I needed to know what he was thinking. Not just because it was my duty as the mission commander but because I was curious and hated to admit it. Lacking any visual representation of Nance, I instead leaned against the surface of the bubble and kept my eyes on the Nova homeworld. They hadn't even told us the name of the planet.

"Well, think about it." Even though Nance was a disembodied voice, I could picture his craggy face and gray-shot beard, which had gotten progressively thicker in the last few weeks since we'd left the hibernation pods. "Antimatter isn't something you're gonna scatter around in hundreds of power plants—it's too volatile, too dangerous. No, it's something you'd put in a central location, under guard, with lots of safety protocols, right? And you'd want the fuel tightly controlled too, because just a kilogram or so of the shit could destroy a city. That means a very centralized power system, controlled either by the government or some corporate oligarchy, like the Corporate Council turned up to eleven."

I nodded. That made sense.

"It seems to be an issue with uplifted species," Dwight pointed out, his avatar rubbing its chin thoughtfully. "The Tahni are a prime example. They were elevated to sentience and given technology they hadn't earned, shaped into a society designed by the Resscharr, which to them is just as good as being told how to live by the gods themselves. Their society becomes monolithic and resistant to change. The same can be said for the Qara and even the Grey and the Confederation. Even though the Confederation putatively had a representative government, it was actually an oligarchy."

I snorted a humorless laugh.

"Well, given the last couple hundred years of history on Earth, I doubt we're in any position to criticize some other government for not being representative enough. The Commonwealth has been an oligarchy from the beginning... or maybe a plutocracy."

"Where did a Marine grunt like you learn all those big words?" Nance asked, laughing.

"Well, I'll tell you a secret," I said, grinning, knowing he could see me even if I couldn't see him. "When I applied for OCS, I originally wanted to be a Fleet officer... but MilPerCen told me I was too intelligent to meet the requirements."

"I'd tell you that you were being insubordinate, Captain Alvarez," he replied, "but you're in command, so..."

"Yeah," Vicky scoffed, grabbing my arm, "you're so much in command that you can't even manage a private moment with your wife."

"It's getting late anyway," I said, taking her hand and pulling her back toward the hatch. "Let's go to bed." I glared at Dwight's image. "Unless we're going to have an audience there too."

Dwight popped out of existence on the screen, leaving a last word as if he were the Cheshire Cat.

"Sleep well."

———

"I hate this shit," Lt. Commander Esmeralda Villanueva admitted, fingers tapping on her control yoke. "One slip-up, one malfunction in that ancient piece of shit, and we'll be burning at nine gravities to catch back up to the *Orion*, and we won't even be able to micro-Transition ahead of them and wait, because the damned Nova said they'd blow us up if we use the Transition Drive in their systems."

I said nothing, knowing she was right but not wanting to dwell on it. The trip between the two spacecraft was nerve-wracking enough without adding worst-case scenarios to it. I generally didn't get motion sickness, but there was something about the relative motion of the two ships in the main viewscreen and Intercept One, the cutter we were flying the transfer in, that was totally screwing with my inner ear.

Unfortunately, Villanueva wouldn't shut up.

"It's the damned gravity drive that's the problem," she went on. "We leave the *Orion* with all that built-up momentum, and if it was another reaction-engine ship accelerating at one gravity it would be no problem. We can do one gravity. But that stupid Predecessor drive doesn't have any inertia, and if we hit it with this momentum we'd be crushed into a thin, fine paste. They have to use that weird tractor beam shit to arrest our momentum, and as long as it works perfectly, we're fine. But I don't trust that alien shit."

"Yeah, I got that impression," I told her, putting a tone of finality into the words that I hoped would give her the hint.

She grunted and gave me a sour expression, probably aware that she outranked me and yet also aware I was the acknowledged mission commander anyway. Maybe I should have promoted myself to colonel just to stop all the awkwardness, but that seemed like a real douchebag move and I was sure it was against the UCMJ somehow, even if we weren't totally following that anymore since Colonel Hachette had died and I was the only one stupid enough to take his place.

Villanueva hit the comm control as our cutter grew dangerously close to the Predecessor ship.

"Lilandreth, this is Intercept One. We're ready for rendezvous."

"Yes, Commander Villaneuva, I have you."

Lilandreth's voice was very human, and that was no accident. I'd heard Resscharr speaking their own language to each other and it was something no human throat could manage. I was sure the opposite was true as well, that no Resscharr could have spoken any human language... without modification. Lilandreth had been modified through nanotech surgery that was still decades or even centuries beyond us, and the process had left her not just able to speak our language but with a sonorous, pleasant tone that might have come out of a professional actor or singer.

"You may cut your engine now, Commander," Lilandreth added.

Villanueva chewed her lip and hesitated, but then snarled and slapped at the throttle control. The distant rumbling of the cutter's fusion drive faded away, a background noise I hadn't really noticed until it was gone. What *should* have happened when the fusion drive stopped thrusting was that the *Orion* and the Predecessor ship should have pulled away, leaving us alone in the darkness. What actually happened was that the pale-green glow surrounding the alien vessel expanded to engulf us.

The first time I'd done this, I'd expected the view on the optical cameras to take on the same green tint, but once we were inside, the color cast disappeared and nothing changed... except we were matching velocities with the cylindrical ship. The gravitic field it generated from the micro-black hole at its heart pulled us in gently, sliding the cutter through what had appeared to be a solid hull and into the hangar bay. The lander we'd stationed on the alien ship sat forward of us, held solid by metal support arms that seemed to have grown out of the deck beneath it. Because they had.

The cutter settled in with a barely perceptible lurch and a gentle sway as the landing gear sank a few centimeters into their hydraulic mounts and then rebounded.

"Well, we're here," Villanueva said, though she still didn't seem happy. "And getting back to the *Orion* will still be the hard part."

"You want to come up to the bridge?" I asked her as I unstrapped from the copilot's seat.

"I'll just stay here, if it's all the same to you," she said, slumping in her seat, arms crossed like she planned to pout until we were back on the *Orion*.

The trek up to the Predecessor starship's bridge was even stranger than the flight over. The Predecessors' idea of an elevator involved stepping off into an open shaft and letting the gravity control deliver me to my intended destination. How the hell it *knew* where I wanted to go, I wasn't sure.

The interior passageways of the ship were also green, a deeper shade than the external hull, and the color scheme grated on my nerves. I didn't envy the lander crew I'd assigned to the place, and possibly Dr. Skinner, though I wasn't one hundred percent sure if it would have the same effect on someone of his species.

"Cameron Alvarez," Lilandreth greeted me as I stepped onto the bridge. "Welcome to my ship."

The bridge looked nothing like any human or even Tahni vessel I'd ever seen. In fact, it reminded me of the officer's lounge on the *Iwo Jima*, except for the paint job. And the Resscharr furniture designed to accommodate a biped with digitigrade legs. It was funny how accustomed I'd become to Lilandreth's appearance since we'd first encountered her people. I wouldn't have imagined I could get used to talking to what was basically a bipedal, intelligent dinosaur, but there you go.

"Thanks for having me," I told her, not commenting on how the whole bit about calling it *her* ship had sounded. I nodded to Lt. Gunderson and his flight crew, who were stretched out in well-padded recliners that had grown out of the deck right in front of my eyes during my first visit to the ship. "You all settling in okay, Mark?" I asked Gunderson.

"I suppose, sir," he said, barely looking up from his 'link screen. "The food here sucks and there ain't much in the way of entertainment, so as soon as you see fit to rotate another crew in here..."

"I'll see what I can do," I told him, "but don't expect relief until we're through the next gate."

"I meant to discuss that with you, Cameron," Lilandreth said, waving me to a chair that had suddenly sprouted up beside her own. It wasn't as if the deck had changed shape to produce it, it was more like I'd looked away and it was just suddenly *there*, a magic trick.

It creeped the hell out of me, but I pretended it didn't and sat down. It's hard to describe what Lilandreth did with respect to that twisted Resscharr furniture, but *sit* didn't quite do it.

"From what the Nova told us before we embarked," Lilandreth went on, "it seems as if their home system is the last in their little protectorate. The other side of that gate is the beginning of what they refer to as *the Wild*."

"The Wild, huh?" I repeated, raising an eyebrow. "That's not all ominous or anything."

The chair, I discovered, was as comfortable as it was mysterious, and I tried to make myself relax.

"I'm uncertain if it's a commentary on the dangers in those systems or merely a description of their attitude toward them. They do not venture beyond their borders. In fact, they seem to have no intellectual curiosity about what lies past them at all."

I frowned.

"That doesn't sound like the people who freaking invaded a whole planet just because the Confederation violated their territory."

"Indeed." She made a motion with long fingers no human could have. "If I were to hazard a guess, I would say they're not curious or worried because they know there's nothing on the other side that could threaten them. And nothing worth having."

I sighed, running a hand through my hair. It was getting too long, starting to curl. Everyone was letting themselves drift too far out of regulation, and that was probably my fault. This was going to be a long trip, and as much as I loathed the idea as candy-ass Sergeant-Major games, I knew I was going to have to start cracking down on the grooming standards before we turned into a gaggle.

"Tell me something, Lilandreth," I said, watching those amber, liquid eyes and trying to read anything resembling human emotion in them. "Once we get there, to the remnants of your people, do you plan on staying with them?"

"If they'll have me." Her shoulders moved in an elaborate, sinuous shrug. "There remains the possibility that they might see me as corrupted, primitive. Or that they may still hold the philosophical differences between their faction and ours against me."

"What if they do?" I wondered. "Will you come with us, back to the Commonwealth?"

Lilandreth eyed me sharply.

"And what do you suppose your government would do with a creature such as myself?"

Warmth flooded my face and I winced.

13

"Yeah. They'd stick you away somewhere secret where they could study you, and if they ever let you out, it would be to pull off some propaganda campaign. So, what *would* you do if it's a worst-case scenario?"

She didn't answer immediately and, for a moment, I didn't believe she was going to. But then she motioned toward the gate ahead of us, a glowing blue dot on the main sensor screen.

"That is what lies ahead of us, and there's no point in thinking beyond it without further information. I've read much of your literature since I've been among you, you know?"

I blinked at what seemed like a non-sequitur.

"Do your people *have* literature?" I asked her. I hadn't considered the concept of Resscharr writing books.

"Not as such," she admitted. "We preserve histories, technical data, theories. We have no tradition of recording legends, myths, fictions. And we certainly have no such concept as your many holy books. I find the whole idea fascinating." Her head tilted as she regarded me, and I had the sense she was looking at me the same way a zoologist might examine some new species of insect. "You follow one of the major Earth religions, do you not? Christianity, if I recall correctly."

"Yeah." I didn't trust myself to say more, not wanting to get into a theological debate with a six-thousand-year-old alien.

"Then you should be aware of the Bible. I read several different translations of it a few weeks ago, when I had a few hours to spare. There are vast differences in the nuances of the words chosen, but for sheer poetry, I doubt any of them could do better than the one you call the King James Version."

I shrugged, not knowing what she was talking about. I'd always read whatever Bible was handy in the military entertainment systems.

"There's a verse that is in all the translations," she went on, "but it's most memorable in the King James."

She closed her eyes as if calling back the memory, and when she opened them, she quoted the words like an old fire-and-brimstone preacher. And with each word, a new prickle of dread passed over my skin, for it was the exact same verse my mother loved to quote, though filled with so much more foreboding from Lilandreth's mouth.

"Take therefore no thought for the morrow: for the morrow shall take thought for the things of itself. Sufficient unto the day is the evil thereof."

[2]

"We should give that ship a name," Nance grumbled, staring at the glowing green cylinder on the main screen of the *Orion*'s bridge.

"Like what?" Vicky asked, chuckling. "The CSS *Dildo*?"

I frowned at her and she put a hand over her mouth in mock embarrassment. We'd had a brief talk about tightening things back up to military standards, and she'd agreed it was important, particularly with the Vergai recruits among our Drop Troopers. But that started with us.

"Anything's better than calling her 'the Predecessor ship' every time we have to talk about her," Nance insisted, not seeming to take offense at the joke, or at least still more incensed by the affront to his sailor's superstitions than his authority.

"The Resscharr," Dwight pointed out, "don't have a tradition of naming ships. They consider them tools, as your people might think of a cargo truck or a hopper. It is their opinion..." maybe the pause there and the subtle hint of bitterness in the words that followed were my imagination, but maybe not, "... that only living things have souls, that only a soul deserves a personal name."

Oof. That was hitting too close to home for the AI. Maybe he and Lilandreth had buried the hatchet, but that didn't mean he forgave *all* the Resscharr. I decided to try to change the subject.

"Speaking of Resscharr traditions," I said, "does it strike you that the Nova are totally unlike anything else we've seen from them? I mean, they're bipedal, but I wouldn't call them humanoid."

"Yeah, the Resscharr are kind of like the Old Testament God," Vicky agreed. "Creating man in His own image." She gave me a sidelong look and I knew she was thinking about Lilandreth's Biblical reference, which I'd told her about earlier.

"They had to work with what they had on hand," Commander Yanayev suggested.

I blinked at her suggestion, not because I disagreed but because the Helm officer almost never engaged in the idle conversation on the bridge while she was on duty. The tall, blonde woman was as professional an officer as I'd ever encountered, concentrating on her job to the exclusion of all else.

But then again, we *had* been at this for years now, not even counting the time spent in stasis. If we hadn't got our asses lost out here, Yanayev would have been the captain of her own ship by now.

"They probably had whatever life was on the Nova home-world," she expounded, glancing around from her station. "And this was the best they could manage."

"Maybe," I said, unconvinced, leaning against the safety railing just behind Nance. I spent more time there than I did in my official command chair. "Or maybe they made them different on purpose. I mean, look at what happened with the Tahni, and even the Qara. They both got in trouble because they believed it was their destiny to be the heirs of the Predecessors. Maybe the Resscharr just wanted someone who would do what they were told."

"Hopefully it won't matter," Wojtera, the Tactical Officer, mused. He didn't look up from his station though. He would be the one responsible for responding to threats and wasn't taking it for granted that the Nova wouldn't prove to be one. "They're pulling back from around the gate."

The gates didn't operate by themselves, of course, any more than the ones back in the Cluster. There were two ways to expand the jumpgate's wormhole, the easier one being a thermonuclear explosion in just the right place, the more efficient one being a high-powered laser feeding a constant stream of energy into the event horizon. The Nova opted for the more efficient option, and like us and the Tahni they kept that laser going with a huge space station and solar collectors dozens of kilometers wide. Probably automated, but I got the sense that if they could have gotten the whole station farther away from us, they would have.

"We're being hailed," Lt. Chase said, looking between Captain Nance and me. "It's the Nova."

"Put it on the screen," I told him and got a dirty look from Nance. Maybe I should have let him give the order, but it was more fun to get the dirty look. I think we both kind of liked the game.

Though maybe I should have specified audio only, because the Nova were not pleasant to look at. Entirely hairless, their skin was slick and rubbery, purplish, and worse, they didn't wear any clothes other than a spare harness that held whatever a talking octopus needed to go about its day. And when I say that, it's because I had no idea what sex any of them were, since their sexual characteristics were as nonexistent as their noses.

I assumed it was on one of the warships shadowing us, since

there'd be too much of a lightspeed delay from anyone on the planet. Though maybe they didn't expect or want a reply.

When the Nova spoke, the voice was slurping, gurgling before the translation program kicked in.

"Earth vessel *Orion*," the Nova said. "With this gate, you leave our territory. We wish you well on your journey, but we strongly caution you not to attempt to return through the wormholes. You will be fired upon, and even with your superior technology, we will swarm you with every vessel we have and you *will* be destroyed. We do not wish to see you in our space again."

And maybe they *didn't* want a response, because the screen went black immediately after he finished the statement.

"Well, that was all smiles and sunshine," Chase commented. I stared at him with narrowed eyes. It was one thing for Yanayev or Wojtera to put their two cents in, but Chase was the *Comms* officer, for God's sake. I really had to get things back under control.

"Keep us on course," I told Nance. He smirked in a way that told me to go teach my grandma to suck eggs without saying it. I frowned at Chase. "Did they send a message to the Predecessor ship as well?" The Nova hadn't mentioned her in the transmission.

"Yes, sir," Chase confirmed. "Laser, tight-beam. We can't read it from here."

"Probably told Lilandreth to put a good word in for them with the Predecessors," Vicky guessed, then took a sip from the bulb of coffee she'd brought with her from the galley. I'd passed on the opportunity and now wished I hadn't. I stifled a yawn and went back to my chair, strapping in. Had to show a good example.

"Two minutes to the gate event horizon," Yanayev reported.

My eyes snapped up to the screen. I hadn't thought we were

that close but, as always, things rushed up at the last second, turning from distant to frighteningly close in an instant. The event horizon of the gate was a blurry twisting of space around the edges of the wormhole, unbelievably huge, big enough to let through a fleet.

And in the middle of it all was nothing. Darkness. Nonexistence.

"Wish we had any drones left," I murmured, and Nance's head came around at the comment.

"We could have sent an Intercept through," he suggested without much conviction. I shook my head.

"They're ready for launch. It's not as if we could turn back."

I just couldn't shake the feeling that there was a *reason* the Nova didn't go past this gate. That feeling was overwhelmed by the gut-wrenching twisting of reality that came with the transition through the gate. I squeezed my eyes shut against a flash of color, and when I opened them again... there was still nothing.

Darkness. Space. Emptiness. A distant point of light barely brighter than the other stars. I looked to Wojtera.

"Are we picking up *anything*?"

"Umm..." the Tactical officer shook his head, peering at the sensor readout as if it was as empty as the optical view. "We got a cometary halo pretty far out and... a white dwarf?" Disbelief brought the last words up an octave and twisted his expression into a deep frown.

"What?" Nance barked, leaning forward in his chair to look over Wojtera's shoulder. "That doesn't make any Goddamned sense!"

I shared a look with Vicky and she shrugged.

"For those of us who didn't study stellar evolution," I said, motioning to both Nance and Wojtera, "why doesn't that make any sense? I mean, I assume that tiny little white dot there..." I pointed at the screen, "... is the dwarf? What makes that so unbelievable? All I remember about white dwarfs is that they're dead stars, right?"

"Yeah, yeah," Nance said, talking with his hands the way he did when he got impatient. "It's..." he sighed. "You tell them, Dwight. I've lost the patience for it."

"If you ever had it," Vicky commented around a sip of coffee.

"A white dwarf is a stellar core remnant composed mostly of electron-degenerate matter," Dwight informed us cheerfully. "It's small but massive, about the size of your Earth but with a mass equal to your sun. Its low luminosity comes from the emission of residual thermal energy, as no fusion takes place in the star itself. White dwarfs are the final evolutionary state of stars whose mass is not high enough to become a neutron star or black hole, which includes over ninety-seven percent of the stars in this galaxy." He didn't have to pause for a breath, but I think he did it because he liked imitating us. "After the hydrogen-fusing period of a main-sequence star ends, it'll expand to a red giant, during which it fuses helium to carbon and oxygen in its core by the triple-alpha process. If a red giant has insufficient mass to generate the core temperatures required to fuse carbon, an inert mass of carbon and oxygen will build up at its center. After such a star sheds its outer layers and forms a planetary nebula, it will leave behind a core, which is the remnant white dwarf..."

"Okay, got it," I interrupted the AI. "So why is that so weird? Sounds like it's pretty common, though I've never heard of a jumpgate opening up on a system with no planets before."

"Well, that's part of it!" Nance exclaimed. "There hasn't been a single gate we've gone through on this trip or in all the Cluster that ever linked up to a system without habitable planets."

"Things could be different here..." I began, but Nance, as he'd already indicated, wasn't in a patient mood.

"Did you miss what the big computer brain just said? Planetary nebula. The expanding star leaves behind planetary nebula. There's barely a cometary halo here! Where's all the excess matter?"

"Couldn't it have... escaped the system?" Vicky suggested. I was surprised she didn't know all this already. One of the things I loved about her was that she was as obsessive a reader as I was, and between the two of us, we tended to stay informed about a wide variety of subjects. Apparently, astrophysics wasn't one of them.

"How many billions of years do you think this thing has been around?" Nance scoffed.

"From analysis of the star's thermal output," Dwight put in, "I would estimate that it's not old enough for the planetary nebula to have either dissipated or been pulled into the white dwarf."

"Well, what could have caused it then?" I asked, starting to get impatient with all of them. "Why isn't there a planetary nebula?"

"That's the *point*." Nance threw his hands up. "I have no idea! There's no natural reason it shouldn't be there."

"Dwight?" I asked, pleading.

"I'm afraid Captain Nance is correct," he admitted, his avatar at the corner of the main screen imitating Nance's gesture. "There is no logical explanation, and I don't have enough data to even hazard a guess."

I sighed.

"This feels like one of those situations where I should be more worried than I am, but right now, I don't see anything we can do except go on through the next gate." I looked over at Wojtera, eyes widening as I had a horrible thought. "There *is* an exit gate, isn't there?"

"Oh yeah, I got a reading on it already," he assured me.

"We'll have to open it ourselves, of course."

"I think we got that covered," I said. I nodded to Chase. "Get me the..." I sighed. Nance was right, that ship needed a name. "Get me Lilandreth."

Chase fiddled with his controls, and honestly, while I had a fair idea of how the rest of the bridge stations worked, communications for me remained a black box. I could ask one of the others to connect me to another ship, but trying to figure out how to do it myself was a mystery. Chase shot me a thumbs up and I touched the control on the arm of my chair.

"Lilandreth?"

"I read you, Cam."

"Have you figured out how to use the gravity drive to open the jumpgates?" I asked her. We'd discussed it before we launched, but there'd been no opportunity to experiment, not with the Nova so touchy about us deviating from our course or basically doing anything they didn't approve of ahead of time.

"I have. It's a fairly simple operation. Would you like me to take the lead? If there's a threat on the other side of the next gate, the shields on this vessel are better suited to surviving it."

"It's a tempting offer," I admitted, chuckling, "but the truth is, I want you to hold the gate open until we get a chance to scout the other side with an Intercept, then keep it open until the *Orion* goes through. If there *is* a threat, I want to be able to back out and regroup."

That was what I was telling *her*, anyway, though I could see by the look Vicky was giving me that she'd already figured out the real reason. I liked Lilandreth, maybe even trusted her to a point, but with that ship, she could just leave us behind, and by the time we got the gate open from our end, she'd be long gone. And if it was just her on the ship I don't even know if I would have minded, but we still had people on board, and I was sure they wouldn't want to be dragged along on Lilandreth's quest for personal fulfilment.

"As you wish, Captain Alvarez." I couldn't tell if she sounded disappointed or not, nor was I sure she'd allow me to see it if she were. "I will maneuver into position and wait for you to launch your probe."

I looked at Chase and he nodded, confirming that the connection was cut.

"How long till we reach the next gate?" I asked Nance. I could have asked Yanayev directly, but I'd pushed the envelope far enough and figured he needed a little ego stroking at this point.

"If you want us to decelerate and wait for a probe," he said with a shrug, "then it's gonna be a solid twenty hours. Of course, we *could* have the Intercept Transition ahead of us and check out the gate while we keep boosting, come through the gate at full speed and not waste time."

I couldn't help but grin, though I truly wasn't trying to make fun of the man's impatience.

"We've been at this for coming up on ten years, if you count the time we've spent in hibernation," I reminded him. "I don't think another few hours is going to make the difference. Let's take it slow and cautious."

Vicky snorted a derisive laugh.

"Since when have *you* ever done anything slow and cautious?" Which brought a quiet chorus of chuckles across the bridge.

"I'm getting older and wiser," I said, settling back into my seat.

"Older anyway," she agreed.

"Helm," Nance ordered, "execute turnover and start braking burn at one gravity. We've been boosting since we arrived in Nova space, and it's going to take us a solid twelve hours to slow down." He smirked at me. "Since *somebody* has suddenly decided we need to be cautious."

"It's your ship, Captain," I reminded him. "And it could be your mission any time you want it, since you're the ranking officer here."

Which was unfair, considering we'd hashed through all this literally *years* ago, though it felt more like months to me because I'd spent most of it in stasis. But it seemed like Nance needed a refresher every once in a while that I'd be more than happy to turn this whole fiasco over to him.

Nance raised his hands in surrender, the way he always did.

"Naw, that's okay, *sir*," he assured me. "I'm happy being a ship's captain. I'll stick to where my strengths are."

Yeah, I wish I'd taken that advice. I was just a Marine, a Drop Trooper. Looking at the distant glint of that bewildering star, I knew I was in way over my head.

[3]

"There it is," Wojtera declared, which was redundant since we could all see the world on the screen.

I'd seen it in the transmissions from Intercept Two after Brandano had gone on his scouting mission and cleared the way for us, though that had been from much farther away. It had been a living world, once. That much was clear from where the oceans had been... and what was left of the cities. Most of the time, even on Earth, the signs of civilization were invisible from orbit. The megacities like Trans-Angeles weren't even dots seen through the portal on a space station in low Earth orbit, everything man had built merely a futile afterthought from a God's-eye view.

That wasn't the case here. The Predecessors might have been life-givers back in the Cluster, creating habitable worlds and ecologies where before had been bare rock, but on this world, they'd created a city so huge it took up most of a continent. *Had taken.* The buildings were still there, but the oceans were gone, evaporated away, and the atmosphere was...

"... barely existent," Wojtera continued the report I'd only been halfway listening to. "Maybe a tenth of an atmosphere, and most of that's sulphur dioxide. Temperature on the surface ranges from -45 to 65 Celsius between day and night, and I'm not detecting any energy readings at all. There's nothing alive down there." He motioned at the sensor screen. "No indication of any spacecraft in orbit."

"Cam," Lilandreth transmitted, her voice coming over the bridge speakers, "we have a view of the planet's moon from our position and there are the remnants of facilities there, but there are no signs of habitation. They're background-cold, and there's not much left except wreckage."

I looked automatically at the glowing avatar on the screen that indicated the Predecessor ship hanging off the terminator of the planet, much closer than we'd dared so far. We'd stayed far enough away to be able to Transition out if we needed to, but Lilandreth's ship with its gravity drive could get away from trouble faster than us.

"What do you wanna do?" Vicky asked me, and I did a double take, something about the way she was sitting striking me as odd until I remembered we were still decelerating at a tenth of a gravity for orbital insertion... if that was what we intended. The light faux gravity was enough to keep us all in our seats, but her shoulders seemed unnaturally relaxed. "We could just head to the next gate. If there's no energy signatures down there, we probably won't find any records. And there's certainly no one alive to answer any questions."

She was right, her argument was logical... and yet. Curiosity called to me, the need to see with my own eyes.

"Is there any significant ionizing radiation on the surface?" I asked Wojtera. The Tactical officer peered carefully at his board, fingers dancing through menus before he turned back to me and shook his head.

"Nothing beyond normal background stuff."

I realized I was chewing my lip and stopped. It wasn't a

good command look, but I was too used to leading from inside a battlesuit.

"I'm going down to the surface with Intercept One," I decided. Vicky glared at me, and I raised a hand to mollify her. "In my suit... with the command team. Notify Villanueva to expect us in a half an hour. Lilandreth, you still there?"

"Yes, Cam."

"Meet Intercept One in low orbit. And get into your combat suit. I want you down there with us."

"As you wish."

She didn't seem enthusiastic, but then again, I wouldn't be that eager myself if it were a dead world that had once held humans.

"Didn't we just talk about how you were older and wiser?" Vicky wondered, arms crossed over her chest. "*I* should be going down there... if anyone does."

"There's no threat," I insisted. "I know you should go but, I just..." I struggled to put it into words. "There's something fucky going on."

"*Fucky?*" Nance repeated, an eyebrow shooting up. "Is that a Marine thing?"

"It's a Trans-Angeles hood rat thing. When you were about to rip some Topsider's fabricator code from their 'link at the train station, but you just *knew* the TAPs were monitoring and you just kept walking." I unstrapped, pacing carefully so as not to bounce to the overhead with each step, and pointed at the main screen at the gray, lifeless hulk below us.

"Something is *fucky* about all this shit, and watching a narrow slice of the picture through someone else's gun camera isn't going to tell me what."

"I don't like flying in the back of this thing, sir," Sgt. Wajda grumbled. "It's like trying to squeeze a whole platoon into a fuckin' two-seater runabout."

I had to admit, seeing the entire command team—what we used to call the headquarters' team before I became mission commander and not just Drop Trooper CO—squeezed into the utility bay of an Intercept cutter was amusing. A three-meter-tall Vigilante battlesuit had to stay hunched over, a tall man in a child's playhouse, and although it wasn't the most comfortable thing for the Marine inside, I'd been a hell of a lot less comfortable in my life.

"It was either this," I told the NCO, "or I could have gone in just a spacesuit and brought a squad of Force Recon with me."

"Force Recon!" I couldn't see Wajda, but the outrage in his voice bristled like a dog on alert. "What use would those damn straight-legs be on a world with no atmosphere?"

"Which is why you and your team are here instead, Sergeant," I soothed the man.

For all the good *they* would do. There was nothing alive on the planet, no energy sources to power automated defenses. I should have just gone alone, but I knew Vicky would have blown a gasket at the thought. She was aware of how I felt about being the mission commander, how I didn't intend to be sitting on the ship like Hachette, pulling everyone's strings from tens of thousands of klicks away, but she was using duty as a way to make sure I didn't go off without her.

Which was fine. I didn't feel right going into combat without her. And I also definitely understood the sentiment that she didn't want me going off and dying without her there, because I felt the same way. That didn't mean it was the right thing for everyone else. If I got myself killed, they needed someone who could take over and do a competent job, and that meant Vicky, whether she liked it or not. Nance had turned down the job because he had a solid handle on his own abilities, and there just *wasn't* anyone else with the experience for this other than the two of us.

Trying to put aside the internal debate, saving those arguments for when Vicky cornered me alone on the ship once I got back, I tied into Intercept One's external cameras and watched the dead world rushing up at us.

I'd seen Predecessor architecture before, on Decision, was prepared for the mind-bending surreality of it. Twists and curves where my human sensibilities expected straight lines and sharp corners, towers that stretched kilometers into the ever-twilight sky, well beyond the material capabilities of even the Commonwealth. More than any other oddity, though, was the unending, Moebius-strip interconnectedness of all of it. I couldn't look at the cityscape and determine where one building ended and another began, as if inside the entire city was just one continuous structure. It wasn't, not really, not if it was anything like the city on Decision, but even from the inside, it had been difficult there to tell where one room separated from another.

So different from anything human, and yet we and the Resscharr had evolved on the same world, under similar conditions, from the same DNA building blocks. What would a civilization that was *truly* alien even look like? We still didn't know. The Skrela had been engineered from a truly alien species, but that world was gone, and all we'd seen of them were drones, biomechanical robots. Everything and everyone else we'd come across had either been human or engineered by the Resscharr. From Earth DNA in most cases, though possibly not with the Nova.

And the Nova hadn't let us peek into their society. Frustrating.

The lower we sank into the continent-sized city, the more worried I became that we wouldn't be able to find a landing site.

There was nothing flat below, no open fields, no parking lots or any sign of a spaceport, just elevated walkways laid across the buildings without conscious pattern, vines in the jungle, a barrier to anything that wanted to reach the surface.

"You seeing this, Lilandreth?" I called over the suit's comms.

"I am," she replied from the cockpit. I suppressed a chuckle at the image of the two-meter-tall Resscharr crouched down behind Villanueva and her copilot, just as out of place there as we were here in the utility bay. "If we can't find a suitable landing spot, your suits could drop using the jump jets. I could ride on your shoulders."

I winced at the thought. It was possible, and from experience I already knew that her combat suit would protect her from the heat of our exhaust. But the Marine officer in me rebelled at the countless safety violations the whole process would involve and, beyond that, getting back on board a hovering cutter with Lilandreth hanging off my back would be... problematic.

"Wait one," Villanueva interrupted. "I see something a few klicks ahead."

In a few seconds, I did too.

"Wow." The word slipped out unbidden.

While I hadn't been able to tell where one building started and the next began, now I had no such handicap. Something had plowed through the roof of the continent building... something *big*. The lower we descended, the larger it appeared, growing from what I'd originally estimated at a hundred meters to nearly a kilometer across. It split a huge section of the city in two, a swathe of destruction with a charred, empty hole hundreds of meters wide and just as deep, spiderwebbing out from splintered piles of rubble to monoliths of detached material, cracked and crumbling but holding together. For now.

Nothing moved down in the wreckage, not even a bit of

tumbling debris, but what captured my attention, and probably Villanueva's as well, was the flat, open space down in the center of the devastation.

"Can we touch down there?" I asked her.

"One way to find out," she said, the whine of the engines changing pitch as she put the cutter into a hover. "If nothing else, I can get you low enough to jump out just a few meters off the ground."

Which wasn't quite as unworkable but I was still hopeful for a flat landing spot, though it was hard to make out the bottom in the shadow. Villanueva must have been more confident than I was because she didn't hesitate in our descent, and I barely had time to switch off the feed from the external cameras before we thumped and banged into as soft a landing as was likely possible under the circumstances.

"Yeah," Villanueva said, and if I couldn't see her lopsided grin, I could certainly hear it, "I think I can touch down here."

"Good job. Make sure your crew is buttoned up and drop the ramp for me."

I was used to the footfalls of the Vigilante echoing hollow against the boarding ramp, but here the sound was muted, a dull thump, matching perfectly the dull, muted light. The Vigilante's HUD was a complex, sophisticated system that blended together optical with infrared, thermal, and sonic sensors into a seamless composition, theoretically indistinguishable from what I could see with my naked eye on a sunny day. Yet somehow, I could always tell when it was dark. Maybe it was psychological, but a thin veneer of artificiality hung like gauze over the image when the system was forced to overly enhance a dark background.

As if there wasn't enough of an unreal haze over this whole place.

The ground was almost perfectly flat, though the black,

grainy surface under my feet gave a few centimeters with each step, like the lunar regolith. The Vigilante shifted from side to side like a toddler learning to walk as I moved to the side, making room for the rest of the team to file out. There were only four of us in all: me, Sgt. Wajda, and two corporals. It was half what the headquarters squad had started with, but attrition had sent those NCOs to the main part of the company. I could have pulled some of the Vergai from the new troops, but the point of the command team was to have people I trusted watching my back, and the Vergai company was still a work in progress. Though I sure as hell wouldn't say that in front of Vicky.

Lilandreth bounded down the ramp behind us, her moves lithe and animalistic, seemingly unbound by the gold-chased combat suit. It was more than a spacesuit, protected by a personal force field that could take more damage than a Vigilante despite being thin as aluminum foil. I fervently wished that when the Resscharr at Decision had enhanced our battle-suits, they could have included those personal shields in the improvements, but they'd lost the ability to produce them in the millennia they'd been stranded and isolated.

At least they'd gifted us the new energy cannons, bigger and more powerful than the handgun Lilandreth carried in a chest holster. I doubted we'd need them on this trip. Black ash stretched out hundreds of meters around the ship, and the massive expanse of destruction surrounding it was daunting in its size and sameness.

"Which way?" I asked Lilandreth, realizing it was probably a stupid question. She couldn't know any better than me. Nevertheless, she pointed off to the right of the nose of the cutter.

"This place is larger than Decision," she said, "but there's a pattern to the layout. This way would be the center of this node."

I had no idea what a *node* was, but I motioned for her to lead, the Vigilante's vicious left-hand claw mimicking the motion I made with my biological arm, guided by the cables plugged into my 'face jacks.

We walked in silence, even our footsteps muffled by the ash until we reached the debris field. Lilandreth paused there and we looked back at the delta shape of the Intercept, farther away than I'd thought it would be for the short hike. It rested at the center of the cut, and I frowned at a thought.

"It wasn't a kinetic strike," I realized. "There's no crater."

"No," Lilandreth agreed. "This was a gravitic weapon. One of ours, and a quite powerful blast to do this much damage. This city was undoubtedly shielded."

I frowned, staring at her.

"You're saying your people attacked their own city? Why the hell would they do that?"

"The Resscharr were forced to devastate entire living worlds to eradicate the Skrela," she reminded me. "We assumed the Skrela hadn't reached the Reconstructors, but that may have been... overly optimistic."

Lilandreth wasn't human and was usually very deliberate with the words she used and the tone she gave them, but the misery and disappointment dripped off the statement like blood from a wound. Only concerned with what this meant to us, to the goal of getting the crew home, I hadn't considered how it would feel to her. She'd abandoned her people to search for the hope of something greater, and if all we found was ruins, she'd be totally alone.

I said nothing, just followed her through the rubble, sections four or five meters long shifting under the battlesuit's feet, my jumpjets activating automatically for a split second when the armor sensed there was a chance it was about to topple over. I resisted an urge to throw my arms out for balance, knowing that would only shift the rubble beneath me even more.

"All right, screw this," I decided. "Hang on tight, Lilandreth."

I grabbed the Resscharr under her arms and hit the jets, riding a billowing cloud of smoke and dust for a good three hundred meters before the rubble evened out into mostly bare floor. I hadn't bothered ordering the others to follow my example, knowing they were smart enough to realize it on their own, which was another reason I preferred experienced Commonwealth Marines for my guard rather than the Vergai noobs.

I set Lilandreth down, the red halo where the heat from the jets had spread harmlessly across the surface of her personal shield fading slowly. Past the rubble, through the sections where all that remained of the wreckage had been burned into ash and formless hunks of carbon, things began to take shape. Bits of furniture, shards of crystal that I recognized as the inner workings of Resscharr electronics, and the unmistakable shapes of energy weapons. The smaller handgun like Lilandreth was carrying, the design unchanged after thousands of years, and the larger, cylindrical carbines such as the Resscharr on Decision had given to the Vergai lay scattered where they'd been dropped... centuries ago? Millennia? God alone knew, because nothing about this place was telling us.

The first mummy was beside one of the rifles, its long fingers outstretched, reaching for the weapon in death. It was obviously a Resscharr from the deep chest and backward-bending knees, though it looked wrong to my sensibilities without the sweeping mane of feathery hair, which might have been burned away in the conflagration. As if the appearance of the single corpse had flipped a light switch in my perceptions, dozens of others cohered into recognizable forms as I scanned around the first.

Then hundreds, piled up in the open spaces between wall sections. Then thousands.

I'd mistaken them for wreckage from the building, but the oddly twisted limbs revealed the truth. As far as I could see into the open center passage of the structure, bodies were stacked like cordwood.

"Hail Mary, full of grace," Wajda murmured, not realizing his comm line was open, "the Lord is with thee; blessed art thou among women and blessed is the fruit of thy womb, Jesus. Holy Mary, Mother of God, pray for us sinners, now and at the hour of our death. Amen."

I hadn't realized he was Catholic, but I echoed the prayer under my breath. These weren't humans, but they were thinking, feeling beings, more advanced than us.

Something had slaughtered them like sheep.

[4]

"I don't think we should go any farther," I told Lilandreth, setting her down again, another ten kilometers deeper into the endless structure of the city. "I think I can get a dead-reckoning lock on our location, but we've already lost comms to the Intercept."

Not to mention, I could barely see a damned thing. The suit's optics was great at intensifying light... when there *was* any light. This deep into the complex there was none, and although the computer was doing the best it could with thermal and sonar, there was also very little heat in here and next to no heat differential, other than us. The atmosphere was so thin that sound waves didn't travel far, which left lidar and radar. And the lights attached to our helmets, which got used once in a blue moon. They weren't something a Marine wanted to activate in combat because it was like hanging a target around your neck, but the main problem with them in here was that they only illuminated exactly what I was looking at.

Mostly, what I was looking at was one corpse after another.

Exactly what we'd been seeing the entire trip into the place, and the view hadn't changed.

"This doesn't make a damned bit of sense." Not Wojda this time. The NCO had fallen silent since his spontaneous prayer for the dead. No, this was Corporal Fujita, a woman of few words most of the time, so I listened to them now that she'd bothered to speak.

"Why?" I asked her. "I mean, other than the fact that we're standing on a planet full of dead people."

"They haven't been shot," she explained, gesturing with the muzzle of her energy cannon. "Look at the bodies. They're all in one piece, mostly. Some crushed bones but no burn-throughs, nothing missing. And Jesus God, sir! There's gotta be... what? I mean, we've seen probably hundreds of thousands. Are there *millions*? All of them just fallen down? Most of them were armed, but who were they shooting at? And how did they die?"

"It has to be the atmosphere," I guessed. "If they didn't mostly die by violence, then they had to have suffocated."

"And how the hell did that even happen, sir?" she demanded as if I would know. "How does a planet lose its atmosphere fast enough to kill millions of people in their tracks?"

"Lilandreth?" I asked. I looked over to her, though my face was just as invisible to her beneath the featureless mask of my helmet as hers was turned away, staring deeper into the grave this planet had become.

"It's possible," she said after a long hesitation, "that a gravitic weapon could have been used to strip away the atmosphere that quickly, though it would have to be one powerful enough to rip a planet apart. And if someone were to render the planet uninhabitable, I don't see the point of not simply destroying it entirely."

Her voice was back under control now, as if she'd let the emotion slip through before and wouldn't make the mistake again.

"This..." Lilandreth went on. "This seems to have been something different. I can't explain it, but it's not something the Skrela could have done. Or *would* have."

"There are no Skrela bodies in here," I pointed out. "No sign of them anywhere outside either. And you don't think your people would have done this. So who would?"

Lilandreth turned to me, the light on my helmet illuminating her face through her visor. She didn't blink despite the piercing beam from my headlamp—I guessed the polarization protected her eyes.

"This is a strange land, Cameron Alvarez. The Reconstructors chose it because none of us had ever ventured into these far reaches of the galaxy before, because they thought the Skrela wouldn't know to follow them here. They came here for safety, but I believe they discovered another enemy. Perhaps one even more dangerous than the Skrela."

"Hey!" Fujita again, but this time she was another half a kilometer farther into the structure. She waved with her left-hand claw. "Come take a look at this!"

I sighed, dreading not just the embarrassment of getting lost in the depths of this place but also the entire haunted-house vibe. I pushed down mental images of all the tens of thousands of dead Resscharr coming back to life and trying to rip us apart and bounded over to where Fujita stood, light shining down on something lying amidst the bodies.

It was a Resscharr, that much was clear from the construction of the corpse, just like all the others... except for how they had died. No suffocation or radiation exposure or whatever other esoteric fate had overtaken the hordes of other Resscharr had killed this one. The corpse rested flat on its back, arms spread like Christ on the cross... rib cage exploded from inside, leaving a gaping hole where organs had once been. The eyes were gone too, popped from inside, and streaks of black ichor stained those ancient, dried cheeks.

"What the *fuck*?" Wojda exclaimed, the first words he'd said since the prayer, ironically. "What could *do* that to someone?"

"More importantly," I added, staring down at the dead Resscharr, "what *would* have?"

———

"You were right, Alvarez," Nance said, stroking his beard. "This is *fucky*."

The images we'd taken with our suit cameras floated in the Op Center's holographic projection, more remote and not quite as nightmarish as it had been when we'd been walking around among them.

"I've done the calculations based on the size of the city, its carrying capacity," Dwight said, his avatar leaning against a virtual wall in the projection, "and it could have housed over a hundred million inhabitants comfortably."

"And they're all dead," I said.

"We don't know that," Captain Nagarro objected.

The Intelligence officer hadn't been down there but she'd had hours to go over the data we'd brought back, so I didn't dismiss her opinion out of hand like I wanted to. That wasn't a reflection on her personally—honestly, I didn't know her that well. It was more a function of how badly I'd been screwed over by Fleet Intelligence during the war.

"The city's enormous," she pointed out. "It covers most of a small continent. You only got to see the part of it close to the damage, and look here." Nagarro pointed a slim, graceful finger at the projection, at a handgun on the ground. "Most of these people were armed. For all we know, they were soldiers. It might be that area was the focus of the... battle or confrontation or whatever. We didn't detect any ships present, so the rest of the population might have been able to escape."

"It's a fair point," Vicky agreed, shrugging. If there was a bright side to the gruesome find, it was that she hadn't been in the mood to scold me for putting myself at risk again. "Is there any way we can get a look into other parts of the city?" She eyed Lilandreth, who hadn't said a word since she'd arrived on the *Orion*. "Maybe with your ship's sensors?"

"No," Lilandreth said, her denial flat and final. "If there were something generating heat or power, if there were life signs, perhaps, but the bodies are the background temperature. If the ship's weapons were functional, I might be able to bring down the roof of the structure at another point and still be able to preserve what was inside, but your energy cannons will merely destroy whatever is beneath."

"Damn," Nance muttered, shoulders slumping. We had gravity in the Ops Center despite the fact that we were still in orbit because it was inside the rotational drum, and it made for better sulking. And pacing. I was too tired for that, but Vicky hadn't stopped since the images had come up on the screen.

"It doesn't matter," Lilandreth said, making a slashing gesture. "They're all dead. I feel it inside. They're my people, and I sense their absence. However many were on this world, they all passed in... whatever this was."

"She's right about one thing for sure," I cut in. "It doesn't matter. Whether a million or a hundred million died, something killed this planet." I tilted my head toward Dwight's avatar. "Do you have *any* idea what could have stripped away the atmosphere quickly enough to kill people that way?"

Dwight's every move, every word, was calculated, and I had to remind myself of that, but his expression of puzzlement surely seemed honest.

"I have one. However, I will be the first to admit that, on the surface, it appears impossible."

"I'm getting used to impossible," I told him.

"If any gravitic or energy weapon had been used to do this, it would have created a huge thermal bloom that would have scorched the entire planet, would have turned the city to ash despite the defense shields."

"We already know what *didn't* do it, Dwight," Nance snapped.

"I merely say this to indicate my reasoning, Captain Nance," the AI replied mildly. "Even if, for instance, the micro-singularity in a Resscharr ship had broken containment, it would still have caused utter destruction in the city. The *only* possibility I can calculate that would have produced this effect... is a wormhole to Transition Space occurring within the atmosphere."

"It's not possible for a stable wormhole to form that close to a gravity well," Nance protested, sounding outraged.

"Which is why he said it was impossible," I reminded the captain absently, not looking at him, my eyes fixed on the dead planet. "Just like the way that one guy died down there. Something blew his chest and his eyes out from the inside." When I looked down from the screen, everyone in the Ops Center was staring at me, and warmth filled my face. "I think it's connected," I told them. "I don't know why."

"Do we keep following the gates?" Nance asked, getting right down to the heart of the matter. This was the decision only I could make.

I rubbed at my eyes, slumping back in the chair.

"Do we have a fix on our position?"

"Oh, yeah." He didn't seem happy about it. "If we head straight for the last system on the map, it'll mean a solid year in hibernation."

"And there's no saying we'd avoid this danger just bypassing the intervening systems," Nagarro added, always eager to state the obvious. Tension filled my shoulders and I nearly said something smartassed, but Vicky had stopped her caged-lion pacing behind my seat and she squeezed my shoulder as if she'd read my mind.

"No," I agreed instead, covering Vicky's hand with my own in gratitude. Sometimes I *needed* to be reminded that I was the commander, not some straphanger anymore. "We have to keep going. But I want an Intercept scouting every gate from now on, no matter how much time it takes. Like I told one of our people before we left, this is a marathon, not a sprint."

"We're kind of ignoring the elephant in the room though," Vicky said. I twisted around to look at her and she shrugged. "I know no one wants to think about it, but we're counting on the Reconstructors to still be around so they can tell us how to reach the Northwest Passage, how to get home. What the hell do we do if they're not here anymore? If they're all dead?"

She was right, I really *didn't* want to think about that. But that was part of being the leader, having contingencies and sharing them with the chain of command in case something happened to me. This wasn't some shitty ViR movie where the commander kept the big plan secret for no good reason, just to spring it on everyone at the last second.

"We'll have to wait and see what opportunities present themselves," I stressed, meeting each of their eyes. "But worst-case scenario fallback plan is, we cram all the hibernation chambers into the Predecessor ship, abandon the *Orion*, and use the gravity drive to get back to Earth."

I winced in anticipation of the outrage that would cause, and I wasn't disappointed.

"Abandon the *Orion*?" Nance burst out, shooting up from his chair, gesticulating like a used hopper salesman. "Put everyone on a *broken* alien ship? For at least... what? Ten years in hibernation? Are you crazy?"

"He's right about that," Nagarro agreed, eyes wide, looking as if I'd slapped her in the face. "That ship wasn't working right *before* we damaged it in the battle. If anything goes wrong, we don't have a prayer of fixing it, and we could all wind up stranded a dozen light-years from the nearest system..."

"Then I'd love to hear an alternative plan," I told them, raising half out of my chair, palms on the table. "Because just to remind you, ladies and gentlemen, we can't go back unless you want a war with the Nova. And without the Northwest Passage, there's no Transition Line that leads us back into the Cluster. Our only other option is to settle on a planet out here, and if we were going to do *that*, then by God we should have fucking done it back on Laisvas Miestas where we had tens of *thousands* of other humans to keep us company and make sure our descendants had adequate genetic diversity to survive."

That quieted them, as I knew it would. We'd gone through all this before, put it to a very non-military vote, and everyone had agreed to take our chances trying to find a way home.

"It's a huge risk, I know," I went on, sighing and settling back down. Nance did as well, though his arms were crossed in sullen resistance to the idea. "And I pray to God it doesn't come down to that, because that'll mean I've failed spectacularly at being your commander and everything has gone to shit. But Vicky is right, we have to have a backup plan, and that's mine." I turned to Lilandreth. "Would it work?"

"Barely. Perhaps. It would take weeks to transfer the hibernation pods, food, water, and other necessities for those who would have to stay awake. And of course, at least a third of you would need to be awake at all times, which means you would all experience over three years subjective time on the journey. Another thing I wonder if you've considered is that there may or may not be any habitable worlds along the way. This wouldn't be like Transition Line travel, where each line is, by necessity, anchored to a star, or like the jumpgates, where they are all linked to living planets. The most direct route may take us through nothing but empty space." Lilandreth regarded me coolly. "Are your people prepared to spend over three subjective years confined to my ship?"

"No," I admitted. "But if it turns out to be the last option, they'll have to be." I rose from my seat. "First things first. Lilandreth, our lander will take you back to your ship. Captain Nance, once she's returned, set course for the next gate."

I nodded toward the slaughtered Resscharr on the screen, and the sight of the ancient mummies, dead in an instant, their very atmosphere stripped away through some arcane twisting of the laws of physics, sent a shiver up my back.

"There's a mystery to be solved here, but first things first. It's our job to make sure that doesn't happen to us... and that we all get home."

[5]

"We're getting a transmission through the jumpgate, sir," Lt. Chase reported without a trace of enthusiasm.

I didn't blame him. Only my own commitment to duty kept me sitting straight upright, my expression carefully neutral. We'd hit two other systems since the dead world and found... two more dead worlds. Not identical, of course. That would have been too neat. No, these had been destroyed in different ways from each other, different than the first.

The second system we'd visited hadn't been a grave so much as a funeral pyre. The one habitable—or what had *once* been a habitable—was scorched black, only turned rubble where there'd once bloomed another city as massive as the first. That had been easier to explain, Dwight had assured us, a case of a containment breach on a Predecessor gravity core. A big one, bigger even than the one on Lilandreth's ship, its explosion had done exactly what Dwight had described, burned the entire outer crust of the world to a crisp.

The third wasn't *technically* dead. There was still an ecosystem, still liquid water and plants and animals. Small ones. But the Reconstructor colony was squished flat, as if a giant hammer had fallen out of the sky and pounded it to dust. Gravitic weapons again, but this time deliberate, focused, rather than what might have been an accident on the scorched planet. Someone had decided to rid the planet of the colony in this most direct and dramatic way possible.

What we'd found on the moon base of that world was even worse in some ways. More bodies, hundreds of them, preserved in the vacuum after the base was ripped to shreds. They hadn't died from the vacuum though. Each of them had exploded from the inside, just like the one Resscharr in the continent city. I was grateful I hadn't led that scout mission personally. It was bad enough seeing it on video from the Force Recon squad I'd sent in.

After the first system, everyone had been subdued, full of trepidation. I hadn't tried to keep the footage secret because shit like that *always* gets out, and it's worse if command tries to hide it. I'd learned that from the other side of the equation, and I hoped the experience hadn't been wasted. I'd once heard it said that intelligence is learning from your own mistakes while wisdom was learning from someone else's mistakes, and I hoped I was at least wise enough to benefit from this one.

But after the second and especially the third, a general malaise had settled in on the *Orion*, not, I thought, at the idea of a new enemy. An enemy was something we could handle. We'd fought humans, Tahni, Resscharr, Quara, and Skrela on this expedition and never shrank from any of them. No, what was bringing everyone down was the realization that with each dead world we found, our prospects for finding the way home dwindled.

This go-around, Commander Brandano had drawn the short straw and taken the scout mission through with Intercept Two and, presumably, he was reporting back.

"Let's hear it, Chase," I told him, once I was sure Nance

wasn't going to order it himself. Even he had shrunk into himself in the last few weeks of dead ends, his eyes lacking their usual jealous intensity when I gave his crew orders. He barely looked up from his chair when Brandano's face flickered to life in a corner of the main screen, cutting off a tiny sliver of the coruscating jumpgate just below the green glow of Lilandreth's ship as she held the wormhole open.

Brandano, unlike Chase, Nance, and the rest of the bridge crew, was *not* apathetic and disinterested. His expression was a Kick addict who'd just taken a hit, eyes wide, mouth twisted into an eager smile.

"Cam!" he exclaimed when my image came on his own screen. "I mean, sir...." It had been difficult getting Brandano to think of me as his superior, despite the fact that he'd been one of the original group who'd backed me against Hachette when the colonel had begun his downward spiral into grief and despair after Top's death.

"What's your report, Commander?" I asked him, some of his excitement infecting my own mood, impatience making me fidget in my seat.

"We have life signs, sir!" he told me. "Energy readings, habitation on the third world out from the primary!"

A murmur went up from the entire crew, even Yanayev, and Captain Nance did nothing to quiet them, instead looking to me expectantly, waiting for me to ask the questions he wanted answered.

"Send us your readings, Commander," I told the pilot. "How close have you gotten?"

He had *orders* not to risk being spotted, but I knew exactly how it was when an officer was away from his high command, on his own with his own judgement for his guide.

"I, uh..." his face reddened. "I wasn't detecting any active sensors, so I made a low-orbit run. I got some images of what looks to be an active city."

"Pull them up on the screen, Chase," I ordered. No use keeping everyone in suspense... and to be honest, I wanted just as badly as anyone else to see them.

The sensor readout streamed down one side of the projection, meaningless and unreadable for me without the interpretation of Wojtera or Dwight, and I ignored them for the moment. What interested me was the video that followed.

The world wasn't distinctive from any of the dozens I'd seen in my travels.... and how odd did *that* sound in my head? Not that many years ago, I'd been sure I'd die in Trans-Angeles, killed by the TAPs or the gangs. But now one planet was much like another, and the greens and blues and brown and just a touch of white at the poles were the least miraculous thing about this living world.

The crucial thing was the part of this world that *wasn't* natural, the part the Reconstructors had built. Like the ruined city on the airless world, this one was visible from low orbit, a glistening jewel sparkling in the noonday light of the G-class star. It wasn't dead like the other one though. There was power inside, and the power was a light shining from within it, a faceted jewel... but an imperfect one. That much could also be seen from the sky. Parts of the giant city were dark, not dead but dormant, long swathes of it, mostly in the center away from the open courtyards and the edges.

The parts I would have expected to be occupied by someone who hadn't built the place and couldn't repair it. I'd seen the like before, on Yfingam when we'd first arrived, and I had a feeling in my gut what we'd find there.

"Captain Alvarez..." Dwight began, but I waved him to silence.

49

"I know. There's only one way find out for sure though. Captain Nance, if you'd please... take us through."

———

"No, I'm going," Vicky insisted, jabbing a finger into my chest. "And if *you're* going, you're going to be in your Vigilante and stay in the middle of the platoon."

"There's no reason to take a full platoon," I insisted, rubbing at the sore spot on my pec where she'd poked me. The woman had sharp fingers. "If the people down there are hostile and well-armed, it won't be nearly enough. And if they're not, we're just going to scare the shit out of them for no reason."

"Don't care," she said, waving the objection away and stalking back down the passageway toward the armory. "It's bad enough that you're going in person again instead of sending me, like you should. We're not going to take a chance of you getting yourself killed and *me* having to be in charge."

I snorted, knowing that wasn't what she was worried about but also knowing this wasn't an argument I'd win, certainly not by giving her an order. The old saying was, a commander should never give an order he knew wouldn't be followed, and that went double when dealing with my wife.

"All right," I conceded, "but I'm going to have to get out of my armor at some point. They're going to want to talk to a person, not a faceless suit of armor."

"How the hell do *you* know what they're going to want. You haven't even seen any of them yet!"

I was in the middle of trying to come up with a line of reasoning she wouldn't be able to refute and picking up my pace to get to the armory before we stopped decelerating and lost gravity when two men with skin tanned so dark it was almost golden rushed up to me. One was tall, one short, one with long hair and the other sporting a close-cropped beard. They wore Commonwealth Fleet utility uniforms, though not well, like new recruits at basic training who hadn't quite gotten over being civilians.

"Cam!" the tall one called, then pulled up as if catching himself. "Uh, I mean... Captain Alvarez. Is it true? We found something and you're going down there?"

"Yeah, we've found an inhabited world, Jay," I told him, shaking my head at the incongruence of his lips not moving in concert with the words I was hearing.

Neither Jay nor Bob spoke English, of course. We'd taken them with us from the Confederation just a few weeks ago, and though they were both trying to learn our language, it wasn't much beyond "which way to the bathroom?" at this point. Thankfully, Dwight had programmed a translation program into our 'links, though that meant the English version of what they were saying followed a half-second after their mouths moved.

"Can we go?" Jay wondered, motioning between himself and Bob, who nodded agreement.

The weren't actually called *Jay* and *Bob* either. Those were the names Dwight had given us to replace the much fancier, more flowery appellations they were given at birth in the Confederation. But the translator worked both ways, and in the ear buds they both wore, they heard their given names.

I stopped mid-step and goggled at Jay.

"What?" I blurted. "Why would you want to go down with us?"

"Because, dude," Jay insisted, spreading his hands. "We've been stuck in this ship for weeks and like, we ain't done *nothing*. We've been trying to learn our job in engineering, but Chief Moretti won't let us do anything until we pass his tests... and learn your language. That's takin' a while, and until then, all we can do is sit in our compartment and study."

"We're going freaking nuts, man," Bob added. He was a man of few words.

"Yeah, but we both can handle a gun now," Jay went on. "I mean, we've actually been spending a lot of time in your simulation range." He winced. "Maybe too much time. Studying your language gets boring. Can we go?"

My first instinct was to say no, and I almost did. Though both of them had proven their worth during the fight against the Nova—and against their old boss, Frost, who'd caused the war—neither was a Marine, and they definitely didn't have any experience contacting aliens. The absurdity of that thought was what made me change my mind. Of course they had experience contacting aliens. They were the first ones *we'd* contacted.

I exchanged a look with Vicky and she shrugged.

"Okay," I told them, "you can come down, *but...*" I interjected quickly as the two of them started to celebrate, "... you're going to be part of the security crew for the drop-ship. Which means you both stay with the bird when we touch down and you'll be under the command of the crew chief. You copy that?"

"Yes, sir," Jay insisted, coming to attention like a child playing soldier.

I sighed.

"Don't make me regret this," I warned them. "Follow me to the armory and grab yourself some body armor and carbines."

"We'll do exactly as we're told," Jay insisted, the two of them falling into formation behind us. "We promise!"

I rolled my eyes at Vicky, but she just shrugged.

"You were the one who always wanted kids."

[6]

They didn't run.

I'd expected them to run when the drop-ship roared in, an aerospacecraft the size of a building falling out of the sky at the southern edge of the city, directly out of their primary star at midday. This was where we'd detected the most activity, including crops being grown and cattle being herded outside the walls.

There was no cockroaches-fleeing-the-light panic this time though. The bipedal figures stood from their tasks and stared up into the sky, their outlines becoming clearer as we descended.

"You were right," Vicky admitted. The words could have been whispered from beside my shoulder, even though she was across the dropship's troop bay from me.

"I know I'm right," I told her, the corner of my mouth quirking up.

"Don't let it go to your head, Alvarez," she smirked. "I've been there for all the times you were *wrong* too."

"We're touching down, sir," Watson called back from the cockpit. "No sign of hostile intent yet. They're just... standing around."

"Copy that," I told him. "Make sure the Intercepts stay on high cover."

And not just because I wanted to make sure Brandano and Villanueva were watching our backs. If the cutters came in too low there was the chance these people could scatter, and we needed them to talk to us.

"Lilandreth," I said, "you're up front with me."

I'd barely got the words out before the landing jets bellowed so loud, even the noise cancellation of my headphones and centimeters of BiPhase Carbide armor couldn't keep the soul-rending shriek from drowning out my thoughts. The massive ship settled down into its landing gear and the turbines whined down to virtual silence. I touched the control to cut loose my magnetic anchors.

"Open the ramp, Chief," I told the drop-ship's crew chief, clomping across the heavy deckplates to meet Lilandreth.

When I stood next to her in just my utility fatigues, the Resscharr towered over me, looking down her nose as we spoke and making me feel like a child. Not in the Vigilante. I was nearly a meter taller than her when I was in the battlesuit, the roles reversed, a waiflike tweener standing beside her older brother, the linebacker on his high school football team. It was an illusion, of course, since her armor and weapons were nearly as effective as mine. She wore no helmet this time though. We needed her face visible.

"I don't know how they'll react to me, Cam," she reminded me as the ramp rumbled downward. "They may see you as advanced, as superior and mysterious since you come out of the sky. But if they see me..."

"We don't want them to be terrified," I countered. "We need to talk to them to get access to the city."

Daylight poured in through the open ramp, throwing our elongated shadows behind us, and I waited for Lilandreth to step down ahead of me. She was hesitant, and I could understand. Faces not too different from hers stared back at us.

These were Resscharr. Not the Predecessors, not even the Reconstructors who were their descendants. No, these were very similar to the Resscharr from Yfingam, degenerate, sunken into primitive squalor. They lived in this city, but they couldn't repair it, could only use what was left, just like the fortress on Yfingam.

"I don't see any weapons," I called back to Vicky as my suit's footpads touched dirt. "Hang back with the rest of the platoon unless we see a threat."

"I will," she acknowledged. "For now."

I'd thought, just as Lilandreth had, that these degenerate Resscharr would have been awed and terrified by the ship, by my battlesuit, but as we approached closer to the nearest of them, a group of older males trying to keep a herd of cattle from scattering, their eyes weren't on me, weren't on the ship. They were staring at Lilandreth.

"Cam..." she said, trepidation in her tone.

"It's okay. Even if they get violent, they won't be able to hurt you." I hoped. True, none of them appeared to be armed, but all it would take was one who'd managed to figure out a leftover energy weapon and hit us in just the right spot...

The murmur that went up from the gathered crowd grew into a buzz as we grew closer and more of them crowded around, and now I was beginning to worry myself.

"Talk to them, Lilandreth," I urged her. Hopefully, their language hadn't changed since they split from the other Resscharr.

"My friends!" Lilandreth called, raising her hands to get their attention, my on-board comm systems translating her words automatically. "My brothers and sisters of the Resscharr! I greet you in the name of the people of Decision!"

I thought they might be confused at the sight of another Resscharr, or perhaps comforted. I did *not* expect what actually happened. Starting with the nearest and working back like a wave through the others, all the way back to the city walls, the gathered Resscharr fell to their knees and then flat on their stomachs, bowing to Lilandreth, chanting as they did. I couldn't make it out at first, the words spoken into the dirt and grass as they prostrated themselves, just a vague rhythm of a phrase repeated over and over.

Half of them rose from their bellies to their knees, hands raised into the air—the females, I thought, though it wasn't easy to tell with the Resscharr—and with their heads tilted back, the words of the chant clarified enough for the translator to make sense of it.

"The daemon has returned! All praise to the daemon!"

If I was taken aback, Lilandreth was totally dumbfounded, stopping in her tracks, gaping at the other Resscharr as if they'd all grown extra heads.

"Keep moving," I urged her. "Let's get past them before they start swarming you and asking for selfies."

She didn't ask what that meant, which was just one indication of how stunned she was, and she didn't argue, which was another. Lilandreth stepped carefully through them, as if she was afraid of being touched, afraid of *contamination*, while the care I took when I walked was based more on a desire not to crush innocent civilians into bags of broken bones.

Neither of us had anything to worry about, as it turned out. The Resscharr stayed a respectful distance away from Lilandreth, which worked just as well for my Vigilante. Though if I had to make a guess based on the interactions I'd had with Resscharr in the past, I would have said they were more afraid of her than me.

The edge of the city was different here than it had been on

the dead world, the internals bare to the outside, as if someone had found the controls for the external freight doors and cranked them open before everything had fallen apart. Whatever had been the original purpose of the rooms we approached, now they were used for food storage and separation, stalks of some kind of grain piled up in the corners with large, wooden casks in the center next to what looked like a giant version of a metate.

Bits of crushed grain flour had spilled on the floor beside it, the rolling stone discarded on the floor. The Resscharr who'd been grinding the grain had rushed out to see the drop-ship and stayed for Lilandreth, leaving the entire food prep area deserted. Grain crunched under my boots, crushed to a paste finer than the metate would have done. No one came out to investigate the noise or the commotion, and we passed through without seeing another living soul, as if all the Resscharr who lived in the city were gathered outside.

It took a lot to strain my sense of reality anymore. After fighting in an interstellar war, traveling most of the way across the galaxy and back, and finding out that the remnants of the dinosaurs had evolved into superintelligent humanoids who'd created all the living worlds in the Cluster and filled them all with life based on Earth DNA, there just wasn't much that could freak me out anymore.

For some reason, the empty corridors did it. We knew they had to be in there, which meant they were hiding from us somewhere in the shadows, monsters from a child's nightmare. I pressed on despite my trepidation, sensing that the leader of this group would be deeper inside. The next few chambers were stacked high with cordwood, and at their center were fire rings built from stone and cooking grates put together from scavenged metal, the floor around them charred with repeated use. I idly wondered if the ventilation system was still active, taking the smoke away with it, or if it just naturally drifted back out the open doors.

I expected it to get darker as we progressed, but it didn't. Light came from somewhere, though I couldn't pinpoint the source, the same as it had been on Decision. It was as if the walls themselves produced light, diffuse and soft enough that even the thermal sensors in my helmet couldn't pick up the source. But it was still getting power from somewhere, probably a gravitic reactor based on a micro-singularity, buried deep under the ground, capable of lasting for millennia without maintenance.

That reactor could have cooked food, provided heat, probably even processed raw plant and animal material into food for them if they'd known how to operate it. Which meant they didn't, that they'd lost not just the art of building and repairing technology but even the knowledge to use what remained.

The... well, I couldn't call it a *room*, because they didn't have rooms, per se, but it was a separate section just past the fire rings. The next section was bare of any utilitarian purposes, no wood for fires, no food, no storage. One shape sat at the center of it, a statue surprisingly human in concept, something I wouldn't have been surprised to see in the center square of a city park back on one of the Commonwealth colonies.

Except that it was of a Resscharr.

Not one of these poor souls, lost amidst the technological magic of their betters. This was a Predecessor, probably one of the Reconstructors. The features were lifelike enough that the confidence, the superiority in the expression was clear even to a human like me. The Resscharr's hands were raised similar to the way the primitives outside had raised theirs in response to Lilandreth, palms out, fingers spread. That was where the realism ended. Waves like stylized sun rays radiated out from the fingers, extending nearly a meter out from the four-meter-tall statue.

At the feet of the Predecessor was another Resscharr, this one smaller, closer to actual size. Maybe. It was hard to tell because the prone alien's rib cage was spread wide open, its chest empty, just like the victims on the last planet.

"What the hell?" I muttered aloud.

"I don't like this," Lilandreth said, her voice filled with a fearful dread I hadn't heard from her before.

"You are the daemon."

We both spun at the voice, though a spin in the Vigilante took a bit longer than it did for Lilandreth, unencumbered by a couple tons of armor. It was another Resscharr, dressed in the same strips of leather and multicolored cloth as the workers outside, except this one wore a glittering silver pectoral, other bits of gold and silver woven into his feathery mane.

"You are the daemon," he repeated, "and I am Gandish, the Elder of the Remainders."

He was older, the mass of hair shot with gray, which was something I hadn't seen among any of the Resscharr before. Even the primitives on Yfingam were eternally young, cared for by the guardian AI left in the fortress to watch over them. Not here. Not this male. Gandish was stooped over, leaning on a heavy staff carved from polished wood and inset with unfaceted gems.

"I have not heard this term before," Lilandreth told him, the hint of a quaver in her voice. "This *daemon*. What do you mean by it?"

"You are one of these," he said, motioning with his staff at the statue. "A daemon of the ancient days, one who could slay their foes with a thought, who led our people to greatness against all others! The daemon Carpashia left this place in such a ship as yours in the time of our great-grandfathers, taking with him the best of us and promising to return." The old male grinned broadly, revealing a mouthful of yellow, cracked teeth.

"You have come from the skies just as Carpashia did. You have returned to take the rest of us to conquer other worlds just as he promised!"

Lilandreth didn't reply to the other Resscharr, staring at me as if somehow I should know how to reply or even what he was talking about.

"What do you mean," I asked, counting on the translator to make sure he understood, "by slaying their foes with a thought?" If he meant *anything* by it. It could be nothing but a superstition, some legend passed down over the centuries. But I had a nagging suspicion that there was more to it than that.

"It is what our fathers and father's fathers told us," Gandish said, as if there could be no other explanation. "That the daemons were as gods, conquerors who trod the stars beneath their feet."

"Great," I sighed. "All kinds of useful data there. Dwight, you getting any of this?"

Nothing. I'd been afraid of that. No signal was getting through this far, just like last time.

"What do you expect from me?" Lilandreth demanded, almost outraged at Gandish's attitude. "You think I'm supposed to take you away from this planet?"

"Away from the slaves," Gandish agreed eagerly, his staff banging against the floor as he approached her. "Away from the rebels who've supplanted your power and seek to rule the Remainder out of spite!"

"Slaves?" I repeated, shaking my head. "Rebels?" I hissed through my teeth, getting tired of this, and cracked open the Vigilante's chest plate, leaning out and looking Gandish in the eye. "Who are the rebels?"

The old Resscharr's eyes went wide.

"You are not one of us! You are of the animals of the old world!"

"Yeah, yeah," I said, waving the accusation away. "But the slaves, the rebels... what do *they* look like? Like me?" I tapped a hand to my chest. It could be Tahni, or even humans he was talking about. The Resscharr had brought both races out of the Cluster, either as individuals they'd kidnapped or, more likely, just as genetic material.

"No, not like you," Gandish scowled, his expression as dismissive as if we humans didn't even rate the title of slave. "The slaves. The unquestioning... and yet they *did* question." He ranted, free hand waving, staff banging a rhythm against the ancient tiles. "We created life, built worlds, moved the very heavens, yet we could never find a servant we could trust! They betrayed, they disappointed, they died away... none were worthy!"

Lilandreth's gaze was fixed on the statue.

"Captain Alvarez," she said, finally, "I wish to go back outside."

"Right," I said, settling back into the suit, sealing the plastron. The interior lights flickered to life, and I synched myself back with the input from the external sensors.

Gandish followed us out, the click of his staff an insect chirping at the edges of my consciousness. The soft interior light gave way to the harsher glare of afternoon sunlight, the tomblike interior silence replaced by chatter of the Resscharr farmers and herders. I noticed children among them this time, something I hadn't seen on the way in. The adults ignored them, not having the same fondness for children as humans or even the Tahni, and I'd begun to wonder if it was because they'd been functionally immortal for so long.

Humans had, until very recently, been very short-lived, and maybe it was more important to us to have a replacement generation.

The young ones were miniature versions of their elders,

looking just as serious and self-important even in their leather and rags. None of our people had left the drop-ship, just as I'd ordered, which was half a miracle. I'd expected Vicky to charge in after me once I'd been gone ten minutes, as edgy as she'd been.

"Everything okay in there, Cam?" she asked, her armor at the front of the platoon, lined up like chess pieces in the yawning gap of the rear ramp. "You find out anything?"

"Nothing coherent," I told her. "Fairy stories about gods who conquered worlds with their thoughts and some kind of slave rebellion. Anything going on out here?"

"That's a big negative. The civilians are keeping their distance, and the Intercepts haven't seen anything else moving on the whole planet."

I grunted. It was nothing I hadn't expected, but the whole situation was maddening. We'd come this far, yet nothing we'd found was leading us anywhere. They'd *followed* me out here, and I was letting them down.

"Alvarez, you copy?"

That was Nance, his transmission relayed down to us by one of the Intercepts, and I glanced upward at the sky by instinct, as if I could see the ship sitting in high orbit.

"Yeah, I copy, *Orion.* Any news?"

"We've got company. Sensors have detected ships coming through the outsystem wormhole. They're heading this way."

Oh, shit.

This could be it.

"Are they Predecessor?" I asked, perhaps a little too eager, imagining the Reconstructors rushing into the system to come check on the intrusion. We just needed a chance to talk to them.

"No."

Nance's tone wasn't grim or worried... more curious.

"They're Nova."

[7]

"They still not answering?" Vicky wondered, fingers tapping on the console of the drop-ship's cockpit. Watson shot her a glare of obvious annoyance but said nothing.

"Nothing so far," I told her, then took another bite of the ration bar.

We were both out of our suits, as was half the platoon. Fifty percent security for the moment, since there was no obvious threat from the Resscharr and the Nova wouldn't arrive in orbit for an hour.

"We've hailed them in the Resscharr language," Dwight put in, his voice coming over the cockpit speakers, "but we don't *know* the Nova language because they never spoke it to us. They only used the Confederation dialect."

"Well, that's not working out too well for us, is it?" I grumbled. The rat bar tasted like cardboard, but there was nothing else. We hadn't figured we'd be on this world for more than a few hours. I washed it down with a swig from a bulb of water, tossed the wrapper into a recycler next to Watson's chair.

"Maybe we should prep for takeoff," he suggested tautly,

looking as displeased with our situation as I was. "Just in case things go sideways."

"Yeah," I acknowledged grudgingly. "But we *need* to talk to the Nova. If they're out here, they might know where the Reconstructors are, or even where to find the Northwest Passage."

"Hey, um, guys?" Jay said, sticking his head up from the short line of steps to the cockpit. He and Bob looked distinctly out of place in the light body armor they'd been issued from the stores of ship's security, like it was a costume they were wearing to a party. "I was just outside checking the landing gear for Chief Sackett, and that old dude, like the shaman or whatever he is? He's wanting to talk to Lilandreth. She, like, told me to go get you."

Deciding it was probably useless to remind Jay that he took orders from us and not Lilandreth, I chugged the last of the water and chucked it before checking that my sidearm was loose in its holster, then headed down to the ramp. Vicky came with me, of course, and so did Jay and Bob, probably because they realized they had an excuse to do something more exciting than guard the ship.

Two squads of empty Vigilante suits stood motionless in their gantries, the Marines who usually crewed them either stretched out catching a catnap, chewing rat bars, or buried in ViR games on their 'links. It took a lot to impress Drop Troopers, particularly these. Maybe, I thought, we should have brought the Vergai recruits like Vicky wanted. They would have been suitably nervous and impressed.

"We gonna get into a scrap, sir?" Corporal Kohl asked me as I passed by, not even looking up from her 'link.

"I'm hoping not," I shot over my shoulder at her. "But then, you know the old saying..."

"Yes, sir. Hope in one hand and shit in the other, see which one fills up faster."

Lilandreth was already outside, right at the edge of the perimeter the two squads on alert had set up at the foot of the ramp. It was the only approach to the ship not covered by defensive turrets when we were on the ground, and more than one energy cannon was pointed at Gandish as he glanced around at the metal giants in obvious discomfort.

Lilandreth looked up at our approach and waved us over to her.

"Cam, Vicky, Gandish has something to tell us."

Gandish scowled deeply, giving us a dirty look.

"Oh, yeah," Vicky said dryly. "I can see he's just eager as hell to have a conversation."

"Tell them," Lilandreth snapped at the older man. Whether or not he still believed she was a daemon, Gandish complied.

"There is an oracle in the center of the city," he told us. "It speaks when it will, giving us warnings of imminent evil, as if we had the arts of our great-grandfathers or the power of the daemons and could do something to stop the danger."

"It's a sensor suite," Lilandreth translated the translation, making an impatient gesture for Gandish to get along with the explanation. "Likely hooked up to satellites still remaining in orbit either around this planet or perhaps the moon."

"What is the oracle telling you?" I asked, cutting across Lilandreth's impatience with my own. "We know there are ships coming. Are they from your kind, the Reconstructors?"

It was a long shot, of course. Nance already said the ships were Nova design, but I had the wild idea that the Nova had been given the ship technology by the Reconstructors, so maybe the Resscharr technology had regressed here right alongside their culture. Gandish scoffed at the idea.

"There have been none of my people who have traveled the

heavens since the daemon Carpashia took the last of the old ships away from here. No, this is much worse. These are the slaves, the Unquestioning. They've returned to this place, and every time they come, they bring devastation and death."

"Well, shit, that's the worst of all possible worlds right there," Vicky said, giving me a bleak look. I shook my head, prickling running up the back of my neck.

"This doesn't track. Why would the Nova let us pass through here if they were already active in this part of the galaxy? They made it very clear we weren't going to see them again."

"They were lying," Vicky declared with a shrug, as if it was the most obvious thing in the world. "Everybody lies."

"Oh, man," Jay interrupted, then flushed when Lilandreth, Vicky, and I all turned to look at him. "I mean, like, we've been dealing with the Nova for a long time. The Confederation, I mean. They were cold-blooded, tentacle-headed assholes, but they never tried to lie to us. They said they were gonna kick our asses if we went where they told us not to, and that's exactly what they did. No deception required, you know?"

"Yeah," Bob added succinctly.

"Well, just because they wouldn't lie to us," I said, "doesn't mean they'd tell us everything. Vicky, get everyone armored up and in covered positions using the city for cover." Gandish's eyes went wide with alarm as Vicky sprinted back up the ramp, probably at the prospective of us fighting his bogeyman rebellious slaves in his city. "You should get your people deeper inside the city," I told him. "Make sure you're not in the line of fire just in case."

"The daemon will protect us!" Gandish insisted, looking to Lilandreth. "She's come just at the time we need her!"

"I am of the people who your kind abandoned to flee to this place," Lilandreth snapped at him. "We were at war with an

enemy who sought to wipe us out of existence, and you Reconstructors left us to our fate rather than stay and fight. Even if I
had the powers you attribute to me, why would you assume I'd
come to help *you*?"

Damn, that was cold. Gandish's face fell, and he staggered
back a step as if she'd slapped him. I felt bad for the Resscharr,
though I wasn't sure if I should have. I touched his arm and he
flinched away.

"Get your people to safety." I motioned back into the city.
"We'll try to talk to the Nova, keep things peaceful."

I'd tried to be comforting, but it didn't land. Gandish pulled
away from me and yelled at the other Resscharr, his words
slurred and loud enough that the translation circuit couldn't
make them out. Whatever he said, it was enough to spur the
farmers and herders into action. Shouts and cries of alarm were
the soundtrack to their frantic scurrying as they hauled baskets
of grain into the storage room or drove their cattle ahead of
them.

I hadn't had a chance to get a close look at the animals
before, my brain just automatically identifying them as cows.
They weren't, though they were vaguely bovine, having more in
common with bison or water buffalo, large and ornery and not
taking kindly to the chivvying into the building.

"I'd hate to have to clean up all that shit," Bob said
fervently, watching the animals trot onto the dirt-smeared
floor.

I'd figured Gandish would have preceded them into the
cover of the massive megacity but he hung back, glaring at
Lilandreth and me.

"There is no safety with the Unquestioning," he spat. "No
negotiation, no peace. The Unquestioning do not talk, they do
not make peace. They seek to rule us and all we used to control.
If you are indeed a daemon, you will slaughter them before they

can do the same to us. If you're not..." Gandish sneered. "You'll die alongside us."

———

"I don't like leaving you here," Watson insisted, her voice small and distant behind the earth-shaking rumble of the drop-ship's belly jets. "We could just get the hell out, take you with us."

I shook my head in the privacy of my suit, standing against the hot blast of gas and debris from the ship's takeoff, an oak facing the storm.

"It's too late to run," I told her. "They'd intercept us in orbit. The *Orion* says they've already launched landers."

"Why don't we just blow the shit out of them then?" Watson asked, a petulant whine to the question.

"Because we're not at war with them," I reminded him, "and the last time we saw the Nova we were on good terms, *and* they were devoted to upholding the wishes of the Predecessors above all else, enough that they would have died right to the last if we hadn't shown them Lilandreth. We can't kill them in cold blood just because we're afraid of them. If nothing else, we don't have the firepower to fight their entire fleet."

"Yes, sir." The ship shot up into the sky and lurched forward.

"Just find a safe place to hole up," I told Watson. "If we need a dust-off, we'll call you."

"I'm with her, by the way," Vicky told me, her Vigilante stomping up to the scorched circle of our landing zone. "We should get the hell out of here."

"So you've told me," I agreed. "But we came here to get information, and we're not going to accomplish that mission if we run away anytime there's danger."

"Don't lecture me, Street Boy," she said, although there was

68

a fondness behind the jibe. "You know I'll follow your lead, just don't expect me to be happy about it." Her Vigilante's articulated left hand pointed at Lilandreth, who stood between us, her energy pistol held loosely at her side. "But dammit, Cam, *she* shouldn't be here."

"This world belongs to my people," Lilandreth said, and I blinked, wondering how Lilandreth had managed to tap into our private channel. "I will not run and hide when one of the species we created threatens to take everything we built."

And I boggled again at that, just as much as at her interruption.

"Didn't you just tell Gandish you *didn't* feel obligated to defend his people, that you felt like the Reconstructors abandoned you?"

Lilandreth shrugged.

"The man is delusional. He thinks I'm some sort of god and I had to get it through his head that I wasn't going to save his people through some miracle, that he was responsible for their safety, not I." She tossed her head in an inhuman gesture. "Besides, what he has said is senseless. The Nova we encountered were utterly devoted to the Resscharr. Why would they allow us to even come this way only to attack us? No, me being here will only help to convince these Nova that they need to help us."

"I'd feel better if you took cover," I told her. Again, that toss of her head, the feathers of her mane whipping through the afternoon air like the diving strike of a predatory bird.

"When I was a passenger on your ship," she said, "I followed your orders. My ship is now my own, as is my fate. I accede to your suggestions when I agree with them, but I am no longer under your command. I will do as I think best."

And I, of course, could *try* to make her do what I said at my own risk. I *thought* I could take her with my armor and weapon but I didn't know for sure, and I'd probably wind up hurting her, which I didn't want to do. Or getting hurt myself, which I *really* didn't want to do.

I would have asked Vicky for advice, but Lilandreth had already demonstrated that I couldn't do it privately.

"Fine, it's your life." I switched to the net for the Intercepts. "Brandano, Villanueva, what's our situation?"

"We have three Nova landers on their way to your position," Brandano told me. "We're shadowing them but we haven't taken any aggressive action yet, per your orders."

Yeah, thanks, Brandano. I needed the reminder that those were my orders. No one seemed particularly happy taking them at the moment.

"Vicky," I said, "please go back with the platoon and keep overwatch on us."

"I should be out here with you," she grumbled but did as she was told, hopping back into the city with a blast of her jumpjets.

That order I was sure of. If things went bad, the platoon needed a leader I could trust... and so did the mission.

She'd barely disappeared into the recesses of the city walls when the landers came into focus, white spheres riding plasma flames down from orbit, Christmas tree ornaments hanging in the blue sky. The three of them landed in a perfect diamond formation only a few hundred meters from where Lilandreth and I stood, the blast of heat and scouring spray of dust and sand spattering against my armor and lighting up Lilandreth's personal defense shield in a hemisphere of energy.

I wanted to run, wanted to join the rest of the platoon back under cover, but I held my position because if I didn't, Lilandreth would have confronted them herself. The blast of the drives had barely died away when the boarding ramps extended downward from ten meters above the drive bells, broad cargo doors sliding open.

Through them loped the Nova mecha. They weren't quite the same as the Tahni mechs I'd encountered during the war. Those had been massive, top-heavy, loaded down with long-range weapons and armor, slow and ponderous, designed to be mobile artillery. These were purposed differently, part of a military philosophy that had evolved in an alien mind. A *dumbass* alien mind, in my opinion. A huge, metal target made sense for an artillery piece meant to hang back behind the front lines and take long-range potshots, but the Nova intended these lithe, lightly armored machines to be a combination of armor and infantry, for all that they were ten meters tall and impossible to maneuver as quickly as a battlesuit.

Still, there was something impressive about the sight of dozens of them pouring off the boarding ramp, plasma guns scanning back and forth on their shoulders. They spread out around their ships into a semicircle, slowly expanding our way. And at their center, a toddler among adults, was a single Nova on foot.

Well, sort of foot. Their arms and legs had evolved from tentacles and even though they, unlike the cephalopod creatures from which they'd descended, had developed an endoskeleton, the way the Nova walked spoke to their aquatic origins.

He came to a halt only twenty meters away, his mecha maintaining a respectful distance the same distance back from him.

"You speak the language of the Resscharr?" he asked. I *thought* it was a he.

"We do," I told him. I cracked my chest plate and clambered out, unplugging my 'face jacks. "I'm Captain Cameron Alvarez of the Commonwealth military. We come from a federation of systems far away from here and are seeking our way home. I'm human," I added, remembering he probably would never have seen anything like me.

"Why are *you* here, Remainder?" the Nova snapped at Lilandreth, not bothering to give me his name or place of origin in return. That was a bad sign. "And where did you find those ancient relics?"

"I am not a Remainder," she said, drawing herself up. "Nor am I a Reconstructor. I am from a world called Decision and I traveled here with the humans. I seek to find others of my species who've not sunk so far as the pitiful creatures here who still dare to call themselves Resscharr."

The Nova commander stared at her for a moment, the mouth that was almost part of his neck working soundlessly before the translator on his belt responded in the Resscharr language.

"You say you are not of this part of the galaxy?"

"I am not," Lilandreth confirmed. "I am of the Predecessors, those you swore to serve."

The Nova commander snapped something in his own language and stepped back, and I just knew in my gut what was going to happen next. I turned and threw myself into my suit just before the mecha opened fire.

[8]

I couldn't think of any good reason why I wasn't dead.

I should have been. The plasma guns were pure hell, particularly for a poor, unarmored son of a bitch like me who didn't even have to get hit square-on by one of them to get killed. All it would take was the thermal bloom from ten meters away to cook me like a brisket. I squeezed my eyes shut, my fingers curled around the edge of my Vigilante's chest plate, and waited to die.

I opened them again to see Lilandreth standing in front of me, her defense shield glowing as bright as a setting sun, plasma coruscating off it in showers of sparks.

"Hurry!" she bit out, her voice strained as if she was having to hold the shield in place with her sheer will.

I didn't need any urging. Skin came off my elbows and shin on the way back into the suit, but it sure as hell beat the alternative. I'd never tried plugging in one-handed before, but the 'face jacks slid into the sockets like I'd done it a million times while I slammed the plastron shut with my other hand. The suit revived and I hit the jets almost before the sensors were up, grabbing Lilandreth around the waist, ignoring the crackle of static in my HUD from the interference of her defense shield.

I flew by instinct, no more thought to direction than *away*, unable to see clearly with the external sensors blinded by the residual electrostatic charge cascading off her armor's force field, unable to talk even if the comms could get past the interference. I could have stayed up as long as I wanted, but that would have involved the two of us being skeet for the Nova shooting team so I went down, hoping like hell I wasn't landing right on top of the enemy shuttles.

I hit uneven ground and stumbled forward, dropping Lilandreth so I wouldn't wind up stepping on her. Like reality had been saving up all the bad news to drop it on me at once, the sensors and comms came back online right as I hit the ground on my shoulder and plowed a furrow into the dirt.

I was a kilometer away and God knows how, because I didn't think we'd been in the air long enough for that, and by some miracle I hadn't flown toward the enemy. I hadn't flown toward friendlies either. I was around the curve of the city walls, somewhere north of where I'd been a moment before, far enough that I couldn't see the hemisphere of the Nova landers past the convex shape of the Resscharr city. Far enough that the outer doors were closed on this side.

"... under attack!" I couldn't tell where the transmission was coming from, couldn't identify the voice through the static, but somewhere above me, thunder cracked and lightning flashed from cloud to cloud.

Proton cannons, or maybe Nova plasma guns. There'd be no air support for now, not with the Intercepts engaged by the Nova spaceships. And if they were attacking the Intercepts here in the atmosphere, they had to be going after the *Orion*.

"Does anyone read me?" I called. "Vicky? Watson?"

No one answered and I rolled the Vigilante over on its side, pushing to my feet. Damage alerts flashed yellow in my HUD, a few hitting red... and one of them was the comms. The receiver was barely operational, but the transmission antenna had been burned right off of the backpack.

"Fuck," I hissed, not worried about it sounding unprofessional coming from an officer because no one else would hear it.

Lilandreth. Where the hell was Lilandreth?

Oh, shit.

There she was, lying face down in the dirt, unmoving. My instinct was to grab for her and I had to remind myself that I was in the suit. Extra gentle, moving the articulated claw like a pair of tweezers, I turned her over. The force field didn't even flicker, burned out by the sustained plasma blasts she'd absorbed trying to save me, and the armor beneath it was blackened, spiderwebbed with cracks.

The field had kept her alive, but some of the damage had leaked through, a nasty burn across the left side of her face and neck seeping red through cracked skin. Her eyelids fluttered, nictating membranes fluttering beneath them, and she stirred, grasping for a weapon she'd dropped somewhere along the way.

"Can you hear me, Lilandreth?" I asked over the external speakers, since my transmitter was fried and I had no clue whether her receiver was still intact. "Wake up! We don't have much time."

In truth, I had no clue whether the Nova were hard on our heels or otherwise occupied. The sounds of battle echoed off the trees facing the city, thunder rolling across the fields from the discharge of energy weapons, black clouds rising even above the towering walls. I had to get back to Vicky and the others.

"I..." Lilandreth trailed off, her eyes open but unfocused as she tried to roll onto her side. "I will try."

"Thanks for saving my life," I told her, offering my arm to let her pull herself to her feet. "I know that had to hurt."

"It was unpleasant." She sounded a little more coherent, stumbling upright, steadying herself against my armor. "I don't understand. They seemed prepared to talk until they found out where I was from."

"Yeah, that was weird," I agreed. "Come on, Vicky and the platoon are engaging them, and I don't know how long..."

The roar of atmospheric jets drowned out whatever I'd been bout to say, a shadow passing across the sun, and I leaned back to look up. It was the drop-ship, coming in hot, its coilguns spitting out hundreds of rounds per minute, a staccato backbeat to the scream of the drives. Incandescent streaks of plasma sought out the massive aerospacecraft, but Watson had a fighter pilot's soul and he barrel-rolled the drop-ship away from the incoming fire, raking the enemy positions with his guns before the drop-ship disappeared behind the walls of the city.

"Hang on," I told Lilandreth, slipping an arm around her and kicking the jumpjet controls.

Nothing happened. Nothing except a red flashing that warned me the jet exhaust ports had taken a hit and needed maintenance before it could be used again.

Damn. That was bad timing.

"Jets are out," I told Lilandreth. "Gonna have to run. Stay behind me."

That was only fair, since she'd burned out her shield taking fire for me. It also meant I couldn't keep an eye on her while she ran because the rear sensors and cameras had gotten burned out of my helmet at the same time as the transmitter. I lumbered into a lope, the Vigilante gaining momentum with each step until it reached a gallop that tore up turf and scattered debris. There were no paved areas outside the city walls, as if the Reconstructors had decided that everything they needed could be included inside the massive building and they needn't disturb any more of the planet than they had by leveling most of a small continent.

It slowed me down, kept me from running at the full capability of the battlesuit's artificial muscles, but I couldn't have gone full speed anyway, not with Lilandreth trying to keep up. I stayed at under twenty klicks an hour, which felt like crawling, and I imagined the platoon rushing on board the drop-ship under fire. Vicky would be in agony, knowing that I was out here alone, that she was leaving me behind, but also burdened by the responsibility to the rest of the Marines. They'd be slaughtered if she waited for me.

The right thing to do was to evacuate, then circle back around and try to pick us up. Vicky might have been a little mouthy about following my orders, but she *always* did the right thing. Which meant we didn't have but a few seconds.

It wasn't enough. We'd just come back around the curve in the wall when the belly jets of the drop-ship roared again and the massive lifting body shape leapt into the sky. I skidded to a halt, staring at a field of destruction. Nova mechs were scattered in pieces, their dead describing the outline of where the drop-ship had touched down... their dead and ours. There were two battlesuits down, burned into slag by the Nova plasma guns, so mangled they weren't even transmitting an IFF signal for me to receive.

The sight of them kicked me in the gut. There were so few of us left, and everyone who fell made it seem more like none of us would ever make it home. A half a dozen Nova mecha turned as one, noticing the two of us, and suddenly the one I was worried about not making it home was me.

The jets were gone, there was no cover to be had and only seconds before those mecha incinerated the both of us in a wave of plasma that outshone the sun. I had one place to hide, and it was inside. Turning, I grabbed Lilandreth around the waist and hauled her off her feet. Changing directions meant planting a spiked footpad and pushing off the dirt and into the nearest open entranceway into the city walls.

One step was all I had on the Nova, and that wash of plasma I'd feared chased us into the open chamber, blasting apart stacks of gathered grain in a whoosh of flame that filled the room. One thing I didn't know about grain. It's explosive. The concussion couldn't penetrate my armor but it did throw me off-stride, the heat stealing my breath away, singing the bare skin of my hands, conducting even through the BiPhase Carbide and insulation.

The suit wasn't supposed to fall. There were all sorts of fail-safes in place, and if my foot hadn't come down on an uneven, shifting surface of stacked grain, they might have worked. The last of those were the jumpjets though, and those weren't operational.

I fell. Hard.

It shouldn't have hurt that bad, not with the armor cushioning me, but the blast impelled me forward head over heels and my back slammed against the floor hard enough to drive the air from me and leave my vision covered with stars. Thought clawed its way through a haze of concussion and I slammed an arm against the floor, rolling back over, getting my feet beneath me. Lilandreth had slipped out of my grasp when the explosion hit and she sprawled across sacks of ground grain twenty meters away, just inside the doorway. She wasn't moving, and I couldn't tell if she was dead or alive.

I shifted my weight for a lunge toward her, but a Nova mecha ducked through the entrance first and I fired out of instinct. The actinic energy from the Resscharr-tech gun speared through the leering, rounded face of the machine, breaching the cockpit where the Nova pilot manipulated the controls with wormlike, boneless fingers. Nothing was left of him but ash and, lacking his guidance and already off-balance, the mecha toppled like a felled redwood between Lilandreth and me.

78

"Dammit!" I yelled, barely able to hear my own curse through battered eardrums.

The room was piled high with grain and crops, and there was no space to go around the mecha. I couldn't even see Lilandreth, much less reach her. I'd have to climb over the damned thing...

Or I would have, if it hadn't been for the three other mecha who barged through the entrance before I could even move. They fired before they'd even cleared their own fallen comrade and the collapsed mecha wilted and flared under the twin blasts of plasma, saving me from the same fate. I fired back, hosing the back end of the mecha with my own weapon, but there was no way I could get to Lilandreth without killing her myself. I screamed wordlessly inside my helmet, hating these Nova, hating myself. I ran.

I left her.

[9]

I hated drinking hot water.

It had happened way too many times in my military career. The battlesuit was well insulated, of course. If it wasn't I'd have been dead twenty times over, burned to a crisp. But the insultation wasn't perfect, and it could get as hot as a convection oven inside the suit. Hot enough to bring the temperature of my hydration reservoir to the level of bathwater.

It was disgusting, but I sucked it down anyway and tried not to throw up. I *could* have fired up the reactor and cooled the interior down, and the water with it, but I remembered very well what this place looked like from the air on the thermal and spectroscopic sensors. The suit's reactor wasn't as hot as it used to be when it had been powered by the breakdown of an artificial isotope, but even the Resscharr-tech reactor would stand out like a pole star.

I'd found a dark corner, somehow. I had no idea where I was in this place or what they'd used this closet for, but I'd been able to squeeze the Vigilante into the narrow doorway and shuffle it back ten meters toward the rear wall before I shut it down and cracked the chest plastron. Then I'd broken out the medical kit.

That was typical after a battle in the suit. There was just so much heat the armor could dissipate, and you always got burned. I had a nasty one on my neck where the suit had taken the hit that had killed my comms, another on my hip where the jets had been disabled, and I hadn't felt either of them until I'd climbed out of the suit.

I'd felt them *then*, all right. You'd think I'd have gotten used to it after all this time, but that turned out not to be the case, and I clenched my teeth against a moan until I got the smart bandages into place. Local anesthetic soothed the pain and I sagged against the cool, faux-stone surface of the wall, breathing again.

That taken care of, I clambered back into the suit and yanked open the small compartment on the righthand side. The pulse carbine stood out as if asking to be used, a frustrated Marine begging to deploy. It wasn't ideal in this situation—the cartridge-fed laser had a hell of a thermal signature, and using it would scream to every Nova in here where I was. But it was better than harsh language. I strapped on the tactical vest and checked the spare magazines in the chest pouches, then unfolded the stock of the carbine and attached the sling to the vest.

Enhanced-vision glasses were in a pocket of the vest, and I slipped them on. The dark closet brightened, although the new light didn't reveal much about the bare walls. It *did* let me see the damage to my suit. Nothing too bad except the jumpjet vent. The armor on the backpack had melted and immediately rehardened, partially obstructing the right side of the vent. It was about ten centimeters long and four centimeters wide and curled like a feather.

Patting the vest along the side, I found the utility knife sheathed there and pulled it out. This was *probably* a waste of time, but if the shard of metal hadn't hardened *too* much... I tried the blade first, but it bounced off with a *tink* of metal on metal, so I reversed the tool and slammed the butt of the knife against the shard. It moved, so I hit it again, then a third time, and the brittle strip broke away and clattered to the floor with an appalling noise.

That *might* not be the only problem with the jets, but I'd at least tried. Now I had to try to find Lilandreth. Assuming she was still alive. My 'link had kept a dead-reckoning record of my course into the city, so at least it could tell me which direction I should go to get back outside, even if it had no idea where anything else was inside the city. I checked it. I had to go back out for fifty meters the way I'd come, then take a turn to the left.

The closet had a sliding door that had been open when I found it, but I'd pushed it shut once I'd gotten inside, and it proved a lot harder to move with my bare hands than it had with the suit's muscles. I slung my carbine and braced my feet against the far wall and tried again. The strain overcame the anesthetics and my neck and hip flared up like wildfires in the forest, but the door slid open just enough for me to squeeze through.

The illumination in this part of the city had been dimmer than the statue room where we'd met Gandish: not completely dark, but more as if the background lights were malfunctioning after all this time. With the goggles on, it might as well have been midday. Coming through in the Vigilante, I'd been obsessed with finding a hiding place, but now, scanning more carefully, I noticed things I hadn't picked up on before.

There wasn't much left of whatever the Reconstructors had done with this place, and after seeing what Lilandreth's Predecessor ship could do, growing its own furniture and even control stations to suit the needs of the operator, I had a hunch that the city was organized the same way. Things grew where the Reconstructors had wanted them to... and once they were gone, the furniture and maybe even some of the internal walls had disappeared.

The Remainder had moved in and built their own. Stones gathered from outside the city had been piled up to form a semi-circle around furniture handmade from local wood. The chairs and beds were similar to what I'd seen on Decision and on the ship, except cruder, misshapen, as if it had been crafted by a child out of cardboard. The room held no sign of recent habitation, no scraps of food or clothing, and I wondered if the Remainder simply moved from place to place inside the city as the spirit moved them. Or maybe they moved in order to hide from the Nova. I wondered where they were hiding now and whether it was far enough.

Watching for the Nova, the Remainder, or any sign of my own people, I tried to think. It wasn't easy. The smart bandages did a great job on pain, but that was a double-edged sword because the built-in anesthetic muddled my brain. Not much, just enough to be noticeable, enough that I had spell things out in my head instead of just knowing them intuitively.

What did I know for sure?

More than I knew the laws of physics, more than I trusted in fusion or the speed of light in a vacuum, I knew Vicky wouldn't abandon me, not if she had any hope at all that I was still alive. Nance couldn't make her, Watson couldn't make her, Brandano couldn't make her. Not God Himself could make her leave me here. I knew it because I'd do the same thing.

Which meant she'd likely have Watson drop her and the rest of the platoon somewhere far enough away that they could infiltrate back through Nova lines and pull me out. She wouldn't risk the ship because she knew it might be the only way we had out of here, which meant it could take them hours to get back here.

Of course, that all depended on what was happening out in

space. The *Orion* could take several Nova ships on her own, but I had no idea how badly we were outnumbered... and the Predecessor ship was useless without Lilandreth to fly it. We'd *tried*, but none of our people had been able to interface with the ship. Lilandreth had insisted it was because of the damage the vessel had taken during our battle, but I had a suspicion she'd rigged the system herself to make sure she was the only one who could control it.

Not that it would have mattered without weapons, and those were inoperable even if Lilandreth had been on board.

The Intercepts would probably be helping the *Orion*, and we hadn't launched any assault shuttles for this operation. That had been my call, one I'd made with the thought that their limited mobility and range would be a liability compared to the Intercept cutters. It was still true, but if they'd been around they could have provided air support Vicky would badly need. For a while. Until the Nova shot them down.

What did all that mean? I had a hard time putting it together, except that it meant I had time to look for Lilandreth before they came back to get me. What did it mean for the Nova? Would they expect it? I didn't think they would. They probably expected us to retreat. They didn't know us, not these Nova. That was something else I'd considered.

These weren't the same Nova we'd faced before. If they had been, they'd have already known about Lilandreth. The Nova we'd fought against with the Confederation and the Grey might not have even known these guys existed. I pushed that line of thinking away, filed it for later consideration. It wouldn't do me any good right now.

Something moved at the edge of my vision, and I ducked below one of the interior half-walls, the brain-twisting partial dividers the Resscharr seemed to have used for aesthetic purposes, since they didn't have any other discernable function.

They also screwed with my depth perception and threw crazy shadows in random directions, and if this was a false alarm, it would be the fifth since I'd set out to backtrack my way to the exit.

It wasn't. The inhuman shuffling scrape against the floor told me that much. I'd heard it before when we'd met the Nova back in the Confederation to negotiate our passage through the wormhole network. They were in here. Not the mecha, just dismounts, moving on... tentacle. A bunch of them, and not that far away. Dropping to one knee, I brought the carbine up to my shoulder.

They were gonna see me, I was sure of it. They'd pop out from around the next wildly curving section of half-wall, and maybe I could get them all before they got me but maybe not.

The half-dividers fooled me again. I caught a glimpse of them passing around the other side of the decorative half-wall but they were heading off to my left, not even glancing back this way. There were a *lot* of them, more than I could have taken if they *had* seen me. A good two dozen, most of them armed and armored like soldiers, wearing absurd, shining breastplates like Spanish Conquistadors and conical, metal helmets, boxy devices I assumed were rifles of some kind cradled in their tentacles.

It was like a bad science fiction ViR movie put together by AI, and my first instinct was to snicker at the ridiculous image... until I saw Lilandreth. The Nova had stripped away her armor and secured her wrists and ankles with shackles, and two of the soldiers carried her between them, forming a litter with their tentacles. She was alive, at least, or they wouldn't have bothered restraining her. I didn't see any obvious wounds besides the burns she'd suffered earlier, but she was only semiconscious, groaning softly though not struggling against her Nova captors.

Holding my breath, I waited for them to pass. A glance

backward to make sure they weren't being trailed by more troops, then I padded after them. I was no kind of Force Recon commando, had very little formal training in stealth or CQB, just one-on-one sessions with Top once we'd signed onto the *Orion* mission. I drew on everything she'd taught me, walking toe-heel, setting each step down carefully, avoiding the *tap-tap* of the soles of my boots on the hard floor. Another trick she'd taught me was to watch the legs of the people I was tailing rather than staring at the backs of their heads. Things might be different for the Nova, but when it came to humans or Tahni, unconscious awareness of peripheral vision cues gave people a sixth sense of when they were being watched.

So wrapped up was I in *not* staring at the Nova that I almost missed Gandish waving at me from a niche between decorative half-wall dividers. His expression was urgent, or at least that was how I interpreted it after my experience with Lilandreth and the other Resscharr, his eyes flickering between the Nova soldiers and me as he waved toward the hidey-hole.

I hesitated, reluctant to give up on following the Nova for fear of losing Lilandreth but very aware that Gandish could give me up to them if he wanted. I cursed under my breath and dashed across the thirty yards of open space between us, praying none of the Nova would cast a look behind them and spot me.

"Human," Gandish hissed, grabbing at my arm. "The Nova have taken the daemon!"

"No shit," I blurted, motioning the way the soldiers had gone. "That's who I was just following! Why did you stop me?"

"We've been watching them," he explained. "They've already sent a force ahead to the Ghost Nexus."

I stared at the Resscharr silently for a moment.

"The *what*?" The translator had chosen the words, of

course, but this was one of those times when I suspected there was a cultural disconnect that the software couldn't reconcile.

"The Ghost Nexus," Gandish insisted. "It's a place forbidden to the Remainders, closed off entirely by Carpashia, but somehow the Nova have reopened it." He tossed his head, his thinning, graying mane of hair whipping against the bare, gray wall beside him. "This is very bad. We were told the Ghost Nexus is cursed, that even going near it could mean all our deaths!"

"What is it?" I demanded impatiently. "What's a Ghost Nexus?"

"It's the place where the daemons are born," Gandish told me, glancing around as if to make sure no one was close enough to listen. "Where they're selected by the ghosts. But those who aren't selected die horribly, torn to pieces."

More myths and legends, though Gandish looked as if he took this one to heart and it scared the shit out of him.

"I have to get there," I told him, rising. "Before they can do anything to her..."

He stopped me with an iron grip on my wrist.

"You can't go that way," he said with the fervor of a religious proselyte. "The corridor narrows! They'd see you before you could get anywhere near them!"

"I'm not leaving her," I insisted, pulling away from his grasp.

"There's another way." He pointed back further into the nook between walls, into the shadows to a low, tight passage I wouldn't have spotted without the enhanced-vision goggles. "Through here. It's a secret way. We can get around them if you come with me."

He didn't wait for me to say yes, just sank down into a crouch that would be impossible for any human—or any other bipedal species with plantigrade knees—to imitate, and waddled through the entrance.

"Shit," I replied, but then sighed and went down to hands and knees and hurried to keep up with him.

I imagined the tunnel being full of dust and mouse-droppings—or the droppings of whatever passed for mice around here—but the goggles were reassuring. The floor was as clean as if a cleaning crew had been through here with a push broom just this morning. Maybe they had. I imagined the Resscharr were pretty serious about keeping their cities clean, and if there was still power...

"Why are you doing this?" I asked Gandish, grunting the question breathlessly, holding the carbine tight to my chest to keep it from banging off the walls. "Why are you helping me?"

He hadn't seemed that eager to talk to me at all before, and Lilandreth hadn't given him any reason to change his mind, as harsh as she'd been to him before. Not that I was ready to turn down *any* help at the moment, but he could just as easily have been leading me into a trap. He'd called the Nova their oppressors, their conquerors, but it wouldn't be the first time someone being oppressed had betrayed their allies in hopes of better treatment.

"You are the enemy of the Nova," Gandish explained, not sounding strained or out of breath at all despite the duck-walk. "They have killed us, enslaved us, and looted the gifts of our great-grandfathers, leaving us with crumbs, forcing to live as the Unquestioning once did. We saw you and your people fighting them, killing them. If the daemon can't kill them, then we would have you defend us from them instead."

Oh, great, *another* bunch of helpless aliens who wanted the Marines to protect them from their big, bad enemies. That never got old. Unfortunately, I needed this guy's help.

"Yeah, okay, we'll do what we can to drive these guys away." Since it fit with what we had to do anyway. "Just get me to the..." I grimaced at the name. "... Ghost Nexus."

The tunnel might have gone on forever as far as my knees and elbows were concerned, and I longed for even the light security armor Jay and Bob had scored, with its hardened elbow and knee pads. My utility fatigues provided little cushion, and after five minutes crawling over the hard floor, the skin was wearing away on my knees. After ten, I stopped trying to keep track of time and considered asking Gandish to take a break.

It was just as well that we reached the end of the line right about then, because it would have made me look like a wimp to ask for a delay when I'd been the one who was all for hurrying up and following the Nova. The side tunnel didn't look any different than a half a dozen others we'd passed along the way, but Gandish took the lefthand turn without hesitation, and after another ten meters we were out.

I was so relieved to be back on my feet, I nearly forgot to check for bad guys before I jumped out of the exit and had to pull back my foot and advance with the carbine ahead of me. To be honest, I couldn't tell much different about this section of the city than the one we'd come from, but Gandish obviously could. He didn't even try to get out of the tunnel, shrinking back instead.

"I can't go with you," he told me. He pointed to the right. "Travel that direction for one hundred meters until you reach an intersection, then turn left. The Ghost Nexus will be where the corridor ends. Good luck, human." Well, at least *that* translated.

Then Gandish was gone, fading back into the darkness. Leaving me alone. Sighing, I jogged in the direction he'd indicated, using my pace count as Top had taught me. Yeah, the 'link would be more accurate but I had to keep my eyes up, and even taking the time to set the distance would have been a waste.

Left at the intersection, and I still hadn't seen or heard

anything. I was beginning to wonder if Gandish had either given me the wrong directions or if he'd been wrong about where the Nova had taken Lilandreth. After all, this area was taboo to his people. He could have been making assumptions about the intentions of the Nova based on his own superstition. I thought that right up to the point where I nearly walked into the back of three of the Nova soldiers who'd set up at the end of the corridor.

Not facing my way but oriented toward a clear wall, as if they were more worried about what was inside than what might be overtaking them. Clenching my teeth against the curse that tried to explode out of me at the sight of the soldiers, I pressed my back against the wall and held my breath. If even one of them turned...

They didn't, still fascinated by whatever was going on past the transparent wall. I slid back along the wall and tried to look past them. Inside the glass, or transparent aluminum or whatever the stuff was, the room was nearly bare. No control panels, no readouts, nothing except for a vent in the ceiling and a one-piece cot that seemed to have grown out of the floor, like most Predecessor furniture. From the vent flowed... something. I could have sworn I saw a glittering rain of particulates, but it was nothing I could pin down, nothing I could focus on even with the enhanced-vision glasses.

Strapped to the gurney, lying beneath the rain of glitter... was Lilandreth.

[10]

I nearly lunged forward, finger tightening into the trigger guard of my carbine until I saw what was on the other side of the chamber. It was a transparent cylinder, and Gandish hadn't been mistaken about there being two approaches to it. I'd taken the secret passage while the Nova had gone the main corridor, which meant most of them were still on the other side.

Over a dozen of them. Some of the soldiers had gone once they'd delivered Lilandreth to the chamber, but there were still seven or eight of them, as well as other Nova lacking armor, dressed in the same basic harness as the commander who I'd talked to before their attack. Officers, maybe, or, given what they were doing, maybe scientists or technicians.

There was a door on this side. The outline was faint but visible, and the security panel was the same as I'd seen in other Predecessor installations and on their ships. If I shot the guards in front of me, I could get through it... just in time for the soldiers to come through the other side and kill me.

I needed a diversion, something to make those guys on the other side look the other way.

A hand fell on my shoulder, and the self-control it took to

keep from crying out nearly caused me to rupture myself. I spun around, finger milligrams away from pulling the trigger of my carbine, until I saw the wide eyes and golden skin of Jay and Bob.

They both looked like they were about to yell in surprise as well, and I put a hand over Jay's mouth, confident in Bob's ability to stay silent. I motioned urgently for them to retreat back the way we'd come, hoping that one of them wouldn't drop their carbine or trip over their own feet. Somehow, they managed to stay quiet until we were back at the intersection and around the corner.

"What the *fuck* are you two doing here?" I demanded, somehow managing to yell at them in a low voice just above a whisper. "Why aren't you on the drop-ship?"

"We, like, kind of *fell out*, man," Jay confessed.

I blinked, looking at them again. They both *looked* like they'd fallen off the back of a drop-ship, their fatigues stained and torn, their armor scuffed and caked with dirt, and both of them had dirt matted in their hair.

"How the hell did that happen?" I wanted to know.

"It was really terrifying, you know? When those Nova dudes attacked, Vicky called for the drop-ship and, dude, when Lt. Watson took off, it was like a bat out of hell." Jay shook his head. "I didn't think a boat that big could maneuver like that! Shit, I was strapped in and I thought I'd get slammed against the wall anyway!"

"Bulkhead," I corrected absently.

"Right, bulkhead. So, we got to the dust-off and Chief Sackett tells us to open the ramp and guard it while the platoon boards." Jay motioned between Bob and himself. "So, we do that, you know? We're standing there at the bottom of the ramp with plasma and energy beams and all that shit going off every-where, waiting for your Marines to get on board. Then, when the last of them is on the ramp, I go to close it... but we get a hit right in the side of the ship from one of those plasma guns and Lt. Watson just hits the jets." He threw up his hands. "The whole damn ship tilts sideways, and the next thing I know, I'm on the ground and the drop-ship is fucking taking off!"

I looked to Bob and spread my hands.

"And how did *you* wind up falling off?"

Bob shrugged and pointed at Jay.

"He's my friend, man. I jumped."

I sighed, shoulders sagging.

"And how did you get *here*?" I waved around us. "Because honest to God, guys, I don't even know where *here* is."

"Oh, that Resscharr priest dude brought us," he explained, waving back in the direction of the tunnel. "After we fell off the ship, we ran in here, obviously, because there was nowhere else to go. That priest dude caught us wandering around and sent us in here, said this was where you would be."

"Wow, Gandish really is desperate." I frowned, slugging my brain into motion. "Here's what I need you guys to do..."

———

Lilandreth jerked against the restraints holding her to the gurney and I flinched in sympathy, a muscle twitching in my cheek. It took everything I had not to jump the gun and go in shooting right then, but Jay and Bob weren't in place yet.

I wanted to curse them for that, blame them for being too slow, but that wasn't fair. It took a long time to get back through that tunnel, I knew that from experience, and they didn't have a guide to help them through. But if there was any way that my urgent and angry energy could make them go faster, well... I was pushing my thoughts through space and pushing them both along.

Lilandreth thrashed, screamed, and that was it. I wasn't waiting a second longer. I'd already made the decision to charge in when the echoing *crack-snap-boom* of pulse carbines sounded faintly from the other side of the transparent chamber. Jay and Bob. Lightning flashed, muted and pale, filtered through whatever material the chamber walls were made out of, and two of the soldiers on the other side staggered before the others rushed forward, their own weapons discharging with a deep-throated boom.

That was my cue. I rushed forward just as the three soldiers on this side sprinted for the door to the chamber, hesitated as if they weren't sure whether they should go inside even to face the attackers, which probably meant they had strict orders not to. I wasn't about to let them.

I'd had a good ten minutes to consider where to shoot them and decided on the gap between the sloping rear face of their helmets and the collar of their chest-plates. It was a vulnerability, but a necessary one if the soldiers ever wanted to look up. I'd synched the targeting reticle from the carbine with my enhanced-vision goggles while I waited and didn't even have to raise the weapon from my hip before I fired.

No kick, of course. No solid projectile to produce recoil. But there was a vibration, the explosion of hyperexplosive cartridges inside the ignition chamber, channeling all that heat energy into the lasing rod and out the crystalline muzzle. It was durable, uncomplicated, and ideal for use in a vacuum, or in microgravity, but it frankly sucked as an infantry weapon. I found out why when the flare of the first burst nearly blacked out the polarization of my goggles.

The laser itself was invisible except where it interacted with particulates like dust, and there just wasn't much dust inside the city. But the heat from the pulses ionized a cylinder of atmosphere, creating a miniature lightning bolt between the muzzle and the poor son of a bitch octopus who I shot. The crackling tube of static electricity didn't *actually* blow his head off his body... it was the laser. But it sure as hell *looked* like it did.

The polished helmet clanged to the floor, weighed down by the head inside it, and the Nova trooper didn't so much fall as collapse in on himself, blood so dark it was nearly black splattering across the floor. The other two reacted in slow motion, as if neither of them had even considered there might be a threat from behind them, and by the time the last of them was halfway turned around, I'd already shot the second.

No decapitation this time, which was just as well, since I didn't need multiple fish heads rolling around the floor trying to trip me up, and by the time the third Nova got turned, I was less than two meters away from him, coming up inside his guard before he could swing the muzzle of his weapon around. He fired anyway, a concussive blast that hammered at my ears and sinuses, punching me in the chest. An echoing explosion battered the wall behind us with a ringing ricochet of debris.

I shut out the noise, the pain, the shock, and braced a hand against the side of the Nova weapon, shoving the muzzle of my laser under the soldier's chin. Just a tap on the trigger, as short of a burst as I could manage, then I threw myself back away from him. Not quickly enough to avoid the backwash of burning blood, and I crouched, spitting out the disgusting, congealed matter. It sucked worse for him.

My shoulder slammed into the door about the same time as the palm of my hand hit the lock plate. If the Nova had somehow secured it with a code or a biometric seal, I would have been screwed, but the door slid aside and I was inside with Lilandreth.

And all that glittering dust. *Shit.* Hadn't thought that part through.

A chill ran up my back, and I wasn't sure if it was psychosomatic or they'd kept the AC cranked up in the lab just like they did in the medical bay on the *Orion*. Or it was that shit coming in through the vent mutating me into an alien slug. Nothing to be done about it now.

Lilandreth's eyes were wide and feverish, staring through me without seeing me.

"Can you hear me?" I asked, checking the restraint straps holding her to the table. "Lilandreth?"

It took a few seconds for me to find the release for the straps, and when I did, I immediately regretted it. Lilandreth thrashed and struck out blindly, and I had to grab her arms and push them down before she connected with one of the wild swings.

"Come on!" I urged, pulling her up to a sitting position, pinning her arms to her side with a hell of a lot of effort. "Snap out of it! It's me, Cam!"

That seemed to calm her down and she relaxed, eyes finally focusing on me.

"Cam?"

I sighed, letting loose of her arms, though I was still ready to duck if she attacked again.

"Let's go," I said, guiding her off the table. She stood, unsteady, supporting herself against my shoulder, and I slipped my left arm around her waist, the right pushing the carbine out ahead of me. "Jay and Bob are drawing them off, but we don't have a lot of time here."

Well, Jay and Bob probably didn't have a lot of time. I had my doubts that they could do anything in a firefight other than surrender or die, but hopefully they could run faster than the Nova.

Lilandreth didn't speak, her breath still coming in short gasps as I half-carried her out the opposite doorway into the main passage. She was heavy. When I'd been in the suit I hadn't realized it, had been concentrating on watching my strength and not hurting her, but now I could barely keep her upright. She had to be nearly a hundred and fifty kilos, and maybe half that was resting on my shoulders. It was gonna be a bad situation if any of the soldiers who'd gone off to chase after Jay and Bob came back before we were out of here.

At least two of them wouldn't be doing any shooting. The two former Confederation mining techs had proven pretty good at backshooting from ambush, which might not have been the kind of reputation either of them had wanted, but it had served us all well this go-around. I assumed they were both dead anyway. Their eyes looked dead, though since they were octopus-people, they might have looked that way all the time. I was tempted to salvage the Nova weapons, but the things weren't built for human hands, or even *humanoid* ones, and I wasn't about to split my concentration enough to figure out how to fire them.

I did pause long enough to put a burst of laser pulses into each of the weapons, not wanting any enemy to come up behind me using a gun I'd left functional. Sparks flew up and pieces melted off, and I jerked away from the spray of molten metal and hoped that would be enough to disable the guns. I'd turned from the dead soldiers back to the passage before I saw the two unarmored Nova who I'd noticed before.

They were cowering in a corner, as if they'd hoped I wouldn't be able to see them, and I pushed free of Lilandreth, aiming the carbine at a point between them. They weren't carrying any obvious weapons, but that didn't mean anything.

"Please, don't shoot!" one of them pleaded in the Resscharr language. "We weren't going to hurt her!"

"Then what the hell *were* you doing to her?" I growled, finger tightening on the trigger.

"We were exposing her to the Transformation Virus," the

other one said. Somehow, despite the fact that they were both hairless, rubber-skinned cephalopod people, I had the sense that this guy was the older of the two. "We're scientists... we've been studying the daemon ever since we found the first records. That's how we knew this lab was here."

"What's the Transformation Virus?" I demanded, losing patience. "Unless one of you starts speaking plain and short right now, you're both going to be doing some transforming yourself. As in transforming from a live asshole to a dead one."

I hadn't met very many Nova, and when I had it had been under very formal and controlled conditions. I'd gotten the impression they were cold and unemotional, devoid of fear or compassion or anything between. Apparently, that was only the case for their high-ranking military officers, certainly not for their scientists, because these guys were scared shitless and it showed.

"It's something that was left over from the war with the Skrela," the older one said quickly, worm-fingered hands raised as if he thought they could block the laser. "A weapon."

"And how the hell do *you* know about it?"

"We were part of the war." He waved at his companion and I wished he wouldn't have, because the sinuous motion of those boneless fingers contrasted with the strange combination of tentacle and skeleton in the arms threatened to make me physically ill. "We were the Unquestioning, the servants of the Reconstructors... they created us to do their bidding, to build their cities and guard their gateways. Then they left us behind once they were done with us." The tone of the translation turned bitter, and I don't know how the algorithm parsed the emotion, but it seemed accurate. "They built a paradise for themselves, and we couldn't be part of it because we were beneath them."

Sighing, I pressed the focusing crystal of the laser against the Nova scientist's chest.

"The point. Get to it."

"The Reconstructors were terrified that the Skrela would follow them here," he said, speaking so quickly the translator could barely keep up. "They found a way to tap into Transition Space without machinery, without a drive field, without a captive singularity... just by using their brains."

"What?" I snapped, nearly pulling the trigger at the very inanity of the statement. "That's fucking ridiculous."

"They did it, somehow," he insisted, arms waggling even more violently. "They used a nanovirus to alter the brains of the daemons, to grow a nexus there that could access Transition Space, funnel mental energy through that dimension, and bring it back to this reality as *physical,* kinetic energy. They planned to use the daemons to fight the Skrela if they came... but the Skrela never came. And the daemons..."

"Destroyed everything," the other Nova finished. "They went to war with each other. Each was hungry for power and couldn't abide any other daemon existing. They brought all of this down to ruin, and all that was left were the primitives of the Remainder."

The bottom fell out of my stomach. If he was telling the truth, that would mean this whole journey had been wasted, that there were no more Reconstructors to help us get home. I wanted to smash the Nova scientist in the face, then on a more rational level, wanted to demand if he knew about the North-west Passage, but neither would help me right now. There was one more thing I needed to know.

"If the daemons destroyed all this, why the hell were you trying to turn *her* into one?" I indicated Lilandreth with a backward wave of my hand.

The two scientists looked at each other as if they felt guilty or embarrassed.

"It wasn't our idea," the younger one said. "We're exiles from the Nova government... they consider us to be heretics, you see. They worship the Reconstructors and consider it blasphemy for any of us to trespass in their space... and when our people originally discovered that the Reconstructors were gone, their empire fallen, they blamed us, forced us out of our homes into this wasteland where we're forced to scavenge whatever we can from the ruins simply to survive..."

He was droning on again, but I didn't need him to finish. The meaning was clear and I closed my mouth, unaware it had dropped open.

"You meant to use her as a weapon," I said, "against the Nova Empire." I was about to ask another question, but the answer came to me from what Gandish had said. "And you couldn't use any of the Remainder because the virus wouldn't work on them... it would just kill them."

"The daemons wiped out any other Reconstructors who had the genetic markers that would allow them to be transformed," the older one agreed, sounding relieved that I'd figured it out. "When our commander heard that she was one of the original blood..." the arms sagged and the scientist stared at the floor. "He didn't ask us if the plan was a good one, he simply ordered us to implement it."

I was ready to leave them there, convinced they were no immediate threat, but the decision was taken out of my hands. I hadn't been watching Lilandreth, sure she was helpless and could barely walk without my help. She proved to be less helpless than I'd thought. I caught a glimpse of her out of the corner of my eye, her long-fingered hands wrapped around the odd, alien grip of one of the Nova rifles. I opened my mouth to ask her what she was doing, but her actions answered me.

I still wasn't sure where the trigger was on the weapon, but Lilandreth knew. She pulled it. The younger Nova scientist was farthest away, so when his torso exploded it showered the older one with blood rather than me, gave me a half-second to stumble backward out of the line of fire. A wordless yell escaped my lips, because that was the most coherent response I could come up with. Lilandreth shifted to the right before my butt hit the floor and fired again.

This time, I was aware enough to observe what the gun did. I didn't think it was a laser, but I couldn't tell if it fired an energy beam or a projectile. All I knew was that it blew the older Nova in half. I stared at Lilandreth wide-eyed, sure she was about to aim the gun at me, but she let it fall to her side.

"We couldn't trust them if we left them behind us," she declared, then her long, striated face clouded over. "And they treated me like an animal. They deserved to die."

I didn't respond, just slowly clambered to my feet, trying not to step in the pooling blood of the Nova scientists.

"It's not safe here," she said, loping down the corridor, suddenly able to walk with no trouble at all.

I followed in silent agreement. It certainly didn't *feel* safe.

[11]

"Do you feel any different?" I asked again. It was probably the third time in the last ten minutes, and I should have felt embarrassed about the repetition, but concern overwhelmed any self-consciousness.

We'd passed through the bottleneck Gandish had warned us about, though there were no Nova soldiers manning it to worry us. What did worry me was that I had no idea where we were going once we passed it. I hadn't come this way, and the dead-reckoning map from my 'link was useless. None of that seemed to bother, or even slow down, Lilandreth.

"I feel fine," she assured me, not looking back. "As far as I can tell, whatever they tried to do to me has had no ill effects."

No *ill* effects, she said, but that wasn't the same thing as no effects. Something about her was different, and it had taken me a few minutes walking behind her before I'd realized what it was. The burns on her neck and face were gone. It might have been that treatment they'd given her. They'd called it a nanovirus, or that was what the translator had said, and I knew nanites were used in the biotic fluid of an autodoc. Maybe the glitter dust shit had healed her wounds as well as... whatever the hell else it had done to her.

Maybe the treatment had given her a better sense of direction than me.

"Gandish said that anyone the virus didn't change, it killed," I reminded her.

"I doubt he qualifies as an expert," she said, waving a dismissive gesture. "His people exist in mythic time and think of the Reconstructors as gods."

Not an unreasonable assertion... except that she hadn't had the chance to talk to Gandish and I had told her very little about him. I was being paranoid. I was *sure* was being paranoid, that all we had to go on was what Gandish and the Nova scientists had told us, and none of those people had ever seen any of it with their own eyes, hadn't even read about it. It was as much legend to the Nova exiles as it was to Gandish. It was just as likely that the glitter dust was harmless, maybe a medical treatment at most.

Yeah. That was it. But my imagination couldn't help recalling the bodies ripped to pieces and that damned statue...

I was so preoccupied with watching our back trail and thinking about how badly things could turn out that I nearly ran right into Lilandreth's back when she stopped abruptly.

"Don't move!"

I knew the voice was a Nova before the translation. There was no mistaking the gurgling, inhuman grunts. There was also no mistaking the one who'd spoken. It was the same officer who I'd spoken to in front of the city walls, I could tell by the curious markings on his harness... and his general imperious attitude.

He stood to the side while four of his soldiers held guns to the heads of Jay and Bob. The two of them looked the worse for wear, burn marks on their armor and half of Bob's hair seared away, blood leaking from a nasty cut on Jay's head and his eyes slightly out of focus. Their guns were gone, and I didn't have to try too hard to figure out how they'd wound up being captured.

"Are you guys okay?" I asked them.

"Oh, you know, man," Jay said, his voice sounding as loopy as his eyes looked. "We've been better."

"Shut up!" the commander snapped, and one of the soldiers nudged Jay's shoulder with the muzzle of his rifle.

"Drop your weapons," the Nova officer went on, gesturing with something that must have been a gun, though I wouldn't have been able to identify it without context. "We've kept your friends alive out of respect for you, daemon, but if you don't submit to us, we'll kill them."

That wasn't an option. I tapped a control on my 'link, turning off the translation circuit. I just hoped that Jay and Bob had been paying attention to their English lessons.

"Guys," I said, "don't reply, but when I move, both of you drop flat."

"What are you saying?" the commander snapped, and I turned the translator back on.

"A prayer," I lied.

Then I dove to the left, hitting on my shoulder, bringing up the muzzle of my carbine even as I rolled into a crouch. I took the one on the far right first, the one who had his rifle in Bob's face. I couldn't be as exact as I'd been when I ambushed the guards on the other side of the chamber, and laser pulses sparked off the soldier's helmet on the way down to his exposed lower face.

The Nova trooper toppled backward and I tried to swing the muzzle to the left to get the next one, but Jay and Bob were too damned slow and weren't going to get out of the way in time.

Then they *were* out of the way. It was as if a giant hand had slammed both of them flat to the ground, just a fraction of a second ahead of a blast from a Nova rifle that concussed the air where Jay's head had been half a heartbeat before. The firing arc was clear and I didn't think about it, just jammed the trigger back and swept the pulse weapon from side to side, riding the lightning through two more of the Nova soldiers.

I would have been too late for the last of them, but Lilandreth was still there, even if I hadn't thought about her in the heat of the moment. The blast from her stolen weapon blew a hole through the last soldier the size of a basketball. I scanned back and forth, hunting for the officer, but he was gone, disappearing round a corner the second the shooting had started.

"Oh, dude," Jay moaned, picking himself up off the floor, hand clutching at his chest. "You didn't have to push me down so hard... I was *gonna* move."

"Push *you* down?" Bob repeated, grimacing at his friend. "You pushed *me* down!"

"Oh, for God's sake," I sighed, grabbing Bob by an arm and pulling him to his feet. "We don't have time for this. You guys know which way to go to get out of here?"

"I do," Lilandreth said flatly, striding past the bodies of the Nova soldiers as if they weren't there.

"And how the hell do *you* know?" I muttered, though I wasn't really looking for an answer. "Where are your weapons?" I asked Jay and Bob.

"Somewhere back that way," Jay guessed, waving in a 180-degree arc back the way we'd come. "I think. They hit us pretty hard and dragged us over here to try to get you guys."

"Just get behind me." It was just as well that they didn't have their guns, because I wouldn't have wanted their pulse carbines sweeping my back every few seconds. I'd been spoiled having trained Marines to back me up for my whole career.

Lilandreth wasn't waiting for us, and I had to jog to keep up with her long-legged pace, which made it harder to watch for threats. Not that I expected them. If the Nova commander had any more dismounts to devote to the operation of getting Lilandreth... *transformed*, I suppose... then they would have been in place guarding her when I'd found her. The Nova didn't seem to put a lot of stock in unarmored infantry and there wasn't room inside here for their mecha, despite the open-concept nightmare of the Resscharr cities.

Lilandreth slowed her pace and I thought at first that it was because she'd been overconfident, that she was just as lost as I was. Until she stopped completely, leaning against one of the partial walls, head sagging as her shoulders heaved.

"What's wrong?" I asked, coming up beside her and offering a hand to steady her. It likely wasn't necessary given that she could rock back on those backward-bending legs like a kangaroo at rest, but the gesture was instinctive.

"Nothing. I am fatigued by the battle and... I believe the nanites have sapped my blood sugar to repair the damage from the burns."

That was plausible. I wasn't a doctor or any sort of expert in nanotechnology, but I did know that the things took energy out of the host's system to repair damage. It wasn't an issue when someone was in an autodoc because the machine replaced the nourishment, but the ones in a smart bandage could drain you. The two I'd put on were making me a little gassed even now, but I hadn't been hurt that bad.

I was prepared to accept that until she screamed and collapsed in a heap on the floor.

———

"What's wrong with her?" Jay grunted, his legs wobbling under the load of half of Lilandreth's weight. Bob grunted agreement, not even trying to talk, sweat beading on his forehead. I was ahead of all three of them, scanning back and forth, the muzzle of my carbine following my eyes.

"The Nova who got exiled out here from their empire," I explained absently, not thinking about how the answer would sound to them, "exposed her to some nanovirus that's supposed to change her into a power-hungry psychic psychopath so they could use her to get even with the ones who kicked them out."

"Hey man," Jay said, scowling at me, "if you don't want to tell us, just say you don't know. There's, like, no need to be rude." He paused, then looked up again. "This *is* the right way out of here, isn't it?"

"I don't know," I told him, not without malice.

The truth was, I had a pretty good idea. I *thought* we were back on the other side of the tunnel entrance, though admittedly that was based on the side tunnels and the shadowy entrances deep within them. I assumed they were the *same* side tunnels, which might not have been a safe assumption, given how brain-twisting the interior architecture was here.

I wasn't certain until we walked up on the statue.

"I hate that damned thing," Bob said. His voice as worn down and exhausted as Jay's, but he still managed to inject it with feeling as he glared at the statue. "Creepy as shit."

Creepier for me, now that I knew what it signified, but I said nothing.

"We're close now," I warned them. "The officer got away, and I'd have to bet he's waiting for us at the entrance with at least a few soldiers with guns... if not mecha."

"And what do you plan to do about that?" Jay wondered.

"They're not going to shoot at Lilandreth," I reasoned. "They need her." I motioned at the statue. "Lean her against that thing."

Using the base of the sculpture as a chair robbed it of some of its mystery, though Lilandreth's condition belied the feeling of normalcy. Her eyes were half open, her breathing settled into something normal now, but she showed no indication she was aware of her surroundings.

I tapped a finger against her cheek.

"Can you hear me?" Adding more fingers, I slapped her lightly and she jerked at the contact. "Lilandreth?"

She responded to the attempt at communication by hunching over and throwing up on the floor. I cursed and jumped back, the black, gelatinous ichor splashing nearly to my shoes. I thought I was going to have to lunge back in and keep her from collapsing into the pool of vomit, but she caught herself on the leg of the stylized, larger-than-life Resscharr and stayed upright.

"I was wrong, Cameron Alvarez," she confessed, her face pale and drawn. "I am *not* simply fatigued. Something is still... active within me. I feel things changing."

"Is there anything we can do?" I asked her.

"I need to get back to the ship. The medical bay there may be able to help me."

"Okay, can you walk? Because I need you to go first. The Nova are probably waiting for us, and they want you alive. You in the lead gives us a couple extra seconds to react."

I felt awfully cold-blooded asking her to do that, putting her life in jeopardy to save ours, particularly when she'd already put herself in harm's way for me. She nodded unhesitating though.

"Okay." I turned to Jay and Bob. "Get her up and stay with her. Wait here until I come back."

"Come back?" Jay repeated. "Come back from where?"

"You think I came in here like this?" I asked him, motioning to my fatigues. "I have to go find my suit." Beat up as it was. "And hope it's enough to get us out of here."

[12]

I'd grown to hate the colors yellow and red. Every time I saw them, it meant that *something* was fucked up. There was way too much yellow and red in my HUD when I started up the Vigilante. The gun worked though, and so did the arms and legs... but the jets. The jets flickered from red to yellow, back to red, the readout beside the display explaining that there was a partial obstruction and the system couldn't allow me to use the jets safely.

Annoying. Luckily, I'd been riding this suit a long time and one of the first things I'd figured out was how to override the safeties. Of course, I might blow myself up, but that was the kind of thing I'd gotten used to risking. The suit's shoulders scraped against the walls on the way out, so narrow was the storage closet, and the teeth-rattling shriek nearly drowned out the staticky thread coming over the comms.

I stopped, listened intently. It was barely audible through the interference of the building, but it was there. It was Vicky.

"Cam..." I could make out my name and not much else for several seconds. "... if you're down there still, we're coming." More static. "... thirty seconds. Be ready..."

Thirty seconds?

"Shit."

I leaned forward and dug my spikes in, gouging the floor and ignoring the scrape of metal shoulder pauldrons against the wall. Five more seconds of it and I was out, bursting free of the storage closet.

The three of them waited for me in the corridor, Jay's eyes lighting up at the sight of the Vigilante like a kid at Christmas. Lilandreth eyed the machine—and me in it—with what might have been doubt, probably thinking of how she'd had to use her defense shield to keep me from being burned to a crisp, undoubtedly wondering how this time would be any different.

"They're coming!" I said, bellowing the announcement over the PA speakers. "The drop-ship is coming in about fifteen seconds and we need to be outside!"

Jay's eyes went from delight to alarm in the space of a second and he clutched my pulse carbine to his chest like a security blanket. I'd passed it off to him, reasoning that I'd be safe inside my armor and he'd probably have a much higher chance of shooting the enemy rather than one of the remaining two of us.

Lilandreth knew what to do even if Jay didn't, and she ran for the light. It was gentler, softer than the harsh glare when we'd entered, well into late afternoon or early evening, but it still stood out in contrast to the diffuse glow coming out of the walls. It was a flare, leading us through the grain storage and processing rooms and out to the yawning openings of the external walls.

I hung back from her a couple dozen meters and wasn't surprised when she was immediately surrounded by Nova mecha. Four of them loomed over her, waddling into position in a semicircle twenty meters away, their plasma guns leveled menacingly. And there was the commander, still farther away, though his voice boomed over what I guessed was some kind of PA system.

"Do not resist us!" he ordered. "We don't wish to hurt you, but you'll either surrender to us or be subdued by force."

"Don't forget option number three," I muttered. Then I hit the jets.

This was that part where I had a good chance of blowing up. It would be quick, at least, which was as much as I could ask for after all these years of putting my ass on the line. The warning system screamed at me, called me a reckless idiot, but it couldn't stop me. If Vicky couldn't, nothing else had a chance.

There might have been an unusual vibration, might have been a strange sound when the jets ignited, but they didn't explode. I'd angled forward before I kicked the controls, and when the jets ignited the suit flew at a slight upward angle, straight through the opening in the wall. The ruddy light of the evening cast everything in a new shade, the silver-gray armor on the mecha glinting red-gold just before I slammed shoulder-first into the cockpit of the closest of them.

I'd taken the precaution of putting in my mouthpiece and it was a damned good thing, because as hard as I bit down on it, every tooth in my mouth would have shattered at the impact. The mecha was a hell of a lot heavier than my Vigilante, but it was also balanced precariously on long legs, and every kilogram of my suit was traveling at nearly fifty klicks an hour when I hit it. It toppled backward, and I would have gone with it if instincts hadn't taken over from my bruised brain and kicked away.

I was cognizant enough to fire off a long blast in the same direction as the jumpjets, the actinic spear of energy piercing through the cockpit just in case the body check hadn't been enough to finish the pilot. He'd been in the center of the formation, and by the time I'd jetted away from the ruin of his mecha, the other machines had already turned their guns on me.

A better-disciplined bunch, an army with training fighting an *actual* enemy with equivalent weapons technology, would have held their fire, would have spread out to improve the angles and avoid blue-on-blue casualties. This bunch hadn't fought anyone except degenerate Resscharr using sticks and stones, and even if we'd been up against the Nova Empire we'd faced in the Confederation, they'd done nothing but beat up on a lower-tech foe.

The other three mecha shot right through where I'd been, and two of them managed to blast the third right through the torso. If anyone had asked me how I knew what was happening when the world around me was a kaleidoscope and everything happened in slices only milliseconds long, I couldn't have told them. I might have said experience just to try to give them an answer, but that would have been a lie. I'd been able to do it since the first time I'd climbed into a suit.

Anyone could learn how to operate a Vigilante, but very few had the ability to turn the firehose gush of information that washed over the operator from the HUD into something useful, something three-dimensional that made sense to a human's instinctive lizard brain. Those were the *real* Drop Troopers, Marines like Top and the Skipper, like Vicky and me.

For me, it wasn't like seeing the readout in the HUD and reasoning through what it meant. I didn't see that readout at all. I just *knew*. I *knew* the mecha that had been to my right when I came out of the building had been hit by both of the other Nova, knew the hits were fatal, that they'd put him out of the fight. I knew that I had to jet into the two on the left, that I had to get between them because by now, they'd have realized they'd killed their own guy. They'd be slower to fire, I was sure of it, despite the fact that they weren't human.

They were. It was a matter of a second, but I'd already lined up my gun before jetting away from the first mecha, and all I had to do was pull the trigger. The mecha didn't fall this time. He'd been standing upright, and when the energy beam ripped through his cockpit he froze in place, another statue, this one commemorating the vanquished rather than the victor.

One left, and this one was panicking, trying to get distance, firing blindly, doing all that at once and not caring that meant he couldn't do any of it well. Plasma fanned out, a light show in the quickly darkening sky, none of it coming closer than ten meters from me, though that was still close enough to raise the suit's internal temperature a few degrees.

He'd made it twenty meters before I managed to target his right hip. The joint came apart under the azure lance and the Nova mecha stumbled, plowed into the dirt under the acrid, black cover of the smoke pouring off the armor. The pilot tried to rise, but I blasted the shoulder on the same side and he collapsed again.

I'd been aware of what was happening around me in a vague, dreamlike sense of understanding, but I'd been laser-focused on killing my immediate enemy, and it wasn't until the last of the four mecha was disabled that I let the details come into sharp relief.

The drop-ship described a wide arc only fifty meters off the ground, pumping coilgun rounds into the mass of Nova mecha pouring out of their landers in reaction to the new incursion. Another sign of amateurs. If it had been my Marines, they would have been out patrolling the entire time, knowing that just because an enemy had performed a tactical withdrawal didn't mean they'd retreated.

That didn't mean we were going to beat them with just the drop-ship though. The Nova landers weren't just spewing out mecha, they were launching fighters. Not space-fighters, not even dual-environment from their design, basically just hoppers carrying armor and plasma cannons, but there were a couple dozen of them, and quantity had a quality all its own.

They were, I realized with a devastating sense of hopelessness, going to reach the drop-ship before it could land. Watson had seen them, had shifted fire to try to take them down, but there were too many. Their plasma cannons might not have had the range of the coilguns but they spoke with an unmistakable authority, and in their wake, the drop-ship shuddered and banked.

Vicky was smarter than I was though, or perhaps she'd just had longer to think about the problem. We didn't have fighters or hoppers on board the drop-ship, but we *did* have a platoon of Drop Troopers, all of them with the Resscharr-enhanced weapons and jumpjets that could stay aloft for an almost unlimited time.

Vigilantes swarmed away from the drop-ship like flies off a carcass, each of them riding a firefly glow. They lacked the aerodynamics of the Nova fighter but their flight paths were more unpredictable, bobbing and weaving like a fighter in the ring. And the energy guns had just as much range as the coilguns. Blue streaks connected the suits with the fighters for a fraction of a second before the disc-shaped craft expanded into spheres of white.

I dared to look away from the light show projected over the evening sky, checking on the others. The mecha had spewed plasma everywhere in their last, wild spasms, and even though I hadn't noticed any of the blasts heading back toward the city, that didn't mean it hadn't happened.

Bob was sitting flat on his ass, a look of utter shock flattening out his broad face, smoke curling off his armor and what remained of his hair, but otherwise looked unharmed. Jay knelt down on a knee, breathing heavy, still clutching the pulse carbine as if he knew he'd screwed up by losing the last one and wasn't about to repeat the mistake. He seemed less the worse for wear than Bob, though still stunned by the battle between the mecha and my battlesuit.

Lilandreth, though, had collapsed again. Her body shook like she was freezing and foam flecked off her lips, and I cursed, knowing I couldn't get out of my suit to check on her, not with the enemy on their way.

"Bob!" I said, and his head snapped up at the blaring from the external speakers. "Go see if Lilandreth is okay!"

She *wasn't* okay, that much was clear, but I didn't want to get into a philosophical debate with him, just have him make sure she wasn't dying. Bob nodded and pushed to his feet, scrabbling across the dirt toward the supine Lilandreth. He wasn't the only one.

I'd known the Nova commander was there when the battle had commenced, but given his quick exit during the fight inside the city, I'd figured he'd hotfooted it out once the shooting had started. I guess I'd underestimated his desire to be the one to retake the empire, because he rushed at Lilandreth from behind the smoking remnants of one of his mecha, his handgun raised, pointed at Bob.

There was no way I could get to him before he fired. Even if my energy cannon had been pointed the right direction, the heat and concussion would have killed Bob and Jay just as surely as whatever the Nova officer was carrying in his hand. I was a few milligrams of pressure from hitting the jets and trying to take him out bodily when a long burst of laser pulses sliced through the Nova commander, chunks of blubber blowing out of his torso, spinning him around.

The Nova officer fell to his knees, the expression on that inhuman face unreadable. If I had to guess, I would have bet that his last words were something along the lines of *this can't happen to me.* Behind the Nova, Jay let my pulse carbine fall away from his shoulder, his face gone pale.

"Good job, Jay," I told him, trying not to show the relief I was feeling that he'd actually figured out how to use the weapon. "Reload and take up a guard position."

And if there were any other dismounts around, he'd have to take care of them, because I had to turn my attention to the battle going on in the air above us. The Nova fighters were engaged with *my* Marines, and I had to help take them down. As long as my jumpjets didn't explode...

I took to the air.

The Vigilantes were holding their own, too agile and maneuverable for the Nova aircraft to get a lock on them, dancing around the plasma bursts and taking down one of the flying discs every few seconds. But a squadron of the enemy fighters had flanked around the right side of the platoon, heading our way. Probably called in by the late Nova commander, meant to take out me.

I was going to return the favor. I'd rather have drawn them away from the others, taken the fight over the expansive city, but I couldn't risk losing sight of the others, not when my comms were down. So I roared straight up into the center of the formation, using the same tactics against their aircraft that I had against the mecha.

And with the same results at first. I announced my presence to the flying discs by blasting a stream of energy through the central aircraft of the four, the lightning burst cutting through the turbofans in its belly and out the upper fuselage in a spray of flame and smoke. The disc wobbled and faltered, tumbling out of the sky, and the others veered wildly, trying to bring their weapons to bear on my suit.

Up close, it was obvious these things didn't just *look* like hoppers—they *were* hoppers, or at least the Nova version of them. Ducted-fan helicopters beneath light armor, no weapons other than the plasma cannon, a utilitarian aircraft probably a lot more effective against lightly armed locals. Not that I was sneezing at them or anything, not when a ball of crackling-hot ionized gas rippled through the air only a dozen meters away. It didn't hit me, not when my Vigilante was swaying like a plumb bob, but it nearly took out one of their own people.

Flying in the suit still felt unnatural to me. I'd spent the formative years of my military career thinking of the jumpjets much the way the 20th-century paratroopers I'd read about had thought about their parachutes, as a delivery vehicle to get us to the ground. Maybe use them to hop out of harm's way in a pinch, but not to turn the Vigilante into an airmobile weapon. With the Resscharr enhancements, though, we would stay up long enough to make that transition, at least with the two platoons of the converted suits we had left. That didn't mean I didn't still think of my Vigilante as a melee weapon.

Leaning forward, I gave the jets a full-power blast and plowed into the cockpit of the closest fighter. It hurt a lot less than hitting the mecha. Those things had thick armor, but the fighters had to worry about load capacity and aerodynamics, and the thin metal over the canopy crumpled like cardboard on impact.

The Nova pilot thrashed and flailed, half falling out of his cockpit, whatever expression might have been on his alien face invisible beneath the mirrored visor of his helmet. And then nonexistent after I smashed my clawed left hand through his head.

At that point I'd worn out my welcome, straining the unwillingness of the Nova to fire on their own planes to the breaking point. I jetted away from the dead pilot and the out-of-control disc just ahead of a wash of plasma, close enough that the turbulence from the superheated swathe of air nearly sent me tumbling right out of the sky.

An instant of panic, out of balance and out of control, before I fed full power to the jets and stabilized about two hundred meters off the ground. I'd picked a bad place to stabilize because one of the two remaining fighters had spun around, about to bring me under its gun, and I didn't have time to maneuver out of the way...

A Vigilante battlesuit dropped out of the air just above the disc and slammed into the cockpit feet-first. The fighter wobbled at the extra weight but might still have stayed in the air if the Drop Trooper hadn't ripped the pilot right out of the cockpit and tossed him into a pinwheel tumble to the ground a hundred meters below.

"Dammit, Cam!" Vicky snapped, her voice crystal clear now that we were close. "Do you constantly have to keep getting yourself into these situations?"

I didn't answer immediately, instead targeting the last of the fighters. It had spun on its axis and tried to run, but it couldn't run faster than the Resscharr energy beam I played across it from top to bottom. And with that, the air battle was over. A quick scan around us showed that every single one of the fighters had been shot down or had retreated back to the landers, and the Marines were touching down all around Lilandreth and the others.

And so was the drop-ship. The coilgun turrets still laid down a hail of fire at the approaching mecha, and this time it was working. The armored column hesitated, recoiled from the fusillade of tungsten slugs, buying us time. Maybe enough time to get the hell out of here.

I touched down beside Lilandreth. Bob was still tending to her but she looked better, conscious and sitting up, though there was something strange in her expression, not pain or confusion but... maybe a sense of being overwhelmed. Bob and Jay covered their eyes to protect themselves from the onslaught of dust as the drop-ship landed, but Lilandreth didn't even try. I put myself between her and the windstorm, hunching over and cracking my chest plastron.

"Are you okay?" I asked, reaching out to touch her arm. Her eyes flashed at me, as if she thought the touch a violation. She settled down, and the overwhelmed look faded into something more coherent.

"Get me back to the ship," she said curtly, using the arm of my suit to pull herself up.

"Everyone on board!" Vicky ordered, tromping up beside us. "We've got about two minutes to clear this LZ if we're going to meet the *Orion* in orbit!"

"What happens in two minutes?" Jay asked her, his hands shaking so bad he had to sling the carbine over his shoulder.

I couldn't see Vicky's face, but I intuited the annoyed look on her face.

"Well, what the hell do you think, boy? We all get our asses incinerated! Get in the fucking ship!"

[13]

Watson raised an eyebrow as I clambered into the drop-ship's cockpit and strapped into one of the spare acceleration couches.

"Didn't expect to see you out of your gorilla suit and up here with us Fleet types."

I was about to say something snarky in return, but Watson chose that moment—probably on purpose—to yank back on the throttle. The belly jets pushed me into the seat and I gritted my teeth against the pressure on my spine as the entire, huge ship shuddered under the sudden boost. The city dropped below us on the cockpit's main screen, though I could still have followed it in one of the side viewers. Stray blasts of plasma followed us upward but nothing came close, the guns on the mecha lacking the range to reach us.

"Keep pouring it on, Chief," Watson urged, none of the strain from the upward boost showing in his voice. "Don't let anyone down there have the breathing space to come up with any bright ideas."

"Yeah, I got ya, sir," the boat's crew chief murmured, not looking away from the coilgun turret controls at his station.

The vibration from the upward boost and then the forward

thrust added to it a moment later drowned out the stutter of the coilguns, but the tactical system's animation on the chief's screen provided a dotted red line connecting the drop-ship to the Nova landing site still dropping away from us.

"We ain't got much ammo left in the turrets," Chief Sackett warned. "Gonna be out of effective range in a couple seconds anyway."

"Okay, break it off," Watson said. He shifted the controls again, performing some arcane gesticulation to the gods of flight, and the pressure shifted from the bottom of my seat to the back as we angled up out of the atmosphere.

"My suit's comms are fucked, Jim," I told Watson. "I'd have been sitting in the back, stuck in the dark, and I wouldn't have been able to look over your shoulder or kibbutz. Where's the fun in that?"

"Yeah, I can see where that would kill you, Alvarez." He turned in his seat and tilted an eyebrow. "Tell me, was this all worth it?"

And with that question the light-hearted banter crashed and burned, and I thought again about the two casualties. I didn't even know their names yet.

"We came for answers," I told him, unable to keep the glum note out of my voice. "We got them. I don't think they're the ones we were all hoping for." I waved it off. "Do we have a reading on the *Orion*? Or the Intercepts?"

"Yeah, we had to coordinate this whole thing pretty damned close," Watson told me, pointing at the sensor readout.

The icon representing the *Orion* was obvious, the shape drawn from the computer file on the Intelligence vessel, and there was nothing I'd seen that was exactly like her. She was heading toward the planet, toward *us*, though I couldn't make out the distance. Farther out, the Intercepts popped in and out of Transition Space, flares of white demonstrating the discharge of their proton cannons as they fired on the Nova ships. It was impressive to watch, but there were at least a dozen of the enemy warships and they were accelerating toward us at an inexorable pace... fast enough that they'd be here before the *Orion* could get to minimum safe Transition distance, I was sure.

"The Intercepts are running interference for us, but that won't last long," Watson went on. "They're trying to give Captain Nance enough time to pick us up."

"Where's my ship?"

I twisted around at the demanding tone and blinked at the sight of Lilandreth hauling herself into the cockpit, Vicky at her heels and out of her Vigilante.

"She insisted on coming up here," Vicky said, hands spread helplessly. "Said I could either let her go or shoot her." She frowned, grabbing at the back of an acceleration couch and pulling herself into it. "You *didn't* want me to shoot her, right?"

"The Predecessor ship is around the other side of the planet," Watson told Lilandreth, eyeing her curiously, though he seemed to ignore the interplay between Vicky and me. "Right where we left her in high orbit."

Lilandreth didn't sit down—she *couldn't*, up here in the cockpit, where all the seats were arranged for humans—but she crouched down and squeezed between seats, slipping her arms through the harness of one of them.

"Take me to my ship," she said, making it sound not just like an order from a superior officer but more like the command of a regent to her underlings. "Now."

"We don't have time for that," Vicky insisted. "The *Orion* is going to rendezvous with us just as soon as we hit orbit. The plan is, we get on board, Transition out, then transfer you to one of the Intercepts and have them take you back to the ship. We're not leaving it behind, obviously—our people are on board!"

"No." Lilandreth's tone was flat, uncompromising. "I need the medical lab on my ship and I need it now." A look of frustration passed across her features, as if she knew she had to give a better reason. "And the Nova have shown the ability to operate Resscharr technology. I fear that if we give them time to reach the ship, they may be able to access it."

And that wasn't a bad point.

"What are we seeing with the Nova landers?" I asked Watson, peering at the screen, trying to figure it out on my own. I'd learned a lot about the operations of ships the last few months—*subjective* months—but it still took me a while to read sensor screens.

"They're in the air," he told me, nodding at the two red dots raising above the surface of the planet not far from the city.

"Coming after us?" I asked him, my cheek twitching at extra pressure I didn't need.

"Chief?" Watson asked Sackett.

"No, don't think so," the older man declared, shaking his head. "They gotta know we're heading straight out of orbit. Their trajectory..." the chief chewed on his lip like a student called out in front of the class. "I'm thinking they're heading for high orbit."

"Oh, damn," Vicky hissed. "They're going for the Predecessor ship."

Lilandreth was right, and that left me with one of those decisions, the kind that always made me regret taking this job.

"Change course, Jim," I ordered, hating the words as I said them but knowing in my gut it was the right thing to do. "We're heading for rendezvous with Lilandreth's ship." Watson goggled at me in disbelief. "We can't let the Nova have it."

Watson sighed, shook his head, but he shifted the steering yoke and dialed back the throttle.

"You're the boss."

"Get me the *Orion* on the comms," I added. And if anything, I hated this part even more. While the copilot pulled up the communications board, I turned to Vicky. "Who was it?" I asked her.

She didn't ask what I meant. She didn't need to, not anymore.

"Channing and Pulaski." The names came out as a sigh. I closed my eyes, setting my jaw against a jolt of pain.

Corporal Ben Channing. He should have been a sergeant by now, but then we all should have been something better, somewhere else if it wasn't for this Goddamned mission. Younger than me, he'd enlisted well after the war. The *Orion* mission had blooded him and he'd been good at his job, good in the suit. He was from Aphrodite, a third-generation colonist, but he hadn't been interested in working for his parents' shipping concern or winding up a crewman on a Corporate Council freighter. No wife, no girlfriend back home, but Top thought he was hanging out with one of the *Orion*'s crew. I'd have to find her and tell her personally.

Sgt. Pulaski was even harder to take. She'd had kids back home on Hermes. Not married to their father anymore and they stayed with him, but she talked about them a lot. I'd heard her tell Top the older boy was about to turn eighteen and she was really hoping we'd get back in time for his birthday, as unlikely as that had seemed. She held out hope. She was one of the people who'd voted to try to get back instead of staying and settling back on Yfingam or Laisvas Miestas.

"What the hell's going on, Alvarez?" Nance demanded over the cockpit speakers. Yeah, I'd expected that. "Wojtera says you're changing course. You know we're on the clock here, right?"

"The Nova are going to take the Predecessor ship," I explained. "We're going to stop them."

"How the hell do you intend to do that? With your little coilgun turrets and a couple platoons of Marines?"

"I need you to launch assault shuttles to cover us. They should be able to take out the landers and give us time to get Lilandreth on the ship and then get out of the system before the Nova fleet arrives."

A long pause, and I could almost hear the muscles in Nance's jaw clenching.

"Look, you're in charge, but this isn't a good idea. I know we have people on board, but they can just abandon ship in the lander and we can pick them up..."

"Lilandreth has been infected with something by the Nova," I interrupted him. "If we don't get her to the medical lab on board the Predecessor ship, she could die. This is my call, Captain. Launch the assault shuttles."

"Yes, *sir*." Skepticism dripped off the acknowledgement, but I knew he'd do it anyway. "I sure as hell hope you know what you're doing."

Yeah. That made two of us.

———

"How close is it gonna be?" I rasped, my mouth dry. There was water somewhere up here in the cockpit, but I didn't want to take my attention away from the screen long enough to find it. The Predecessor ship filled it, growing a soft green, not orbiting the way a normal ship would be. Instead it stayed in place, anchored by its gravity drive to a point in space... or maybe, more accurately, anchored *through* that point in space into another universe.

Watson snorted a soft laugh.

"Too damn close. We'll be getting to the Predecessor ship in two mikes. That'll give us just enough time to dock before the

Nova landers reach firing range... and still leaves us with about ten minutes before the assault shuttles arrive."

Vicky didn't say anything, but I could feel her eyes on me. She wouldn't question my orders in front of everyone, at least not when there was no chance of changing the plan, but she had as many doubts as the rest of them. I turned back to Lilandreth. She was lolling again, her chin down against her chest under the pressure of our deceleration.

"Can you extend the ship's defense shield over us once we dock?" I asked. I wondered if she was coherent enough to understand what I was saying, but then she nodded.

"Once I reach the bridge," she told me. "But the shields... they've been weakened. The same damage that took out the weapons. They won't be able to take much before they overload."

"Oh, everyone's just full of good news today," I sighed. "Can you get us out of orbit with the drop-ship docked?"

The idea had just come to me and I'd already built a plan around it. Use the Predecessor ship to take both of us out of orbit faster than the Nova landers could follow, go meet the assault shuttles en route. Either the enemy landers would break off or the assault birds could blow the shit out of them. The entire plan vanished in a puff of reality with her answer.

"Unfortunately, no. If the ship were fully functional..."

"Yeah, yeah," I grumbled, waving it away. "Then the shields will just have to hold up the ten minutes. Let's hope the Nova want the ship intact in that case."

"What about the platoon?" Vicky wondered. "If they try to board, we could hold them off."

Not a bad plan... but another thought struck me and I grinned.

"Lilandreth, are the shields one-way?"

She frowned at me, her confusion piercing the discomfort she was obviously still feeling.

"I don't understand."

"I know it absorbs fire from the outside," I clarified. "But can you shoot *through* it?"

"It's possible. I'd have to adjust the frequencies, but if I can stay conscious long enough..."

"What do you have in mind?" Vicky wanted to know.

I shot her a grin.

"You know how you always complain about me going off without you and taking stupid chances?"

"Yeah?" She drew the word out into four syllables, eyes narrowing.

"Good news," I assured her. "It's your turn."

"I'd be pissed at you," Vicky advised over my 'link's earbud, "if I didn't know very well you'd be out here yourself if your suit comms weren't broken."

"You know me so well," I agreed, gasping the words out as I helped support Lilandreth. "Just don't fall off."

"What the hell's going on?" Lt. Gunderson asked, rushing forward to take my side of the towering Resscharr, though he left Jay carrying the rest of the load. Gunderson pointed at the holographic projection at the center of the bridge. "Why are there Marines crawling around the outside of the damned ship?"

"Get her to the control platform," I told Gunderson, waving at the command position, not so much a chair as a dais where a Resscharr could stand comfortably at the center of the bridge. "Hurry!"

I rushed ahead and waited there for them, as if there were anything useful I could do there other than stare at the images from the external cameras. As Gunderson had said, there were Marines crawling around the outside of the damned ship. It wasn't as risky as it sounded, since the Predecessor ship had its own gravity field which extended to the surface of the hull. It should keep them safely anchored to the hull even if their magnetic boots didn't hold. That was an iffy thing, because the ship's hull wasn't technically a ferrous metal. Or maybe *any* metal. Lilandreth had never been clear about that.

Vicky led the platoon out into a semicircle perimeter, spreading their firing arc as wide as she could while still maintaining overlapping fields of fire. It wasn't something we'd ever tried before, but that didn't stop her from doing it expertly.

"Do we really think we're gonna do more than scratch their paint out here?" Vicky asked. I didn't have to check my 'link to know she'd kept the question for our private connection instead of the general net.

"No idea," I admitted. "But I do know you'll be just as safe out there as we are in here. If the shields fail, we're all dead."

She sighed like a mother at a naïve comment from her young child.

"It's so cute that you think that's comforting."

"Oh, my, this doesn't look good." I looked around at Dr. Spinner shuffling onto the bridge, his eyes wide.

The little man was from the Grey, the rival government to Jay and Bob's Confederation, though for my part I couldn't tell the difference between their ethnic derivations. His clothing style had been different than theirs, but now they were all in Commonwealth utility fatigues and I couldn't even make out the distinction in their language in the split-second after they spoke, before the translation program took over.

"Dr. Spinner," I told him, "go get the medical bay ready for Lilandreth. She's been infected by a technological nanite virus that's trying to reconstruct her brain and we need to reverse it."

Spinner rocked on his heels as if I'd slapped him but nodded and turned to run back the way he'd come.

"Oh, shit, here they come!" Bob said, pointing at the display.

He'd come along, even though I hadn't asked him to since he was injured and I didn't think he could handle Lilandreth's weight, and I imagined he'd just followed because Jay was going. I had an instinct to snap at him for the breach in discipline, but the image in the display distracted me. The huge spheres of the Nova landers glinted in the sunlight, growing from tiny stars to massive worldlets in their own right.

"Lilandreth!" I snapped, but Jay and Gunderson had already deposited her at the control dais, her long fingers wrapping around the twin handles there.

"I'm working on it," she said. "I'm... feeling better."

Her eyes closed and the handles glowed with internal light, though there was no difference that I could see or feel.

"The shield has now extended to the drop-ship," she announced, eyes still closed. "I'm working on allowing the energy from the suit guns through it now."

"No pressure," I murmured, staring at the ships. "Vicky, how long before they're in your range?"

"Well, I don't rightly know," she admitted. "We haven't done any range tests in a vacuum. I'm sure the inverse-square law hits us at some point, but if I could do math like that in my head, I probably would have gone Space Fleet and not been stuck in the Marines."

"The Nova landers will be in the effective range of the guns in ten seconds," Lilandreth said out of the blue. I stared at her, but her eyes were still closed. "Which will be approximately the same time as this ship will be range of the plasma cannons on the landers."

"Ten seconds, Vicky," I told her, not bothering to ask how Lilandreth knew any of that.

"And will our shots make it out of the shields in ten seconds?" Vicky wanted to know.

"They will," Lilandreth said. And I didn't even bother asking her how she broke in on our private line this time.

"Fire at your discretion," I said to Vicky. "I'd wait until as late as possible though. Once they realize you're out there, they might try to circle around where our guns can't reach."

"You know that thing commanders do where they tell their subordinates things they already know just because it makes the officer think he's doing something useful? You don't have to do that with me."

"Sorry." I winced, wishing I was out there. Because there wasn't a damned thing useful I could do in here. That was a dangerous position for a commander, because it gave them way too much time to think. "Gunderson."

"Yes, sir?" the man asked, snapping to attention, which was out of character for him, probably a sign of how worried he and everyone else was.

"Get your lander ready to launch," I told him. "Take the crew with you." I motioned to Jay and Bob. "Them too. Get ready in case we need to use you as an escape pod."

He nodded, then started yelling, chivvying his own people, as well as Jay and Bob, into motion. I doubted they'd do much good or even be able to get out in time if the ship was in jeopardy, but at least it got them off the bridge and out of my hair.

Spinner. I had to get Spinner on the lander too, once he got the medical lab set up.

"I will not require the medical lab, Cam," Lilandreth said. My head snapped up and I took a step closer to her.

"What?" I asked. Had I said part of my thought out loud, or was it just a coincidence? Now wasn't the time to debate it. "Why not?"

"Because it's too late." Her eyes opened, and when they did the catlike pupils were wider than I remembered, darker, the portals to some ancient version of hell. "There's no reversing it now."

I tried to ask what she meant but my mouth hung open, disconnected from my brain for a moment. Before I could shake free of the fugue, Vicky interrupted my thoughts with a barked command over the general net.

"Concentrate fire on Bandit Two near the drives and open fire!"

Twenty-some streams of azure energy weren't visible for long once they penetrated the Predecessor ship's shields, disappearing into a computer simulation as they collimated on the rightmost of the two ships in the display. Sparks and bright clouds of vaporized metal puffed out from the base of the sphere, near the drive bell for its engine.

"Come on," I chanted, half a prayer. "Come on, come on..."

The Nova waited a half-second longer than I expected to return fire, which I assumed meant they were hesitant to damage the ship since it represented invaluable salvage. But they weren't going to sit there and take fire without returning it, not for long. The plasma weapons were more primitive than the energy guns but were a hell of a lot bigger, and visible for a lot farther from the emitter. I winced at the approach of the fireballs, seemingly in slow motion, bracing myself as if it would be a physical blow.

It was. The gravitic shields absorbed the shots, their faint-green glow blazing into a fiery halo at the influx of energy. But the thing I'd come to understand about the shields was that they transformed thermal and electromagnetic energy into kinetic... and it hit like a sledgehammer. The deck shook beneath me and I grabbed at the edge of the control handles out of instinct, but the ship didn't buck or sway and I kept my balance.

"That was a solid hit," I said.

"Two more volleys will be sufficient to collapse our shields," Lilandreth declared flatly. "The combined fire of your Marines will take another thirty seconds to penetrate the armor on the lander. We won't live to see it."

"How do you know that?" I demanded, denial being the first stage of grief. But yeah, it was still a good question. "There's no way you could tell that just from the ship's systems... not this quick."

"It's enough to say that I know and that I'm correct."

Well no, it wasn't enough, not nearly. But I couldn't waste time arguing the matter, because if she *was* right, then we had to have an alternate course of action. Evacuation. We had to get out of here. No time to get everyone back into the ship... the platoon would just have to jet away from the hull and hang in orbit until the drop-ship came back for them. Lilandreth and I would get out on the lander, and I needed to call Doc Spinner...

My mouth was hanging open, ready to give a half a dozen orders to four different people, my muscles tensed for a sprint to the lander. It probably wouldn't have worked, or if it did, it would have been due to more hesitation on the part of the Nova flight crews than anything I did. But Marines didn't give up. We kept fighting until we were dead, because there was no way of knowing if the next second we'd fought for would be the one that saved us.

That next second saved us. Maybe Lilandreth was wrong after all. Maybe the Nova lander already had damage, or there was an unforeseen weak spot in the armor down by the drive bell. Whatever the cause, the fusillade of actinic energy penetrated something. A flare of star-bright white erupted from just above the drive bell and expanded to consume the entire vessel... and didn't stop.

As if the white flame was spreading across a sea of hydrocarbons rather than hard vacuum, it flowed out over the thousands of meters between the first lander and the second. They were flying close for spaceships, but not close enough that the explosion should have gone that far. Then again, I wasn't a physicist and their ships used antimatter... there could have been a good reason for it.

And it could have been a miracle from God. I was leaning toward that possibility.

"Holy shit!" Vicky yelled in my ear, screeching like her team had just won the World Cup. "Did you *see* that? Did you fucking see it? We took out both of those things! I'm going to hold that over your head until we're so damn old our brains are running out of space for memories... and *then*, I'm going to have the footage from my gun camera running in a loop on a holocube beside our bed!"

My laughter bordered on the hysterical and I felt like I was going to collapse, like the certainty of death and the desperate need to avoid it had been a prop holding me up and now that it was gone I was left with no strength in my legs.

"I don't blame you a bit," I told her. "Bring everyone back to the drop-ship. We still got those Nova cruisers coming in. We have to get the hell out of here... unless you want to try to knock down a cruiser with your suit gun."

"I'm tempted," Vicky admitted, "but I probably shouldn't push my luck."

Lilandreth stood motionless at the control dais, hands clasped together as if we hadn't just had our asses pulled out of the fire by the unlikeliest shot in history. I didn't know how Resscharr celebrated, but I guessed this wasn't it.

"I know you don't like to be wrong," I told her, grinning, "but of all the times to be wrong, this was a good one."

She met my eyes, and a cold shudder went up my back at the sight of those infinitely dark pupils.

"I was not mistaken, Cameron Alvarez." She shook her long leonine head and looked out into the holographic display opposite the world below, into the emptiness of open space.

"Though I think both of us will eventually wish I had been."

[15]

"Damn it," I muttered, sinking into my acceleration couch on the *Orion*. "Just when I thought we were finally out of the shit."

The cluster of Nova cruisers wasn't advancing on our position, but they'd formed a blockade between us and the jumpgate. It wasn't as obvious on the optical feed as it was in the sensor display, where the computer had thoughtfully animated the position of the jumpgate as well as the globular formation of enemy ships between us and it.

"Hey, I did my part," Vicky said, hands raised as if she was swearing off this particular problem.

"I'm never going to hear the end of this, am I?" I asked her, shaking my head. I hadn't brought up yet what Lilandreth had told me, figuring it would be better not to distract from the problem at hand.

"I'd have to estimate that the other side of this gate is one of their strongholds," Dwight ventured, and I glared at his avatar with an expression that mirrored Nance's.

"Gosh, y'think?" Nance asked him, motioning at the blockade.

"We could Transition right past them," Yanayev suggested. "They couldn't do a damned thing about it."

"*We* could Transition past them," I agreed. "But Lilandreth couldn't."

"That thing can accelerate at hundreds of gravities," Nance said. "She could just zoom right through before they could turn and chase her."

"I could," Lilandreth responded over the cockpit speakers, listening in over the comms. "However, I couldn't outrun their weapons, and the shields are depleted...." Her face was in a corner of the bridge's main screen, though looking at her eyes in the projection, I didn't get the same sense of bottomless depths that I had in person. She frowned, her eyes slitted. "It might be worth a try. Though were I you, I'd be more circumspect about barging through the gate blind after Transitioning past them. They might have an ambush set up on the other side of the wormhole."

I shared an alarmed look with Nance, not so much at the prospect but that neither of us had considered the possibility. Then again, I still wore the smart bandages and had the excuse that I wasn't thinking clearly.

"I would suggest," Lilandreth went on, "that I run ahead of you with as much acceleration and speed as I have time to build up, then, once I've distracted them, you Transition in closer to the jumpgate. I'll scout ahead through the wormhole and signal back whether it's safe to pass through."

"If they catch you in a crossfire," Dwight reminded her, his avatar positioned on the screen beside Lilandreth's face as if they were staring into each other's eyes, "your shields will collapse. You could be destroyed."

The AI actually sounded concerned, which surprised me. The two ancient enemies had made peace, but that didn't mean they loved each other, and at times I felt like they could barely stand talking to each other.

"It's a risk," Lilandreth agreed. "But our only alternative is resigning ourselves to being trapped on this side of the gate."

Well, there was one other possibility, though I didn't bring it up. We could abandon the Predecessor ship and use the Transition Drive. But Lilandreth had already shown a willingness to die before she gave up the vessel, and I doubted she'd changed her mind. The hairs stood on the back of my neck as her eyes moved to stare directly at me, which wasn't possible since she couldn't know how her image would be projected over here.

"You're concerned my ship won't survive," she said. "I will send Lt. Gunderson and the science crew back over to the *Orion* before we attempt this maneuver." Her head cocked to the side in an odd expression I couldn't read. "Dr. Spinner has expressed a desire to stay aboard despite the risk, if that's all right with you."

"Yeah, okay." I tried hard to sound nonchalant, but I couldn't shake the idea that Lilandreth had read my thoughts. "Go ahead and send the lander over. We'll cut thrust and match velocities with them."

"Easy for you to say," Yanayev murmured, her expression sour. I knew how much of a pain in the ass it was and commiserated privately, but officially I awarded her a stern look. "Sorry, sir," she added and, knowing Yanayev, she meant it.

"How long is the transfer going to take?" I asked, rubbing a hand over my face.

"Half hour, maybe," Yanayev replied.

"I'm going to run down to the sick bay and get these smart bandages off," I told Nance. "Before I fall asleep on my feet."

"I'll go with you," Vicky volunteered. "Then I'll stop by our storage compartments and make sure Top is taking care of PMCS for the platoon."

And check on the Marines, she didn't say. We'd been at this for a long time now, lost a lot of people, but it never got any easier. I remembered all too well how it been after we'd lost half the company fighting the Skrela. The survivors had been shell-shocked, and instead of getting used to it, it seemed we took it harder now that there were fewer of us left.

We were coasting, our drives off, forcing Vicky and I to use our magnetic ship boots to get around, and I hated using them even more than usual since I felt the pull against my hip with every step.

"We need to find a way to use the Vergai troops more," Vicky said once we were off the bridge, away from anyone who might overhear.

"If we'd used them this time," I pointed out, gritting my teeth against the pull of the burn on my hip, "we'd all be dead. Their weapons couldn't take out the Nova mechs and their jets couldn't have stayed aloft to engage the fighters."

"I'm not stupid," she snapped. "I know that."

She wasn't just being irritable, I should have realized she knew it.

"Sorry," I told her. "I'm running on fumes here."

"You've heard how the Originals talk about the Vergai," she went on, accepting my apology by blowing past it.

The Originals was how the two platoons that were all remaining from the company we'd started off with referred to themselves. Just the term put a wedge between them and the Vergai recruits from Yfingam. They were new, inexperienced, their suits more primitive even than the Vigilantes we'd used in the war, the Vergai volunteers lacking the 'face jacks, forced to use obsolete neural halos.

"Yeah," I replied with a shrug. "They're noobs though. Even if they weren't from another society, they'd still be noobs. Noobs always get looked down on, but the problem here is, we can't solve that problem by mixing them with the Originals because their suit capabilities are just too different."

"So our only option is to get them experience. Even if it's a risk."

I frowned. I wanted to argue with her, because it *was* a risk, not just to the Vergai but to the mission. But I didn't. Because she was right, and having a divide between the two companies was going to be just as deadly as not having the right tech for the mission. We both fell silent as we boarded the lift.

I'd rather have avoided it, but as beat up as I was, I didn't think I could make the hop into the rotational drum without help from the elevator. Most of the drum was evacuated when we were in a combat situation, since we might have to undergo heavy boost and most of the compartments would be aligned the wrong direction. Not the sick bay though. A lot of medical treatments required gravity, so it was the one compartment that actually swiveled on gimbals to keep it either using rotational or boost gravity at all times.

"There's a bigger problem than that," I said once we stepped off into the drum. It was a relief to be just *walking* again instead of pulling my feet up to break the traction of the sticky plates. There was no one in the corridor, but I put a hand on her arm and pulled her closer to me. "Lilandreth."

"Is she still messed up from what the Nova did to her?" Vicky asked, wincing. "I was hoping the med bay in her ship could help her out."

"She told me it was too late. That the changes had already happened and they were permanent."

"What changes?" Vicky asked, eyes narrowing. "Is she going to die?"

"No, I think it's more serious than that." I swallowed hard. "I hate to tell you this, Vick, but you didn't destroy those landers." Her glare was hard enough to melt lead, but I shook my head. "There was no way. Even if there was some weakness in that ship you were firing at, explosions just don't propagate like that in a vacuum. You know it as well as I do."

"Well," she admitted, squirming under the pressure of honesty, "I didn't *think* they did, but I'm not a..."

"Physicist, yeah, I know. Me neither. But she *told* me." I gestured behind us. "You saw those worlds, you saw what happened to them. I told you what those Nova scientists said, what Gandish said."

"You don't seriously believe all that shit, do you?" Vicky asked. "Those are myths! Those Resscharr down there are basically Neanderthals in a high-tech cave. And the Nova exiles are desperate to get revenge against the people who kicked them out. They're..." She shook her head, searching for a metaphor I supposed. "They're the Nazis back before World War Two, hunting down the Spear of Destiny and the Ark of the Covenant because they were looking for supernatural help in a war they couldn't win any other way."

"I'm pretty sure the whole Ark of the Covenant thing was a movie," I confided, "but I get your point. But come on..." I spread my arms. "What else could have done that?"

"Just about anything except fucking magic psychic powers!" she exclaimed, and I checked around us again instinctively. There was no one roaming the passages, but there *could* have been.

"It's not exactly psychic powers. The scientists said it was mental energy funneled through Transition Space, which..." I winced. "Yeah, sounds a lot like magic psychic powers, but there's some convincing-sounding tech shit behind it, and I just don't know how else to explain what happened."

"Unless the lander thing was just a fluke, a weakness, some weird function of their power systems and what they did to

Lilandreth just fucked up her head." Vicky spun a finger next to her temple. "Maybe she's delusional."

We were at the med bay, and I sighed, knowing we couldn't talk about it in here. I didn't believe in keeping things from the crew, but a commander had to lay out the facts in an understandable way, not let the rumor mill run wild.

"I'm not sure," I told her, pushing open the hatch, "that's any better."

Jay and Bob were in the sick bay already, which I should have figured since I'd sent them both this way once we docked with the *Orion*. Neither looked too bad, though seeing them both with their shirts off was something I could have gone my whole life without doing. I wasn't sure whether body hair that thick and curly was typical of their people or if we'd just lucked out, but the two of them could have spent their off hours on the asteroid mine braiding each other's back hair.

"Hey, Cam," Jay said, perking up from where he sat on the gurney beside Bob. "I mean, sir. You doing okay?"

"We'll find out," I said with a shrug, motioning to Dr. Hallonen. "Doc, can you take off these bandages and check me out? I gotta get back to the bridge in twenty minutes."

The older woman offered me a disapproving look as she checked off an item on her tablet with a stylus.

"Just because you're the commander doesn't give you the right to expedited service, Captain Alvarez."

"Oh, of course it does, Doc," Vicky sighed, motioning at her to get on with it. "Just get the damn bandages off him and you can get back to treating these malingerers." She blew me a kiss. "Gonna go check on the troops."

Jay stared after Vicky, looking like she'd shot his dog, and I would have patted his shoulder to comfort him, but not with all that damned hair.

"She's joking," I assured him. "You both did great in there. You definitely saved Lilandreth's life."

"Yeah, man, I hope she's gonna be okay," Jay said, wagging his head with a hangdog frown. "She didn't look so hot down there."

"She's... better now," I said, stripping out of my fatigues as Hallonen rolled an instrument cart over to me. "We're going to be making a run out of this system and she's going to lead the way in her ship."

"I still wanna know what happened to us down there," Bob spoke up. He seemed sullen, depressed, and I wondered if it was the usual post-traumatic stress. It hit people differently, but I'd seen the depression hit people before. "I mean, when you went after those mecha..."

"That was so epic, dude," Jay interjected, laughing, almost manic. And that was *another* way people reacted to combat. "I mean, you took out *four* of those things by yourself! It was crazy!"

Bob glared his friend into silence.

"When you did that," he went on, "I heard what you said but I didn't have time to translate it in my head before I was already on the ground." He looked over at Jay. "I thought *you* pushed me, but you didn't. And I didn't push you. That was weird."

Yeah, it was weird, all right. I was saved from commenting on it by Hallonen ripping the bandage off my hip. The most coherent thing I could come up with was a yelp as I limped away a pace.

"Stop being a wimp," she snapped at me. "Hold still if you're in such a big damned hurry."

I bit back my gut-level response and held still as she sprayed the synthskin over the burn. It didn't need debriding or disinfecting—

the smart bandage had done all that, had started the subcutaneous repair—but barring a few hours in an autodoc, the natural flesh would still take days to grow back beneath the synthetic kind. One thing the synthskin did was patch things together so it wouldn't feel like someone was flaying my hip every time I moved, and I sighed in relief at the cool feeling where once had been abraded heat.

"All right, let me get that one on your neck," Hallonen said.

"Cam," Bob said, unusually talkative but not seeming happy about it, "I don't know if I'm cut out for this. I mean, I'll do whatever job you need me to do on the ship, engineering or whatever. I'll shovel shit for you if you want. But I don't know if I can do the whole soldier on the ground thing."

"Not everyone can," I told him, then winced as Hallonen pulled the bandage off my neck. The burn there wasn't as bad, and neither was the pain. "It's nothing to be ashamed of. I wasn't made to be Force Recon, which was why I wound up in the suit. I doubt Captain Nance would be much good in a gunfight. Or Doc Hallonen," I added as she treated my neck wound.

"I'll have you know I could kick your ass on a live-fire range, Alvarez," she muttered.

"Just because you got ambushed this time though," I continued to Bob, ignoring Hallonen's jab, "doesn't mean you can't learn better with more experience. Granted, this is the kind of experience that can get you killed before you get good at it, but don't feel like you're a failure just because you failed." I chuckled, half from the soothing spray on my neck, half from the point I was making. "I mean, look at me. I've failed at basically every level of leadership, starting with team leader in a squad. The very first time I saw combat, my battle buddy got killed in a situation I should have seen coming." The memory of seeing Lance Corporal Kurita's charred and broken armor was a kick in the gut even after all these years. "You just have to believe that you're doing more good than you are harm."

"Do you still believe that?" Bob asked me.

I thought about that for a moment. If I hadn't come along on this mission, Zan-Thint would have let loose the Skrela on the Commonwealth. I kept telling myself that, because every other step I'd taken had simply dragged us all deeper into this mess. Every move had seemed inescapable, the only right thing to do, and even now, looking back, I couldn't figure out anything I could have done differently.

"You're done, Alvarez," Hallonen told me, slapping me on the arm.

"Thanks, Doc."

I slipped my fatigues back on and took a step toward the hatchway before I turned back to Bob to give him the answer he deserved.

"I guess I have to."

[16]

Space combat is strange.

My idea of war was formed going toe to toe with Tahni battlesuits, shooting at enemies who were close enough to see with the naked eye because that was the range of our best weapon. Missiles that traveled too far could be spoofed, and a suit could only carry so many of them. The missile load lasted maybe two engagements, three at the most, but battles could drag on for hours, sometimes with no resupply. That meant we did most of our damage with the plasma guns, the one weapon that didn't need reloading. And since most of our fights were in cities, we stayed below the rooflines to avoid being tracked by *their* missiles.

We found each other by accident, killed each other at arm's length.

Space combat had no cover, no concealment, not unless you hid behind a moon or a planet, but even then the enemy could find you pretty quick. No, space war was a chess board with pieces millions of kilometers apart. You couldn't strike until you were close, but getting close required foresight, expert moves conducted with perfect timing.

Unfortunately for the analogy I'd built up while sitting on the bridge, waiting for the show to kick off, if this was a chess board, we only had two pieces. Four, if you counted the two Intercepts. Brandano and Villanueva were hanging at station-keeping off our right shoulder, though I wasn't sure what good they thought they were going to do. Intercept pilots always whined about being cut loose, and it wouldn't hurt anything keeping them out there since they could micro-Transition just as well as we could. And hopefully would.

"They're still just sitting there," Wojtera said, shaking his head. "You'd think they'd at least give us an ultimatum or something."

"There's no need," Lilandreth said, her voice sounding as if she was seated just behind me instead of a few thousand kilometers away. "They've sent another part of their fleet around toward the incoming gate to cut us off. In their eyes, we have no choice but to surrender or fight them."

"Are you ready?" I asked her, not asking how she knew about the movements of the Nova ships when our sensors hadn't picked them up.

"I am." She turned in the image on the screen. "Dr. Spinner, are you certain you wish to remain here?"

The camera view changed to the Grey scientist. He was smiling. There was something off about the smile, something vacant behind his dark eyes. I couldn't put my finger on it, and when he spoke, he sounded normal.

"Quite certain. I've dreamed of being in a spaceship going at relativistic velocities, and I wouldn't give up the opportunity for anything."

"All right then." I tightened my safety harness. I wished Vicky were up on the bridge, but she'd told me the Marines needed her back in the troop bay, and it would have been a long trip up to the bridge again anyway. Still, I felt very alone up here without her. "Captain Nance, are we ready to micro-Transition?"

"Ready as we'll ever be." The older man shook his head. "I hope, if I live through this and get home, that I can get a job on a passenger liner or a freight ship and never have to micro-Transition again."

I didn't respond to his griping aloud, but to myself I agreed wholeheartedly.

"Okay, Lilandreth. Go."

Just as Dr. Spinner had never been on a ship going at a good fraction of the speed of light, I'd never *seen* one going at those speeds before, and I stared at the screen carefully. The pale-green glow of the drive field shifted tone and glowed brighter as the cylindrical shape leapt forward like it had been shot out of a mass driver. The acceleration would have turned a human into a squishy, gelatinous blob on the deck if it had been from a reaction drive, but the Predecessor ship used a gravity field projected ahead of the ship to pull it as fast as the... well, honestly, I didn't know the limitations of its acceleration other than I'd been told it still couldn't go faster than light.

The cameras tried to follow it, but the ship was a green streak across the screen, leaving off one side before the focus could shift. I cursed under my breath, more from awe than annoyance, and shifted my gaze to the sensor screen instead. The computer tried to simulate the Predecessor ship the same way it did ours and the enemy's, but there was a difference. I couldn't enumerate it, but it wasn't as realistic, didn't capture the essence of the vessel. Still, it was the best we could do and I couldn't look away. It was unreal, unlike anything I'd seen before... well, except for the other Predecessor ships I'd seen at Decision, and I'd mostly been on the ground for that fight.

"Judas Priest on a pogo stick," Nance said softly. "What I wouldn't give to have a drive like that on *my* ship."

"What *I* wouldn't give if her weapons worked," I shot back. "Then this wouldn't be a problem."

"Eh," he scoffed. "She wasn't invincible even when the weapons *did* work. If she were, we wouldn't have been able to damage her in the first place."

That was fair. It didn't change that I would have felt better if her weapons worked. The green glow was already almost to the Nova blockade, close enough that...

"Micro-Transition," I ordered, then tightened my stomach muscles and gritted my teeth.

"Helm," Nance said with a nod. "Execute."

The first Transition wasn't bad. Not any worse than usual, though I would never get used to that feeling. But to jump just partway down a Transition Line and come back out before the point of no return when there was no gravitational mass to anchor the exit meant we had to Transition back out within a few seconds. Not nearly enough time for the human body—or brain—to shake off the effects of the first jump.

The second one was the same psychological impact as a two-meter-tall gang enforcer kicking me square in the balls. And yes, that had happened. Once. I'd crawled away and, later on, arranged for the TAPs to catch the guy on the train with a backpack full of Kick he hadn't been aware he was carrying. I had no such recourse to get revenge against the laws of hyperdimensional physics, so I just had to sit there and take it.

"Sitrep," I croaked, trying to get my eyes to focus again as I peered at the Tactical display.

"We're twenty thousand klicks on the far side of the blockade cluster," Wojtera said, tone crisp and businesslike as if he wouldn't know what I was talking about if I asked him if he *liked* being kicked in the nuts. "Both Intercepts are with us."

He paused, and I was finally able to get a good look at the Tactical board. There were dozens of Nova cruisers between us and the Predecessor ship, spherical just like their landers but dozens of times bigger, maneuvering to get a better shot at the speeding, green bullet.

"The Nova have opened fire on the Predecessor ship," Wojtera added, as if we all couldn't see the red flares of plasma on the screen. "They're laying down bracketing fire... getting pretty close."

I winced as some of the rounds drifted directly into the path of the ship, exploding like a mine laid out ahead of Lilandreth... and doing nothing. I started to say something, but my mouth hung open. I didn't know a *lot* about physics, but I did know that velocities added together and the plasma blasts hitting a ship traveling at a decent fraction of lightspeed would hit even harder, should have gone right through her shields. They didn't. Instead, she simply plowed through the center of their formation as if they weren't there, shrugging off one shot after another.

She blew by us, moving so fast the ship was a broad, green laser shining through the ever-night, leaving the Nova cruisers gawking in her wake. Shooting right by us and through the jumpgate. Something on the other side of the wormhole held it open, which meant the Nova had forces on that side as well... which was why we didn't immediately follow.

Not that we didn't want to.

"Oh, I think they've noticed us," Nance mused, rubbing at his chin casually, as if the dozens of Nova ships spinning on their axes toward us in an orchestrated motion like a zero-G ballet didn't bother him at all. "How long we got, Woj?"

Which was my clue that he *was* nervous. Nance had gotten a little sloppier about trimming his beard, maybe less strict with his bridge crew, but he always—*always*—called Yanayev *Helm* and Wojtera *Tactical*. He might call the man *Woj* in the mess, but not on the bridge.

If Wojtera was surprised, he didn't show it.

"They're boosting our way. About... eight gravities. That's gotta hurt, but I guess those octopus things are pretty stout. The nearest of them'll be in range in just under ten minutes."

"We're thirty-five minutes out from the gate at one gravity," Yanayev added, and Nance grunted.

Ideally we would have Transitioned closer, but there was a minimum safe distance for a jumpgate, just like there was with a planet. Not as far, but still too far, and the distance chafed at me, but I kept my mouth shut and let Nance do his job.

"Set course for the gate," he said. "Give the alarm for emergency boost and take us to four gravities." Which would take us through in *nine* minutes. Nance nodded to Chase. "Comms, pass the order on to the Intercepts."

"We haven't heard the all-clear from Lilandreth yet," I reminded him, because this was part of *my* job. "If we build up that much momentum, we won't have time to decelerate if she tells us it's not safe."

"We're coming in near the north polar edge of the gate," he told me. "Worse comes to worst, we can adjust course and scoot around the event horizon of the wormhole." Nance made a face. "We'll get some nasty static charges from the edge effects, but it's still doable."

The emergency boost klaxon sounded, annoying and obnoxious both for the sheer clamor of it as well as for what it signified.

"Four gravities acceleration," Yanayev warned, and three hundred kilos plus smashed me into my acceleration couch like a baseball bat.

I didn't *think* my nose was bleeding, but it could have been. Four gravities was a bad spot for me. Two or three Gs wasn't bad, just made things uncomfortable, but I could power through it. If we went all the way to seven or eight, full emergency boost, I usually blacked out and didn't have to endure all of the pain.

But four gravities kept me conscious with a fist wrapped in my lapel, slapped me in the face and told me "no, fuck you, you're going to have to sit here and suffer."

I couldn't even let my mind go hazy, my vision go out of focus to try to make the time pass faster, because I had to pay attention to Comms and Tactical. I couldn't have sworn to how much time had gone by, though I wouldn't have been shocked whether it was five minutes or five hours, the homogenous, dull pain that spread out over my whole body taking up my total attention.

"We're getting a signal," Lt. Chase ground out through clenched teeth, finally distracting me from the discomfort. "From the jumpgate."

"On screen," I told him. It wasn't a stern, commanding order the way I'd intended it, more of a wheeze.

Lilandreth's face towered over us, somehow seeming even larger than the actual size of the projection because of the boost smashing me into my seat. The perspective made her expression seem manic, almost diabolical.

"You may pass through without concern," she declared archly. "This side of the gate is safe."

I would have grimaced in disbelief if I hadn't already been grimacing in utter discomfort. How the hell could the other side be safe when the Nova knew we were coming? Had they sent all their ships through to this system? That seemed short-sighted, though none of the command decisions the enemy had made so far had impressed me much.

"We're coming through," I told her, squeezing the words out from my diaphragm. "But we have the entire fucking fleet about a minute behind us, so don't wait, just get moving to the exit gate. Hold it open for us if there's no existing mechanism."

I had to suck in a desperate breath after expending that

much oxygen. Lilandreth looked disgustingly comfortable, and like Nance, I envied her the gravity drive.

"Do not slow your acceleration when you come through," she instructed. "I'll take care of them."

"What?" I blurted, but the screen had gone dark. "Chase, get her back."

"She's not responding to our hails," he told me after a moment.

"Should we go through?" Nance asked me. *Sure, defer to my authority when you're afraid of being wrong.*

"We don't have any choice. Do as she said, don't reduce acceleration until I give you the word."

The wormhole filled the main screens, eclipsing the empty space around it, swallowing the stars in blackness. It was salvation, at least temporarily, but for some reason the hazy unreality of it terrified me. On the other side was the unknown... and now, that included Lilandreth.

Passing through the gate wasn't unpleasant, not after the micro-Transition, just an unexpected step down off a stoop to the ground by comparison. And on the other side was carnage.

"Jesus Christ," Nance whispered, barely audible over the roaring in my ears. And the screaming inside my head.

The Nova hadn't been reckless or stupid after all. They hadn't sent all their ships across to the other system. They'd kept at least half of them on this side. Every single one of them burned fiercely like leaves dumped into a bonfire, shattered into drifting bits that littered the space in front of the gate. And sitting there, holding open the wormhole for us like it was a mundane task, was Lilandreth's ship.

No other vessels approached her, and if there was anything left alive in this system, it surely wasn't in space. A faint blue sparkled off to the left side of the screen, a planet millions of kilometers away, and according to the Tactical display no ships orbited the world, none lifted off its surface.

"What the hell happened?" Wojtera demanded, nonplussed. "She... she doesn't have any weapons." He looked over at me, despite the strain of the boost. "Does she?"

"You may begin deceleration."

The voice wasn't on the speakers, wasn't in my earbud. It was everywhere, as if it had come from the air on the bridge.

"Where the fuck did *that* come from?" Chase demanded, looking around for the source of the voice. "We didn't get any transmission!"

"It's Lilandreth," I said. I knew what was happening. I didn't want to admit it to myself, but I knew. "Turn us around. Begin deceleration at one gravity. Pass it on to the Intercepts."

I pushed aside the things I didn't want to consider and concentrated on what I could control. The Intercepts didn't have the Resscharr-tech photon drives and would burn through their on-board fuel pretty damned quick if we didn't allow them to cut thrust.

"Helm, execute," Nance said, driven back to the curt professionalism I was used to from him by what was undoubtedly sheer confusion.

The pressure lifted, and I sighed with relief too instinctive to be quashed by the situation. Free fall twisted my guts... or maybe that was just the fearsome knowledge that I hadn't shared with the others. When the steering jets thudded against the hull to turn us, I was half convinced it was my heart beating out of my chest.

The *Orion* turned slowly, inexorably, almost reluctantly, as if the ship herself knew what we were about to witness and didn't want that for us. Nothing could save us from that fate. The Nova flooded through the jumpgate, still burning at eight gravities, willing to accept any pain, any pressure to catch us, to catch *her*.

"She's holding the gate open," Yanayev breathed. "Why doesn't she just close it?"

"She wants them here," I told the Helm officer. "She wants them where she can deal with them."

"Deal with them how?" Nance asked, glaring at me, as if he sensed I was holding something back.

"Watch."

As the Nova came through the jumpgate, it was as if they ran headlong into a physical wall, solid enough to stop even a cruiser the size of an office building boosting at eight Gs. The spectral wall shredded the warships, each erupting in a ball of antimatter destruction, starbursts of energy reaching out to touch the tendrils from the ships exploding around them.

I should have been happy to see it. These Nova were the enemy who'd killed two of my Marines, who would have slaughtered every one of us to get what they wanted. They'd been an unbeatable swarm of massive warships... and now they were a fireworks show, soap bubbles popping as they reached the ceiling. And yet, all I could feel was dread, foreboding that wouldn't be comforted.

The bridge was silent. Not even profanity broke the spell of what we were seeing. No words were spoken, even as the last of the enemy ships erupted and vanished into fiery death. Once they were gone, the Predecessor ship darted from her position beside the jumpgate, moving faster than she had before, as if it wasn't gravity propelling her anymore but pure will.

Lilandreth's face appeared in the main screen, though Chase had made no move to connect her.

"You have many questions," she said. "I would answer them." Her eyes somehow found me, staring straight through to the core of me. "Come to my ship and we will speak."

She vanished from the screen and everyone on the bridge stared at me, waiting for an explanation. They weren't going to get it right now. Not until I had something coherent to tell them.

"Get a lander prepped," I told Nance. "I'll be heading over to the other ship."

"Who do you want to fly you?" Nance asked, but I was already shaking my head.

"No one. I'm going alone."

[17]

The Predecessor ship had always been alien, but now, it felt... haunted.

I stepped out of the lander's hatch with great hesitation, reluctant to leave the shelter of the little ship, as illusory as it might have been. I hadn't come armed, not even with a sidearm, because I knew how pointless it would have been. If Lilandreth wanted me dead, I'd be dead. And there wouldn't be a Goddamned thing I could do about it.

She didn't come to greet me at the ship, and I debated internally whether I might not be better off waiting for her to, but I knew where she was. *How* I knew, I wasn't certain, but she was on the bridge. I didn't remember the walk from the hangar bay to the bridge being this long, and paranoia nagged at the edges of my thoughts with images of the ship rearranging its passageways to keep me lost.

Almost as if the ship had read my thoughts and decided the joke had run its course, the next curve in the corridor opened up onto the bridge. Lilandreth stood at the center of the compartment, and even though her hands were clasped in front of her rather than raised over her head, she reminded me of the statue back inside the Reconstructor city.

"I told you it was too late," she reminded me, not turning toward me, her attention still focused on the central display where a star map rolled by.

"Is..." I coughed, clearing my throat. "Is it what they said? Were those Nova scientists telling us the truth?"

"As they understood it." She finally looked away from the hologram and faced me. I swallowed hard at the sight of her black-hole eyes and nearly averted my eyes, "Their knowledge, of course, was incomplete. They were correct in their assessment of the motivation of my people. They came here to escape the predations of the Skrela, and the one thing they feared more than death, more than dishonor, was the idea of that plague following them here, searching out their last refuge."

"That's why they developed the... virus?"

She laughed softly. I knew her people didn't laugh as a natural reaction, which made it calculated.

"That was where their knowledge was incomplete. You've come to have an understanding of my people, Cameron Alvarez. Do you think their first instinct would be to develop a weapon they would use themselves?"

The Predecessors had created the Tahni to be their warriors against the Skrela, then, when the enemy had advanced too quickly to use them, they'd run, taking humans and Tahni along. They'd established human and Tahni colonies, hoping to continue the program, and when those had proven disappointing, they'd created a hybrid race, the Quara, with the idea of turning them into their soldiers.

"No," I agreed. "I don't."

"Of course not. Instead, they sent the servants they'd depended on for so long, the ones they'd brought along with them." She waved long fingers in the air and gave me a challenging look, daring me to guess. I didn't have to guess. The answer was blindingly obvious.

"The AI."

"Yes." She smiled approval. "The technical aspects of this are beyond not just your personal knowledge of hyperdimensional physics but that of your species. Up until today, they would have been beyond my own. But I will attempt to explain."

Lilandreth made no move, not even a tilt of her head, but the holographic display changed from the star map to a diagram. A saddle shape, not two dimensional, not just three but somehow *four*, though I couldn't explain how that was represented. It was as if the image extended not just off the screen but through time.

"This is a representation of the universe," she told me. "Not a static point in time, but the universe from the beginning to the end."

"I don't see the Big Bang," I told her, frowning at the projection, wondering if I was looking at it wrong.

"You wouldn't. It was outside time and would be impossible to represent in any form that would mean anything to a mortal being. This is what you can experience, what your instruments can measure. And this..." the image shifted to what looked a lot like a reverse image of the first one, the areas that had been dark now light, glowing red, but not just in the gaps of the shape. The red was around it as well as inside it, and I got the sense that I wasn't able to see much of what was there. "... is what you call Transition Space. To your understanding, this is as close as I can come. It would look to you as if it occupies the same space, yet it doesn't. Transition Space is its own universe that merely exists side by side with ours."

"Okay, I get that," I said, shrugging. "That's why we're able to access it, because it's connected to ours. And the speed of light is different there, or something."

"It's not that simple. Unlike our universe, Transition Space lacks the concept of time. It doesn't exist there, which is why the journeys we make through it seem either instantaneous or much shorter than they would be normally. But that's not the only difference." She closed her eyes and sighed, like she was trying to explain nuclear fusion to a five-year-old. "Transition Space is, for want of a better word, a living thing. Not sentient, but still alive in its own way, as if each roil of quantum foam were a neuron in a living brain. This was how the Reconstructors hoped to gain access to its power... by overwriting the neural patterns of a sentience they could control atop it. I can't explain to you the mechanism, but the brain patterns of sentient AIs were *imprinted* onto the neural matrix of Transition Space in the hope that they would help defend the galaxy from the Skrela."

"Oh, I bet that didn't turn out well," I said. The AI were the ones who'd *created* the Skrela in revenge against the Resscharr who'd enslaved them.

"It did not. The AI ceased communication with their masters and the experiment was deemed a failure. That was when the Reconstructors developed the virus... and used it on test subjects among their own people." She tossed her head. "But the AI they'd sent ahead of them weren't dead, weren't simply hiding. I described Transition Space as a living mind, but perhaps a better analogy would be to a quantum computer matrix. The AI had written themselves into the matrix. They knew that the Reconstructors would eventually try to access the matrix, and they set a trap for them."

"How would they know that?" I frowned, confusion over-ruling the dread I'd been feeling. "How do *you* know any of this?"

Lilandreth sighed, obviously exasperated by my ignorance.

"Transition Space is a quantum computer the size of a *universe*," she reminded me. "Imagine how many possibilities you could run through that processor in a fraction of a second. As fast as you could think. It's not omniscience, but it's close as anyone could come. You've been convinced I'm reading your mind, and you're not entirely wrong. I've been running the possibilities of your reactions based on my knowledge of you through the matrix... not on purpose, not just on you. It happens automatically now."

"And the Nova fleet? Was that automatic?"

"No," she admitted, eyes downcast for a moment. "That took considerable effort. You have to understand, turning thought into kinetic energy takes considerable concentration and will. And each time I focus my consciousness so deeply into Transition Space, it gets worse."

"What?" I asked, shaking my head. "You said the AI had set a trap. What is it?"

"The voices." Her reply was so soft I nearly missed it. "The AI... they're still there. They're *part* of Transition Space now. The Reconstructors called them *ghosts*. And whenever one of us gains access to the matrix, the ghosts begin to whisper in our ear, telling us how incredible the power is, how we're gods and deserve to rule. How we shouldn't abide any competitors for our power, how we should crush them and solidify our hold."

"And your people believed that?" I found myself gaping in horrified disbelief and tried to force my expression neutral again.

"They believed it enough that they destroyed each other," Lilandreth told me. "Enough that they wound up distrusting even their most ardent followers and wiping out their own civilization. The last of them died hundreds of years ago, by their own hand, encouraged by the voices."

Well, shit.

"Lilandreth, that isn't you." It was part argument, part desperate plea. "I've known you for a while now. You've come to terms with things that would have driven a lot of other people nuts—human, Tahni or Resscharr. You've made peace with them, and you can handle this too. You don't have to listen to the ghosts. You know what they are, and you can fight them."

Her infinitely dark eyes looked on me with what might have been fondness.

"You don't understand, Cam. Imagine that you're trapped in a cell every day for the rest of your life, and every day your jailer is whispering to you that your life is meaningless and you should end it, that you should kill yourself. At first, of course, you'd scoff at them... but day by day, the whispers would wear at you, break down your sanity. Sooner or later, you'd give in. And I will too. Not today, but someday. I'll hold out as long as I can, but you should be ready for it."

I tried to think of something, a solution, but just threw up my hands in frustration.

"There has to be a way to undo this," I insisted. "We should go back to the lab, see if you and Dwight can figure out how to reverse it."

"The lab there was badly damaged before we came. The functionality to simply release the virus stored there was barely existent. It would be a waste of time." She paused, laying a long, agile finger aside her jaw as if in contemplation. "The only place that might have such equipment still intact would be at the heart of the Reconstructor civilization. A place that would be called Homecoming in your tongue. If it's still intact."

"Then that's where we're going," I declared, not brooking any argument. "Take us there and we'll fix this. I promise I won't let this happen to you without a fight."

"I'll lead you to Homecoming. While I still can."

―――――

"Oh."

That was all Nance could say, and I didn't blame him. I was pretty much at a loss for words myself. No Ops Center this time. Vicky, Nance, Fleet Intelligence Captain Nagarro, and I were all crammed into my office. It still felt strange having an office, much less the largest compartment on the ship, but once I'd taken over from Hachette, I'd inherited it.

For all that I'd fully intended to share everything with the crew, this was different. Maybe what Lilandreth was doing wasn't *exactly* reading minds, but it was close enough that I wanted to keep the number of minds involved to a bare minimum. I hadn't even intended to invite Nagarro, but Vicky had insisted, saying the Intelligence officer had proven herself and I needed to start trusting her.

I wasn't so sure, but she was here and looking just as gobsmacked as the other two. As I probably did.

"We're going to this Homecoming place then?" Vicky said, her words slow and deliberate, as if she was having to force herself to accept that any of this was real.

"That's the plan," I agreed. "It's still quite a ways along the jumpgate route, and we might run into more of the Nova forces."

Nagarro snorted.

"*That* shouldn't be a problem, given what she did to this last bunch." She was trying to sound cocky, blasé, but I'd been around the block long enough to realize it was a put-on, that she was more freaked out than any of us.

"Yeah, except that every time she accesses the..." I shrugged. "... *whatever*, the power, the matrix, whatever you want to call it, she becomes more susceptible to the influence of the ghosts."

"You can't trust her," Dwight said, and I nearly jumped out

of my chair. We hadn't invited him in on the meeting, but there was no way to keep him *out* of it of course. His avatar paced along the confines of the holographic projection above the desk, a virtual caged lion, as if he'd been there all along. Which he had, though not visible to us.

"You still don't trust her, after all we've been through?" Vicky asked, scowling at him.

"It's not that," the AI insisted. "We had our differences, but those are behind us." He glowered at us from above. "It's the Psi Virus."

"The what?" Nance asked, glaring at him askance.

"The Psi Virus. The name isn't exact, but it's as close as your language can estimate."

"And where did you get the term at all?" I wondered.

Dwight's avatar adapted an expression that I thought was embarrassment, or guilt.

"You understand that I've left pieces of my coding throughout the ship, the Intercepts, the shuttles... and your Vigilantes." He raised his hand to forestall the outraged protest ready to burst out of my mouth. "This is not intended to eavesdrop on you or spy on your private conversations. Rather, it's to allow me to gather intelligence when you're in the field, and the major portion of my coding isn't able to convey my consciousness. Part of me was with you in your Vigilante when you were inside that lab, and it absorbed available data from the systems there without your knowledge."

"Well, isn't that just peachy?" Vicky murmured, eyes narrowed as she glared at his avatar.

"You have my word that I would never interfere with your suits. I merely wish to be as well-informed as possible in order to help you reach your goals and return home."

Dwight sounded sincere, but that was the problem with an

AI. He could pretend to show any emotion and we'd have no clue whether it was genuine.

"What did you find out?" I asked him, pushing the concerns aside for the moment. "Aside from what she already told us."

"The data there confirms her account. It also detailed that the virus only infected a certain genetic profile, and of those, only a small percentage were able to undergo the transformation. The others died, horribly. The Remainder leader you spoke to, this Gandish, needn't have worried about infection or death. His people were of the wrong genetic signature to succumb to the virus. I suspect he was working off warnings only half-remembered from the days when the *daemons*, as he called them, still lived. Perhaps the daemons created the taboo in order to make sure no genetic outliers would rival them."

"I suppose that's why the Nova wanted her so bad," I said, nodding. "They had to know it wouldn't work on any of the Remainders."

"Unfortunately," Dwight went on, sighing, "the data also confirmed her dire predictions of what's to come. The incidence of mania among the infected was one hundred percent. There were no exceptions."

"How long has she got?" Nance asked, running fingers through his beard in a newly developed nervous tic.

"The average time between infection and mental deterioration was measured in days, though there were mentions that some had held out for weeks."

"Oof."

"We have to help her get through it," I said, sullen, mulish stubbornness setting into its familiar place in the set of my jaw. "She didn't ask for any of this, and we wouldn't have survived the Nova attack without her."

"She's not evil," Dwight acknowledged. "But it won't matter.

There are some things that just can't be fought. The danger is, once she's gone too far, passed beyond the ability for reason, we may not recognize it. By then, it will be too late. We won't even be able to strategize together because she'll know what we're going to say, know our plans before we do. My advice would be to use the Transition Drive to leave her behind, before she figures out a way to travel back to your Commonwealth."

And *shit*, but that was a possibility I hadn't even considered.

"We're not abandoning her," I said, not letting go of my resolve. "Not until there's no other way."

The others nodded agreement, and Dwight said nothing. He might not have been strictly human, but he knew us well enough to understand when there was no use in arguing. My mind was made up, and I was sure this was the right thing to do.

I should have remembered that every time I thought that, I wound up in deep shit.

[18]

"Sometimes," Vicky confided, whispering close to my ear, "I think this is all a nightmare that I can't wake up from."

I stirred, blinking against the darkness, and turned around in bed to face her. I could just barely make out her eyes, the outline of her face by the soft green light of the chemical strip-light above the hatch of our compartment. My first instinct was to ask what time it was, though the question was even more meaningless now than it usually would have been. We were between jumpgates and the last four systems had been empty wastelands, charred ruins all that was left where there'd once been habitables. I had no reason to hurry back to the bridge until we came to something interesting.

"What?" I mumbled, rubbing sleep out of my eyes. "You had a nightmare?"

Unlike me, Vicky was wide awake, her eyes clear and piercing.

"When we took Top's offer to join this operation," she went on, not bothering to correct my groggy mishearing, "I was kind of eager, believe it or not. I missed being a Marine and I knew you did too. I thought this would be good for both of us. I still thought that, right up to the time we left Yfingam." She shook her head, and in the pale light I spotted the glint of tears. "But now…"

I wrapped her in my arms and, to my surprise, she was shaking.

"It's okay," I said inanely. "We're gonna be okay."

Vicky shocked me again by pushing away, face contorted in a grimace.

"Don't lie to me!" she yelled, loud enough that I was glad the compartment was soundproofed. "Dammit, Cam, we've been through really bad shit! Do you think I'm a child who needs comforting?"

"Everybody needs comforting," I reasoned, sighing as I fell back against the pillow. "I wind up having to comfort the whole damned crew."

Her shoulders sagged and she laid a hand over my arm.

"You're right. I'm sorry, I didn't mean to snap at you. But I don't want comfort. I need to prepare myself for what's actually going to happen. Are we just going to keep moving ahead no matter what until we're all dead? Because I could live with that when the mission was saving the Commonwealth and I'd volunteered to die to do it. We don't have any mission now except getting home… and I just don't see how we're going to do that."

I nodded.

"I've been thinking the same thing. But we can't go back. We made our choice, burned our boats on the shore."

Her quiet sobs broke up into a laugh.

"You and your fucking military history books. You still can't bring yourself to read fiction, can you?"

"I read it," I protested defensively. "You and Top and Hachette *made* me read it. I just enjoy history more. Besides, look at our lives, Vick. What the hell could I read that was stranger than this?"

"Point," she acceded. "But this all reminds me of *The Odyssey*. Years spent wandering, trying to find a way home while everyone around us dies."

"Yeah, well, I don't think I'm as smart as Odysseus." I ran a finger across her cheek, wiping away the track of a tear. "Besides, I don't have to worry about you being courted by a bunch of minor Greek nobles. You'd kick the shit out of them and come find me yourself."

Now she laughed and leaned in to kiss me, though I could still taste the salt of her tears when she covered her mouth with mine.

"You're damn right, Alvarez. Now, make yourself useful and distract me from all this shit before some asshole AI or mind-reading psychopath or just Nance deciding he just *has* to talk to us immediately..."

I had to laugh too as I bore her down beneath me on the bed. That was another difference between me and Odysseus. My Penelope would never have stayed home during the war.

———

"What have we got this time?" I sighed, pulling myself into the chair for what seemed like the millionth time just since we left the Remainder world.

Lilandreth was holding the jumpgate open while Brandano took Intercept One through the wormhole to scout the other side. It was days and days of boredom punctuated by hours of nerve-wrenching tension, and beneath the surface roiled an undercurrent of constant worry. If it had been practical, I would have visited Lilandreth's ship every day to check up on her—and to give her an anchor in reality—but that would have required us to slow down for the transfer, and I felt like getting to Homecoming was more important to solving her problem than indulging my paranoia.

"We're getting a signal through the jumpgate now," Chase replied.

"On screen," Nance ordered, beating me to the punch.

I bit down on the complaint that tried to work its way out. It was possible that, given the secret we were keeping, we might have wanted to be a little more cautious about showing everything on the main screen. But I couldn't say *that* aloud either without letting everyone know we were keeping something secret from them. Which was one of the things I hated about keeping secrets.

The main optical display had shown the shimmering nothingness of the gate, but now half of it switched to a cockpit view of Brandano. The man had a stern, recruiting-poster face with clear eyes and a strong jaw, but at the moment he lacked the confidence and certitude that usually went along with those looks. In fact, he looked very much like he was about to shit his pants.

"Um, sir... we have a situation here."

The view changed from the Intercept cockpit camera to the external video and sensor readouts. Just the other side of the jumpgate, a cluster of a dozen Nova cruisers hung in the blackness, motionless relative to each other and the wormhole.

"Oh, that's unfortunate," Wojtera said.

"They're not attacking," Brandano reported, wonder in the statement as if he hadn't expected to be alive to give us the status. "They're broadcasting a message in the open, in the Resscharr language. It's for Lilandreth."

I looked to Vicky, then to Nance. Both appeared just as lost and clueless as I felt. But if I told Chase to keep the transmission private, the whole crew would know I was keeping it from them.

"Feed the transmission to the Predecessor ship," I told

Chase, "and put it on here live."

It felt like a mistake, but not one I could avoid making.

The transmission was video as well as audio, which was unfortunate, since I really hated looking at the octopus-faced bastards when they talked. This time, the shot showed the entire control center of one of the ships, revealing the nest-like pits in the deck where they squatted against the extreme boost they could endure.

Their commander stood higher than the rest on a podium rather than a pit, his tentacles wrapped around himself as if he were ashamed of his nakedness. That disgusting mouth moved and the gurgling, clucking sounds of their language were lost in the translation they'd sent, then the one Dwight had provided for us.

"Mistress, we would speak to you in peace." He inclined that bald, grotesque head toward the camera. "And in person, if you are willing."

"Why the hell would she do that?" Chase blurted, then reddened as if he'd just realized he said it aloud.

"Lilandreth," I said, knowing she'd hear me whether or not Chase looped her into our conversation. "How do you want to handle this?"

That was also risky. I knew I couldn't order her around—wouldn't have been able to even if she wasn't a telekinetic demigod. But deferring to her would undermine my authority with the crew.

"They're telling the truth," she said, her face appearing on the main display. Chase shook his head and gestured helplessly at his control board, dumbfounded. "I think I should meet with them in order to avoid danger to your ship and crew. Would you care to accompany me, Cameron?"

I carefully didn't let my frustration and annoyance show on my face, though I figured Lilandreth probably knew what I was feeling anyway. There was no way I could tell her no without looking bad, and she knew it. The question was why she wanted me there in the first place.

"Of course," I told her. "I'll head over in a few minutes."

The transmission ended whether I was done talking or not. I sighed between clenched teeth and unstrapped from my seat, motioning to the flight ops officer.

"Get me a lander prepped."

"Flying it yourself again, Alvarez?" Nance called out after me as I floated toward the bridge hatchway. His tone wasn't quite teasing, because there was nothing at all amusing about our current situation, but it was dryly humorous.

"That's what I like about you, Captain Nance," I told him. "You're so damned perceptive."

I'd barely made it to the central hub when Vicky swung out of the bridge level entrance, and the lack of gravity was the only reason she wasn't standing with feet wide and hands on her hips.

"I'm going."

"Why?" I asked, slipping past her, pulling myself into the transport hub. It was faster than the lift, since we weren't under acceleration. "Because to be honest, I don't want to go."

She followed just behind me, keeping pace, speaking up to be heard from two meters back.

"Because I'm tired of hearing about this shit secondhand. I want to see what's going on for myself."

"I know better than to try to talk you out of it," I reasoned, tightening my hand against the padded guide pole to slow to a halt at the hatchway for the hangar bay.

The lander was tucked into a niche near the center, beside Drop-Ship One. I waited for Vicky to emerge behind me, then waved at the ship.

"You drive."

[19]

"Good afternoon, Captain Alvarez, Captain Sandoval," Dr. Spinner said, scaring the shit out of me.

The little man had just *appeared* beside the lander's airlock as I dropped from the last step of the stairs, my hand going to my sidearm before I saw who it was. The hand stayed there as I got a good look at him. The scientist from the Grey Collective had never been what anyone would consider fashion-conscious, particularly since the Grey had gone in big for plain, unadorned clothes for their civilians that weren't too different from the uniforms their soldiers wore. But he'd taken it to a whole new level since he'd been left alone with Lilandreth here on her ship.

The fatigues we'd given him to replace his Grey Collective tunic and loose trousers were stained white with dried sweat, the front fastenings of the shirt undone to reveal that he wasn't wearing a T-shirt beneath it, just as the pungent smell wafting off of him revealed that he hadn't bathed recently. His dark, curly hair was uncut and unkempt, sticking out in random places where he'd slept on it and neglected to do anything about it.

The worst part was his eyes. Not that they were infinity pools like Lilandreth's, but the whites were as red as any Marine I'd intercepted staggering back to base after a colossal drunk, the corners thick with rheum.

No, I take it back. The worst part was his smile, the feral baring of yellow teeth showing plainly that not only was he aware of how he presented himself, but he was happy about it.

"Dr. Spinner," I said, taking a step back from him. "Are you all right?"

"Never been better!" he enthused, surging forward as if he wanted to take my hand. Another step back kept him from securing it and the scientist seemed to give up on the project, his palms raised instead toward the overhead like a Pentecostal preacher praising God. "There's so much pure knowledge here! I could spend the next thousand years on this ship and never reach the end of what there is to learn!"

"Well, that's great, Doc," Vicky said, taking shelter just behind my shoulder against the possibility that the manic little man would try to hug her. "But maybe take a little time for a bath? A change of clothes?"

Spinner looked down at himself as if he'd just noticed his appearance, but the smile didn't fade.

"Yes, yes... but things like that are trivial compared to the secrets of the universe! Compared to service to the Mistress." He waved back behind him. "She sent me to tell you that she's coming, that she'll fly with you to the Nova ship once we're through the jumpgate." Spinner shuddered like he was in ecstasy, eyes rolling back in his head, and I worried he was about to pass out. "How I envy you, to witness her greatness in person! Would that I could accompany you, but my duties keep me here." He shook his head frantically, glancing back as if afraid someone had overheard him. "Not that I would complain! No,

174

they are barely *duties* so much as privileges! If I'd known of the wonders of the Predecessors when I was but a lowly researcher on my world, a shaman casting animal bones and reading signs in the heavens, how I would have prayed for this opportunity..."

The guy was beginning to worry me now.

"We need to get Hallonen over here," Vicky whispered, making a circular motion with her finger beside her temple. Normally I would have worried that would offend Spinner, but the translator wouldn't work for culturally specific gestures.

I nodded. The alternative would be getting Spinner off the Predecessor ship, but we might have to tranquilize him to manage that. I was about to call back to the *Orion* to give the order, but a familiar shudder went through my soul and I reached out by reflex to steady myself against the lander's fuselage. We'd passed through the jumpgate.

The doctor's house call would have to wait.

"Are you prepared?"

And Jesus *Christ* if I wasn't getting sick and tired of the jump scares. I don't know how the hell a two-meter-tall talking dinosaur could be so stealthy, but Lilandreth was just suddenly *there*, right behind Vicky. Vicky's nails dug into my arm through my sleeve, though she kept her face neutral.

"As prepared as we're going to be," I said. "You sure you trust these fish-faced assholes enough to go out there in an unarmed lander?" I knocked on the thin armor of the fuselage demonstratively. It rang hollow.

"You know as well as I do that the armor of this aerospace-craft is not what protects us, Cameron."

"Yeah," I admitted, waving an invitation for her to board the shuttle, "I guess I do."

I just hoped to hell she remembered that we were there too.

"Holy shit," Vicky whispered close to my ear, her hand strategically placed over her nose. "And I thought *Spinner* smelled bad."

I'd experienced the stench before, when we'd met with the Nova back in the Commonwealth and then again on the Remainder world, but I would never, ever get used to it. If someone had left dead fish out in the sun for three days and then drenched the entire mess in fermented cat urine, the stench of that still wouldn't have approached how intensely horrible a ship full of Nova smelled. I breathed through a slitted mouth and debated internally whether *tasting* the stench was worse than smelling it.

We'd been escorted to the bridge by a squad of Nova soldiers, though none of them had attempted to disarm Vicky or me despite the fact we were openly carrying handguns. Neither had anyone pointed a weapon at us. In fact, they'd all averted their eyes from Lilandreth as if they thought looking straight at her was disrespectful.

The smell was almost distracting enough that I didn't notice the layout of the ship, but the peculiar design caught my attention. I guess it was a function of the spherical shape of the cruisers, but the docking bay was at the north pole of the globe, the opposite end from the drives. We'd dropped into the ship through an open hatchway that had closed behind us, pumping atmosphere back into the hangar bay... a lot faster than I'd imagined it would be. Not an efficient method in my estimate, but they hadn't had the need for efficiency.

A dozen of their cargo and troop landers were crowded around our shuttle like bullies on the playground trying to intimidate the new kid, but Lilandreth hadn't looked impressed, much less intimidated. The ship was under gravity... somehow. They lacked the gravitic technology of the Predecessors, so I had to assume that either they'd spun the sphere for centripetal force or boosted it at one gravity just for our comfort. I guessed the latter, since the "down" of the ship was toward the deck of the hangar bay.

I suppose that should have worried me—after all, they could be taking us farther away from the Predecessor ship, maybe even to another gate to kidnap us from the system. But Lilandreth just strode purposefully down the spiraling ramp that led from the hangar bay around the perimeter of the interior hull until we reached the center and the control room there.

The view on the central holographic projection showed that my guess had been correct. The cruiser had left the Predecessor vessel behind and described a lazy arc away from her, heading nowhere in particular, surely not toward the habitable planet.

The officer who'd sent the original message was there on the bridge, though I could identify him only by the markings on his harness and a peculiar keloid scar on his neck. Lilandreth stopped in front of him, arms crossed, waiting expectantly. The Nova commander performed something halfway between a bow of obeisance and a Russian split, then stood straight again.

"Welcome, Mistress," he said, spreading his arms, fingers waggling like they'd never stop moving, even after he was dead. "We thank you for your graciousness in agreeing to meet with us."

"Don't waste my time," Lilandreth snapped. "If you have a point, get to it."

"As you say, Mistress. We have wronged you, attempted to bend you to our will, and for this I would only seek to blame the one responsible, the Commander of the Splinter Worlds, the one you slew quite justly."

"The one Jay killed, you mean," I corrected him. I was certain the translator delivered the words in the Resscharr language, but the Nova commander didn't even glance aside at me, much less acknowledge the point.

"His sins are his own and died with him," the commander went on. "We would not have you judge us all by those transgressions. He sought to use you for our purposes. But we would instead have you use us for yours."

Lilandreth regarded him with a tilt of her head that might have been interest or merely curiosity.

"Go on," she urged.

"We came here as exiles." The Nova officer motioned expansively, including the ship and all the crew in the control room. "Chased from our homes for daring to think we might be destined for more than waiting for the return of those who would never come back. We wanted nothing so much as revenge, the opportunity to go back and right the wrongs done to us so many years ago. Now that you have come though, many of us realize you *are* the fulfilled promise of the return. We would put aside our petty desires and be your servants. We will conquer in your name, put this entire sector under your control and make sure that every Resscharr worships you as a god. And then, if it pleases you, we could accompany you back to the Nova Empire to lay their worlds at your feet as well."

It made sense, I had to admit. They knew what she could do, knew they couldn't defeat her. Joining with her was the only chance to take advantage of the success of their gambit. But I was still stunned by the offer. It was ballsy, daring... and insane. They were tying the very existence of their society on the whims of an alien who they *knew* might go mad.

"Interesting," Lilandreth said, tapping her fingertips together in front of her chin. "Your offer is within the parameters of possibility and thus was not entirely unforeseen, but I estimated the odds of you actually going through with it at no more than thirty percent. I must admit, the concept is not without its attraction. Let me ask you a question in return. You would put yourself at my command, put your existence in my hands... but how far would you go?" She tilted a scaly eyebrow. "Would you risk annihilation at my word?"

A prickle of alarm heated up the back of my neck and I eyed her sidelong. Was she teasing them, playing with the Nova for her own amusement, or was she seriously considering this? Or was she teasing *me*?

"We pledge to obey until the death," the Nova officer vowed, his arms forming a pattern that might have been their equivalent of a salute. "We trust you not to waste us as a resource."

"That's kind of equivocating, isn't it?" Vicky asked, smirking at the Nova. "If you *really* have faith in her, you'd just say 'yes,' and mean it."

The translator for the 'link repeated the words in Resscharr, so I knew the Nova understood her, but he ignored the comment, didn't even give her a dirty look, acting as if she wasn't even there. I had the sense that if we hadn't been Lilandreth's ride, the Nova would have tossed us both out of an airlock.

Lilandreth regarded the Nova officer with a measured stare, as if she were judging his worth.

"I believe you." She held up a finger, forestalling any celebration or oaths of fealty. "However, I need time to consider all the possibilities. I must go back to my ship and... contemplate the situation. I believe you will be useful, but you must be utilized correctly. Give me a few hours and I'll get back to you."

"As you say, Mistress." Again with that multijointed, acrobatic bow.

Lilandreth didn't acknowledge it, simply turned and walked away, leaving us jogging to follow her.

"And I want this ship within flight range of my vessel before I return to my lander," Lilandreth added over her shoulder.

I said nothing, not even in English, as we circled the inner edge of the sphere's hull, the Nova guards scrambling to keep up with us. They *probably* didn't have a translation program for our language, but there was no use taking chances. The journey back up to the hangar bay took a lot longer than the way down, and not just because the cruiser began maneuvering halfway along the arc to turn us back toward Lilandreth's ship and Vicky and I and the Nova guards had to pause to grab onto handholds along the passage and hang on for dear life. Not Lilandreth though. She just stood there, waiting patiently, as if gravity and momentum were mere inconveniences rather than immutable laws of motion.

Even once the thrust was just straight behind us, it was a steep climb up a slick, metal ramp, reminiscent of trying to make my way up the hill to the troop barracks on Hachiman. My quads cramped and my right knee ached a little despite the best efforts of the Commonwealth Fleet Medical Corps. They'd rebuilt the whole thing twice and it *should* have been perfect, but nothing ever was.

I couldn't help but keep glancing back at the Nova guards, wondering if their commander would decide that Lilandreth's answer hadn't been definitive enough and he needed to have his soldiers try a surprise shot to the back in hopes of taking her out before she became too big of a threat. Which would have been bad for her but worse for us, because neither Vicky nor I had any telekinetic superpowers.

The squad of soldiers simply formed a line and watched impassively as we boarded the shuttle. Vicky went to the cockpit and began the start-up sequence, but I hesitated beside the airlock and looked at Lilandreth.

"What are you thinking?" I asked, not trying to conceal my concerns because it wouldn't do any good.

Lilandreth smiled, which I knew was an affectation for my benefit.

"Don't be concerned, Cameron. You worry that I may take their offer, make the Nova exiles my army and try to conquer this part of the galaxy. I wouldn't do such a thing."

I sighed, nodded, grateful that she'd proven my faith in her justified. The ghosts might get to her eventually, but she was still the same Lilandreth I'd known.

But she wasn't done, and when she spoke again, that darkness flashed in her eyes.

"If I were to conquer, I would need no army, would make no bargains to gain one. My followers would declare me god not because they want something from me, but because it would be undeniable, because I am that I am."

The casual blasphemy didn't bother me as much as the undeniable thought that it had lifted from, if not my thoughts, then at least a bone-deep knowledge of me from youth to present. I said nothing, *thought* nothing, keeping my mind and expression as blank as possible. She was a reader and I gave her nothing to read, not so much as a thought flickering across my eyes.

"Everybody, get strapped in," Vicky called back from the cockpit, breaking the deadlock between us. "They're opening the hatch and I'm blasting us out of here as quick as possible. I don't trust these assholes not to take a shot at us for spite."

I didn't want to look away from Lilandreth for much the same reason, and I backed my way into the cockpit and fell into the copilot's seat. Vicky frowned a question at me, but I just shook my head.

"I wouldn't worry about the Nova, Victoria," Lilandreth said, speaking normally from back in the passenger compartment, yet her voice could have been a whisper in my ear. "The Nova are many things, but they're not stupid."

Vicky's jaw tightened, and she pushed the throttle forward as if the roar of the belly jets could shut out the Lilandreth's voice. Could shut out the ghost voices trying to turn her into a monster. But I knew the truth.

Nothing could.

[20]

"Did it go well, Mistress?" Dr. Spinner asked, so close to the shuttle's landing spot in the hangar bay that I wondered how he'd avoided being singed when the belly jets had fired their last blast to touch us down.

"As well as might be expected," she told him, making a shooing gesture to force the dirty little man back as she descended the steps. I wasn't certain she'd actually touched any of them. She paused at the bottom and looked back up at me. I waited in the hatch, ready to close it as quickly as possible, but her smile interrupted that intent. "You and Vicky should come to the control room with me, Cameron. You'll find this interesting."

"We really have to get back to the *Orion*," I told her, pushing the button to close the airlock. Nothing happened except Lilandreth's eyebrow twitched.

"I must insist," she told me. "Besides, you can't make it back through the jumpgate and all the way to your ship in that lander. I'll take you back through myself... afterward."

After what? Vicky mouthed the words at me and I shrugged. But I couldn't close the damned airlock, which probably meant we wouldn't be able to start the engines without Lilandreth's consent. The walls were closing in around us, but I had no answer other than to do what she wanted and hope there was still a way out of this.

"All right," Vicky answered for both of us, pausing halfway down the steps to point at Spinner. "But you keep this rancid monkey away from me. I haven't been poked at by someone this smelly since I was in high school."

"Spinner, go back to the archives and amuse yourself," Lilandreth told him.

The scientist looked disappointed that he wouldn't be accompanying us, but he was, if nothing else, an obedient pet, and he rushed to do as his mistress wished. I guess we were doing the same thing, though we didn't smell as bad doing it. Yet.

"Is that what you have planned for us?" I wondered, staring off after Spinner.

"I don't have to *plan* these things, Cameron," she corrected me, not looking back, just assuming we were behind her still. "I don't have to plan anything. I act and the consequences fall out as they must. The symmetry is beautiful. I wish I could show it to you two." Lilandreth paused and half-turned toward us, and there might have been genuine regret in her expression. "There's so much I'd love to share with all of you. You humans are pesky creatures, you know? Had you not evolved, had you not managed to survive our attempt to extirpate you, we might still cling to our home on Earth. And yet I can't bring myself to hate you, or even resent you. You succeeded where our many creations failed, and you did it without our help. Perhaps that was our mistake, to think we could achieve artificially what necessarily had to happen by chance, by the whims of chaos. And now here you are, resourceful, spirited, wonderfully violent. Not even I, who can draw on the computational power of a universe, could have designed servants so perfect."

Lilandreth didn't wait for our reaction to that, which was just as well, since I wasn't sure whether the bird Vicky shot her would have been greeted with amusement or outrage.

The control room was as active as if it had been crewed the entire time we were gone... or as if Lilandreth had never truly been away from it. On the projection screens, the Nova ships waited, the one we'd boarded now back in its place in the globular cluster formation, lined up for review on a parade field.

Trying to impress the new boss.

"I've really lost all respect for the Reconstructors," Lilandreth sighed, staring at the ships. "I mean, I know they were getting desperate, but these... *things* they created to serve them." Her shoulders shuddered. "It reeks of desperation. It's one thing to be suited to serve, another to beg for it like animals."

She fell silent, her shoulders hunched, and I thought she was angry, raging at her distant relatives for their mistake. I knew I'd read it wrong when the air between us and her began to shimmer as if we were staring at her through a heat mirage in the desert. Having no idea what that signified, I pushed Vicky behind me and backed away a few meters.

The rage wasn't aimed at us though.

The power shot out from her as if she were a lens focusing the photons of a laser, not slicing through our own bulkhead and hull but somehow piercing the virtual layer of the holographic projection and spearing out into space as if the screen were a physical viewport. That was clearly impossible, but I'd grown inured to the impossible lately. However it manifested itself, the energy burst cohered again on the outside of the hull, clearly visible despite the lack of particulates to interact with it.

It moved much slower than light, and yet the Nova cruiser had no chance to maneuver out of its way. I had time to consider that perhaps the visible beam was nothing more than an optical illusion created for our benefit by Lilandreth, that the Nova saw nothing, detected nothing of it until it was too late. Before that notion had bounced from one side of my brain to the other, the cruiser imploded.

It was very much like a singularity had opened up at the heart of the giant, spherical ship, sucking it inexorably into the depths of hell. Perhaps hell didn't want them, because the collapse ended in an eruption, what had begun as metal transformed into white energy and burning vapor, a sphere of destruction.

There was no sound, no shockwave, and yet I went back on my heels with the same slap to the chest I would have felt if the explosion had been a half a klick away instead of a hundred thousand kilometers. Vicky whistled softly, which was a casual reaction given the circumstances, but maybe she was trying to keep from appearing intimidated. I looked between Lilandreth and the screen, waiting for her to finish the job, destroy the rest of the Nova ships, an inevitable secondary effect to the first one going up.

Instead, she smiled at me, so very cold and inhuman, talons of ice clawing at my chest.

"I think I've conveyed my answer to their proposal quite clearly, don't you?"

"Yeah, I'm sure they got the message," I said, my voice hoarse, my mouth dry.

"We'll go back through to the *Orion* now," Lilandreth promised, and even as she spoke the words, the Nova cruisers and the explosion at the heart of their formation dropped away from us, the Predecessor ship pulling away, heading for the jumpgate. "I'm sure they'll be glad to see you return safely." The smile faded and I was glad to see it gone, but what replaced it was dark, turbulent, the same kind of anger that had been a prelude to the storm of destruction a moment ago. "We have much to discuss once you're back. You're a persuasive young man, Cameron. I'll need you to persuade your crew that I'm the only hope you have to return to your home, that only by agreeing to serve me will they have a chance to see their loved ones again."

"I thought you'd decided to stay here," I said.

"This?" She waved a hand around. "This is death and ruin, the sad remains of a once-great empire. The remnants here are more pitiful than the societies I encountered on my journeys with you out of Yfingam. No, your Commonwealth seems much more promising."

Shit. With every second it felt as if my testicles were shrinking back into my stomach.

"I'm sure your people will be amenable. I know just how badly they all wish to be with their friends and family. Though I'm afraid Dwight will have to be dealt with."

"Dealt with?" Vicky asked sharply.

"Of course." Lilandreth inclined her head toward us. "You humans I have some affection for, but the AI... well, you've seen it yourself, haven't you? They've been responsible for every horrible nightmare we Resscharr have undergone in the last ten millennia, from the Skrela to the ghosts that caused the destruction around us. How can you allow their infection into your home systems? How could *I* allow my ancient enemy to accompany us on our journey?" She sighed as if the decision was difficult for her, as if she'd agonized over it during sleepless nights. "No, I'm going to be forced to purge him from your systems, starting with the quantum core of the *Orion* and going down from there to your individual 'links. Every string of code will be eliminated until the AI are no longer a threat to me... or you."

"What about Homecoming?" I asked, shaking my head, not at all surprised by what I was hearing, simply terrified. "I thought the idea was to find the heart of the Reconstructor civilization, find the lab where we could cure you. We can't do that without Dwight."

"Cured?" Lilandreth barked a laugh, throwing back her head as if I'd said something hilarious.

Every show of emotion she'd ever displayed was fake, done for our benefit, and I knew that... on an intellectual level. Believing it in my gut was another matter. In that moment, I could believe it. The cackle was so self-consciously diabolical, it could only be deliberate.

"Cameron, I'm a *god*. Who would wish to be *cured* of that?"

———

"What the hell are we going to do?" Vicky asked me as the lander slid into the docking niche in the *Orion*'s hangar bay.

Neither of us had said a word the entire flight until the gray metal womb of the ship had swallowed us up. The security the embrace of the *Orion* gave us was probably illusory, but if we couldn't talk now, then there simply would be no safe place or time and we might as well give up.

"We tell them," I said, the only answer I could come up with. "We tell them and decide together. This is too big for me to make the call. It's the difference between servitude and survival against resistance and almost certain death."

The magnetic locks settled in with a metallic thunk, and the turning in my gut as I moved to the hatch wasn't just because of the lack of gravity.

"What happened to all that talk about returning to military discipline?" Vicky asked, slapping the airlock control, and maybe part of it was teasing, but part was an honest question. "We running the ship as a democracy now?"

Ouch. That stung, especially from her... and especially since I knew she was right.

I wasn't doing something noble and compassionate by letting the crew make the decision, I was pushing off the responsibility because I had no idea what to do. How could we hope to fight Lilandreth? Even without her being able to predict our every reaction, she still had the power to blow the entire ship apart just using her brain.

"Dwight," I said quietly as I passed through the lock and into the hangar bay. "We have a big fucking problem."

"I'm aware."

I didn't curse, but it took some effort. Vicky just rolled her eyes.

"How? I know Lilandreth wouldn't have let you monitor us remotely through the wormhole. Not the way she feels about you at the moment."

"I was not present as a coherent code section," Dwight explained, though with an impatient edge to his voice that I hadn't heard before. "I simply instructed your 'links to record while you were gone, then downloaded their memory once you were aboard the ship."

"I should delete you myself," I told him, scrambling up into the central transport hub and pulling myself hand over hand. "But I need ideas. Tell me you have one."

"There's no way to attack her directly. She'd anticipate it and destroy us immediately."

"Yeah, we know that," Vicky strained out from behind me. "I thought you were supposed to be the big-brained AI."

"I can't invent possibilities that don't exist. All we can do is react to what she does. Eradicating me won't be as easy as she believes anyway. She's not omniscient. Even with access to the Transition Space neural network, she can only work with information that is actually available to her. She can predict your

189

actions, but only based on the facts she knows about you, what's in your records, what you've told her. As for me... she *thinks* she has all the information on the AI, but we never trusted her people. They know what we wanted them to know."

"She knows enough to hate you," I informed him. "She's going to erase you from our databanks, and the only reason she hasn't already is probably because she knew we'd tell you about it and she wants you to suffer the only way she can make you, by forcing you to contemplate your own mortality."

"You're undoubtedly correct about that. If I've discovered anything about the Resscharr, it's that they have a nearly preternatural ability to avoid taking blame for any sins they've committed. It's why I once believed the only way to keep the rest of the universe safe from them was to eradicate them. I suppose it's poetic justice that one of them now has the power to do the same to me."

"Yeah, poetic," I agreed. "That's exactly what I was thinking, how tragic this was for you."

"I sense sarcasm, Captain Alvarez. Surely this isn't the time for that sort of thing."

Thank God we reached the bridge, because I wasn't sure how much more of Dwight's crap I could take. Though having to explain what had happened to Nance in front of the whole bridge crew wasn't much better. The captain swung around in his chair as Vicky and I floated onto the bridge, having foregone the stability of our ship boots' sticky plates in favor of the speed of free-fall maneuvering.

"How did it go?" Nance demanded, spreading his hands as if I should have told him already.

"Not well." I fastened my seat harness as I talked, mostly out of habit. We weren't going anywhere, but being the one guy not strapped in when the shit hit the fan was painful. "They offered to be her loyal army, she said she'd consider it, and then once we were off their ship, she blew the damned thing up by way of telling them no."

"Shit," Nance commented simply.

"Sir," Wojtera said, facing me with utter confusion writ across his broad, plain features, "how is she doing this? That ship doesn't have any operational weapons."

It wasn't just the Tactical officer staring at me, the entire bridge was, Vicky included.

"The Nova experimented on her down on the Remainder world," I said, deciding to rip the bandage off quickly. "Exposed her to an experimental treatment from back in the days of the Reconstructors. It basically gave her telekinetic abilities." And the rest of it could wait, since it had no bearing on the situation at hand.

"Telekinetic?" Yanayev repeated, eyes going wide. "That's pseudoscientific babble!"

"Not when the Predecessors do it. It's beyond me, but it involves accessing Transition Space and changing thoughts into energy. Pseudoscience or not, we've seen it work... and so have you. It's how Lilandreth destroyed the Nova fleet."

Disciplined or no, there was no stopping the buzz of conversation and the blurted questions that exploded out of that revelation like I'd tossed a grenade into the middle of them.

"Worse than that," I told them, raising my voice to override the chatter, "there's a side-effect to the treatment. It's driving her insane." Complete silence and many horrified stares greeted the proclamation. "And the first symptoms are narcissism. She wants to take us back to the Commonwealth and conquer it, rule it as a god. We can either submit or she'll pop us like a soap bubble, the same way she did to the Nova cruisers. I doubt she would have allowed Captain Sandoval and I back on the *Orion* except she wanted us to convey her demands."

And there it was. Everything out in the open, which meant

it would spread to the entire ship soon. I didn't think it mattered. They'd have known soon enough. As their commanding officer, my next move should have been to reassure them that everything was going to be okay, that I had a plan to get us out of this and all they had to do was follow orders, do their jobs and trust me. I'd once been a pretty good liar but I'd fallen out of practice, and this didn't seem like a good time to start the habit again.

Almost as if she'd been listening in—and she likely had—Lilandreth's face popped onto the screen, bringing a collective gasp from the bridge officers. Not from me. I'd been expecting her.

"Captain Alvarez has presented you with my offer," she said. "I will return you to your homes in exchange for your unquestioning service to me." Her imitation smile was almost warm this time. "Trust me when I tell you, those who swear fealty to me now will be among the most rewarded when I come into my kingdom." Again with the sacrilegious shit. Again, I was sure, aimed at me. "You will rule your own worlds, each of you," Lilandreth promised, not with the manic verve of an evangelist but more with the slick warmth of a salesman. "If you follow me, the masses will bow to you as they do to me and none will have power over you except me. For this, I give you my word." Her long-faced features darkened, the warmth draining away. "But those who would refuse my gracious offer should beware. I prefer willing servants, but I don't *require* your consent." She tilted her head in a shrug. "I am not unreasonable. You probably require time to consider this. I give you five minutes."

The screen went blank, but not as blank as the stares from everyone on the bridge.

"She's starting," Dwight said. His avatar was on the screen, but there was something wrong with it. The edges of the image grew fuzzy, static playing across it. "She's trying to access the system and delete me."

Damn. She hadn't wasted any time, and all I could do was wonder what she knew about me and what she didn't. She knew my military career inside and out, knew about my beginnings as an orphan, my experience in the group homes that were a matter of public record. But she didn't know a damned thing about my life on the street, how I'd stayed alive.

"Lilandreth," I said, the words flowing out naturally, as if they'd been bottled up inside for years and I'd simply released them, "is there any way we could compromise on this?"

I thought she'd ignore me, but in a second her face reappeared on the projection.

"What sort of compromise?"

"Well, you know, me, I'm all for your idea. I mean, why should I give a damn about the Commonwealth? They gave me the choice between the Freezer and the Marines, and I chose the option where I would maybe get out and have a life after. Then I found out that the only reason we had a second war at all was that the Corporate Council was running things and didn't want to lose the threat of the Tahni by taking them out at the end of the first war." I shrugged. "But that's *me*. A lot of the people on the ship are less pragmatic than I am, and I don't want to see them turned into zombies like Spinner just because they haven't taken off the rose-colored glasses, you know? So, I was thinking... maybe the ones who don't want to do this you could just leave behind? They could maybe settle on one of the habitables here where they wouldn't cause you any trouble? As a favor to me?"

I didn't *mean* any of it, of course... well, except the part about the Corporate Council, I guess. But that wasn't the point. We needed to buy time, and one thing I'd learned on the streets, scamming the gangs and the Surface Dweller marks, was that bullies love to have their egos stroked. And doing it was the best way to keep them distracted from pounding me into the ground. The downside to this whole gambit was, I had no endgame, no TAP patrol to call, no back alley to duck into. I was trying desperately to think of one though.

"That *is* an intriguing option," Lilandreth admitted, laying a finger on her cheek. "And doing this would insure your support..."

Whatever she might have decided was lost in a shout of alarm by Wojtera, half the screen shifting to the wormhole as it suddenly sprouted a crop of spherical fruit.

"Nova cruisers!" he yelled. "They're coming through!"

[21]

I was only surprised it had taken this long.

I'd expected the Nova to panic after Lilandreth had destroyed their command cruise. That part hadn't been hard to predict and I didn't even have a universe-sized supercomputer. But how that panic translated into action was another story. They might have run. I'd given it about even odds against the other end of the fight-or-flight response, but if they'd chosen to fight, I didn't see the point in waiting until Lilandreth was back on this side of the wormhole.

Unless it was to gather reinforcements. There were many more of the cruisers than I'd seen the last time we were over on the other side of the gate, and this time they hadn't come to talk. One, then two of them flashed into nonexistence with a flexing of Lilandreth's mental muscles, but the others didn't falter, focusing dozens of plasma cannon blasts on the glowing-green hull of the Predecessor ship.

The gravitic field swelled into a brilliant halo of verdant energy, not overwhelmed but getting close, and I held my breath, praying the Nova would take care of our problem for us. Holding my breath turned out to be a bad choice, because in the next instant every bit of air in my lungs gushed out as the drives ignited and boost pressed me back into my chair with what had to be close to nine gravities of acceleration.

Mercifully, I blacked out.

Transition woke me up... and just as I blinked back to consciousness, we jumped again back into normal space and the rubber-band snap of reality yanked everything in my stomach back up into my throat. I barely had the presence of mind to clamp my jaws shut against the rush of bile, couldn't speak as a jumpgate filled the main screen... then bone-crushing acceleration slammed me into my seat again and I swallowed the mouthful of vomitus just before passing out again.

The vague sensation of passing through a wormhole pierced the crushing, breathless pressure of emergency boost, then another micro-Transition. This time the boost wasn't a nine-gravity bone-breaker, just a generally uncomfortable three or four and I stayed conscious, able to focus on the main screen, on the image of our main gun firing. The blue spear of energy disappeared into a point in space and that point expanded into the fuzzy, vaguely defined circle of a jumpgate. It barely stayed open long enough for us to pass through it and the boost went back to a single gravity.

I sat up, wiping blood off my nose and vomit off my chin, the blaring of klaxons not quite able to drown out the moans and curses from the bridge crew. Some of the more colorful curses were from Vicky as she worked her left shoulder.

"Didn't get strapped in tight enough," she told me when I looked over at her in concern. "Think I dislocated my shoulder, but I popped it back in."

Which was not ideal, but right now she could wait.

"Turn off the Goddamn alarms!" Nance snapped and Chase hurried to obey, his eyes struggling to focus. "Somebody tell me what the fuck just happened!"

"I apologize," Dwight said. His avatar was back, looking none the worse for wear, or at least not as bad as the rest of us. "I'm afraid I took control of the ship. It was an emergency."

"I won't argue that," I allowed. I tried to find something on the navigation screen that could tell me where we were, but the data streaming across it was incomprehensible. "How far did we go?"

"I took us through five jumpgates."

"*Five?*" Nance repeated, disbelief in his slack expression.

"Bridge, this is Hallonen." The woman's voice was strained, her breath hissing into the audio pickup. "We have multiple injury reports coming in. Broken bones, ligament tears, concussions. Are we going to be performing any more unannounced emergency burns, or can I send my people out to take care of the wounded?"

"Dwight?" I asked, eyeing the AI's avatar. "Are we?"

"We should be fine at one gravity for the moment," he said. "Unless we run into any Nova forces. But we'll have to micro-Transition to the next gate. We have to stay ahead of her."

I didn't have to ask who *her* meant.

"Go ahead, Doc," I told Hallonen. I looked around the bridge and noted a couple of people dabbing at cuts or bloody noses. "And once you get the worst cases taken care of, maybe send someone up to the bridge to patch a few cuts and a dislocated shoulder."

"Right."

Cautiously, I unstrapped and took a ginger step, still unsure if I'd picked up any injuries without knowing it. Nothing felt broken, and I leaned against the arm of my chair, fighting to take a full breath with sore ribs.

"Five jumpgates, Dwight?" I repeated Nance's question.

"I micro-Transitioned between safe minimum distances," the AI explained, "and boosted at twelve gravities to get to the safe Transition distance." He shook his virtual head. "I fear it still may not be enough, but going farther at that kind of boost would have badly injured or killed many of you."

"Top, what's your status down there?" Vicky asked, leaning over the comm speaker on her seat's armrest. "Any casualties?"

"Oh, hell yeah, ma'am," Czarnecki growled, his deep bass rattling the speaker. "Got a dozen Marines down with broken bones, four probable concussions. No one dead though."

"Medics should be down soon to take care of you," Vicky assured him. "Provide first aid and hang tight."

"Okay, we're running," I went on to Dwight once I was satisfied the Marines would be all right. "Running's good, but I have to assume from your gloomy demeanor that it's only a short-term answer."

"Lilandreth was distracted by the Nova," Dwight agreed, "but that won't last more than a few minutes. An hour at the very most, if the Nova are smart and don't care if they die in the attempt to kill her. Once she sets out after us, well... you've seen what her ship can do. She can take it right up to the edge of lightspeed and doesn't have to slow down to go through the jumpgates. We've gained hours at most. We have to make the most of them."

"And do *what*?" Wojtera snapped.

I raised an eyebrow at the outburst, but if the Tactical officer noticed, he didn't care.

"You said she's basically a god," Wojtera pointed out, his usual laconic, unflappable attitude completely evaporated in the face of this one last straw. "What are we gonna do when she catches up with us? Beg for mercy again?"

"We have one chance," Dwight replied, and thank God, because I had no ideas. "We have to get to Homecoming, to the Predecessor biotech facility there, and find a way to reverse what's happened to her."

"Unfortunately," I said, frowning at the suggestion, "we don't have Lilandreth to guide us to Homecoming, and I doubt the system is in our nav charts."

"I've deduced its location."

And *that* was another bomb dropping into the middle of us.

"You did what?" Vicky demanded.

"I told you," Dwight explained, smirking, "I listen, I gather intelligence in order to be more effective. I used the record of the jumpgates, the data I gathered from the Remainder world, the data I scrubbed from the recordings on your 'links when you were on Lilandreth's ship... and, in my copious spare time since you arrived, I've been cross-checking each data stream. It's not certain, but I would give it a seventy percent chance that I've found the system."

"How far?" Nance asked, a light of hope rekindling in his eyes.

"Five more gates. Five systems. Unfortunately, I also believe there are Nova forces between us and Homecoming."

"We'll worry about them when the time comes," I told him. "The question is, if we get there, can you actually pull this off? Can you reverse what's been done to her?"

"Unknown." Dwight confessed. "My best hope is to cure her. The backup plan is to find a way to kill her." His avatar raised its hands in acknowledgement. "She doesn't deserve it. She didn't ask for this. But if it's a choice between us and her, well..."

"We try to help her first," I told him. "She risked her life to save mine. I owe her that much. But if it comes down to it, if there's no way to reverse what's been done to her, then yes, our backup is going to have to be killing her. We can't let what she's become loose on the Commonwealth."

"Where are we, Woj?" I asked, suddenly realizing I hadn't

even checked the details of the system we'd been traveling through. "Any threats?"

"Nothing," the man replied, a sullen undertone to his words, though the existence of a plan seemed to have mollified him a little. "No sign of habitation, no energy readings. As far as I can tell, we're alone here." He shrugged. "We have another half-hour before we reach the next jumpgate."

I frowned.

"Chase, tell Dr. Hallonen we only have a half-hour until all the wounded need to be secured. Make a general announcement to the entire crew giving them twenty minutes to get themselves squared away."

"Yes, sir."

"It would help our odds," Dwight put in, "if we could increase boost. My recommendation would be four gravities for ten minutes, two for a half hour, alternating."

I glared at his avatar.

"We already have injured from your last high-G boost," I reminded him. "We start running four Gs ten minutes at a time, three times an hour, we'll have people stroking out."

"What about the hibernation pods?" Vicky suggested. "We put all nonessential personnel into the pods, run a skeleton crew and keep them—*us*—doped up on blood thinners and stimulants to ride out the burn."

I exchanged a troubled look with Nance.

"It should work," he acceded with obvious reluctance. "But I'd ask Hallonen first."

"Vicky, you need that shoulder taken care of," I said. "Head down to medical, and while you're there run the idea by the Doc."

She nodded and jogged off out the bridge hatch. I knew her shoulder had to be hurting pretty bad because she didn't argue with me. I watched her go before I looked back up at Dwight on the holographic projection.

"You're all about predicting odds," I said. "What are the odds that when we get to Homecoming the Nova are already going to be there?"

"Unquantifiable. But what I gleaned from the Nova flagship where you were taken for the... *negotiation* indicates they don't know of its existence. Yet. I'm confident they will be there shortly, however."

"How can you be so sure?" Nance wondered.

"That's obvious, Captain." The look Dwight's avatar affected was grim. "They'll be following *us* there."

[22]

"I'm not looking forward to this," Nance admitted, shoulders sagging as he settled back into his acceleration couch. "Emergency high-gravity boosts are always hell, but this shit..." he tapped a fingertip against the drug patch on his neck, "... always makes me sick as a dog for hours afterward."

I rubbed at the identical patch on my own neck and had to agree. I wasn't a spacer either by trade or nature, yet it seemed my fate to ride high-gravity burns, and they always sucked.

"Look at the bright side," I told him. "At least you didn't have to try to convince Vicky to go into the pod."

Nance laughed.

"How'd you manage it?"

"I told her if she reinjured her shoulder during the boost, she wouldn't be able to suit up if we needed her. If there's anything that can get Vicky to do something she doesn't want to, it's appealing to her sense of duty." I sighed. "Unfortunately, that's not something that generally works in a marriage."

"Shit, if I knew how to make a marriage work, you think I'd have volunteered for this operation?"

The bridge seemed deserted. We hadn't kicked *everyone* off, of course. Yanayev and Wojtera were still around, though not Chase. We weren't launching Intercepts—not least because they wouldn't be able to maintain that kind of boost—so there'd be no other ships to communicate with, and there was no need for anyone to field calls from other compartments or send out warnings, since two-thirds of the crew would be under. Same went for the Flight Ops officer and Damage Control. Not that we couldn't conceivably take some damage, but there wouldn't be enough crew to pull it off unless it was an emergency and we had to wake everyone up.

Lt. Springfield was the only Marine officer staying awake besides me, along with a platoon of Drop Troopers, just in case. Campea had made a case for keeping his Force Recon troops up, arguing they might be needed to repel any boarding actions, but I was pretty sure that if the ship was badly damaged enough that we were going to be boarded, one platoon of Force Recon wouldn't save the day.

Luckily, the next system after the one we'd sowed down for was likewise empty, because if we'd faced opposition there, we wouldn't have had the luxury of doing this at all. We were keeping at one gravity until everyone was tucked in, which I would have been fine with a couple hours ago, but now that Dwight had made me paranoid about both Lilandreth and the Nova, I was sweating every minute.

I tapped the comms control on my armrest and leaned over it by reflex, though that wasn't necessary.

"Doc, we close to being done down there?"

"We're five minutes closer than we were the last time you called me, Alvarez," she snapped. I said nothing, just waited, having gone through this dance with Hallonen before. When she spoke again, her tone was more measured. "Nearly done. I'm not going under. You're going to need *someone* to stay awake who knows how to pull the others out of hibernation, and I wouldn't ask any of my people to go through this torture. We just have the rest of the medical bay crew to put down. Say... ten minutes."

"Thanks, Doc." I grinned, even though she couldn't see it. "And thanks for volunteering to stay up and take the punishment."

"Oh, don't give me that feel-good horseshit, Alvarez," she scoffed. "I know exactly how much punishment *you've* taken because I've had to repair most of it."

I shrugged, not knowing how to respond to that.

"Give me the heads up once you're strapped in, Doc."

A muscle in my cheek twitched and my hand shook as a general feeling of antsy discomfort made me squirm in my seat. The stimulants were kicking in a little early, along with the other affects, and they made me want to try to hit the head one more time before the boost. It was a waste of time, of course. I'd emptied my bladder and hadn't had so much as a sip from the bulb of water tucked into a pocket of my chair. I'd need it eventually, along with the protein bars in the same pocket. We'd planned ahead for that, a half-hour break halfway through the ordeal when we'd drop down to one gravity, though that had provoked an argument with Dwight, who seemed to regard us as being wimpy for not toughing the thing out right to the end.

I checked the time, thought about calling Hallonen again but rejected it, checked the time again. Not much had passed, the stimulants making each second drag by, and I'd just about decided to risk getting up and going to the bathroom despite the unlikelihood of it doing any good when the speaker in my armrest crackled, startling me.

"All right, Alvarez," Hallonen said. "I just slapped on the patch. Let's get this over with."

I squeezed my eyes shut, checked my 'link again. Somehow,

nearly ten minutes had passed. Whatever this shit was that the patch was feeding me, it was the good stuff.

"All right, Captain Nance," I sighed, settling back. "Get us moving."

"All personnel," Nance announced into the PA system, "prepare for emergency boost."

That and the alarm klaxon that sounded next were pretty much a formality. Those of us still awake knew what was coming.

"Yanayev," he went on into the last echoes of the alarm. "Engage emergency acceleration."

A rumbling roar of thunder filled my head, the vibration from the drive building up into a relentless, crushing pressure. Not the overwhelming surge of pain and inevitable blackout of before... though in some ways, this was even worse.

Four gravities was right at the edge, the most acceleration I personally could take without it affecting my ability to think coherently... for a while. But it was enough to be painful, like that old method of execution I'd read about where the victim was placed under a wooden door and rocks were piled on top of it. The ordeal could last for days and was considered a horrible way to die, and after a few minutes of the constrictive force, I was hoping the bastards trying to kill me would just add another rock.

"Passing through the jumpgate in ten seconds," Dwight said, his voice distant and tiny and disgustingly unaffected by the tortuous acceleration. "Recommend reduction to two gravities now."

"Two gravities, Helm," Nance gasped out.

The stimulants had another benefit besides keeping me from passing out after ten minutes in high boost. They also kept me alert, which meant my surroundings hadn't taken on the gauzy haze that usually fell over my vision after a couple minutes at these kinds of acceleration. I was focused on the main screen, saw clearly the glittering play of the energy cannon as it activated the wormhole, expanding the sub-microscopic tear in the fabric of reality into something large enough to allow a ship to pass through it.

The influx of air as my chest was finally able to expand wasn't the absolute flood of relief I usually felt. The stims and other drugs the patch injected me with held back the extremes of agony but also robbed me of the sublime pleasure of their passing. It was a tradeoff I could live with, since it meant I was thinking clearly when the next system cohered into the glowing fusion flare of a star, a living planet close enough that the rich blues and greens were plain on the circle of the world... and the cluster of stars moving fast enough that they couldn't be natural.

"We have bogies!" Wojtera exclaimed, springing into action now that the boost had been dialed back to two gravities. "Thirty... no, thirty-*two* cruisers, coming in from fifty-three degrees relative north, accelerating at six gravities. They're positioning to cut us off from the exit gate."

"How long until we're at safe Transition distance?" Nance asked him just as my mouth had opened to voice the same question.

"Twelve minutes at two Gs," Wojtera answered so quickly that he had to have anticipated the query. "They're going to reach us first."

"Shit," I muttered. "All right, we didn't get all this shit pumped into our blood for nothing. Six gravities to the Transition point and then we micro-Transition. Dwight, plot the jump for us."

Not that I didn't trust Yanayev to do it, but the drug patches couldn't help but affect our thought processes, and I wanted a check from something that didn't have to worry about human weakness.

"I can handle the boost and the Transition if you prefer, Captain Alvarez," Dwight offered, and Yanayev scowled at him.

"No, that's okay," I said. "This isn't Commander Yanayev's first rodeo."

And I would have had to listen to her complain about letting the AI do her job for days afterward... not without justification. There was a reason the Commonwealth didn't allow AI to run our warships, and everything we'd discovered about the fate of the Predecessors convinced me that we'd made the right decision.

I sucked in a breath, shook my arms out to loosen them up, and tried to relax.

"Engage boost."

Four minutes at six gravities didn't *sound* like a long time. A fellow Marine—not *me*—had made the case once to a Fleet Attack Command pilot once in a bar on Eden that he could put up with anything for just a few minutes. The Fleet pilot's response had been delivered with the air of superiority for which pilots were famous, but she hadn't been wrong. Imagine, she'd said, a 450-kilo bull elk sitting on your chest for five minutes. Not only making it nearly impossible to get a full breath, but while the bull was sitting there you had to try to make sense of instrument readings from a display and manipulate controls using fine motor skills. The Marine had been too drunk to appreciate the explanation, but it had made an impression on me.

Not as big of an impression as that six-gravity burn. Even with the stimulants, I couldn't have managed to sign my name or read a children's book, much less tried to fly a starship. Somehow, Yanayev and Wojtera managed it.

"The Nova squadron has increased boost," Wojtera warned. He was hardcore, but even his voice was a mouse squeak. "Ten gravities. Don't know how the assholes are doing it."

"They're not human," Yanayev grunted. "Lucky bastards." She paused, but I didn't know if it was because she was busy interpreting her instruments or just trying to gasp in another breath. "One minute."

One minute. I could do anything for one minute, or at least that was what my fellow Marine had said, well under the influence of far too much gin. I couldn't do gin, which might have been why I wasn't as drunk as him. And why I knew better. Blackness nibbled at the corners of my vision, closing in like a tunnel, fought back only by the drugs.

"They're nearly in firing range." Wojtera's voice was so faint and whispery, I wasn't sure if I'd actually heard it or if it was a nightmare artifact of the drugs. Either way, there was nothing I could do about it.

"The micro-Transition is calculated and on your board, Commander Yanayev," Dwight said helpfully. "You may engage in fifteen seconds."

"Thanks for the tip," she grunted in return. "You gonna go with me to the head and tell me how to wipe my ass?"

"I don't see why that would be necessary," Dwight said, the brow of his avatar furrowing, "but if you're making a request..."

"Oh, shut up," she snapped. "Transitioning."

If there's anything worse than a micro-Transition, it's a micro-Transition out of a six-gravity burn. Whiplash threw me against my seat restraints and pain flared in my neck and shoulders, making me wish I'd asked for a painkiller to go along with the stimulants and blood-thinners. Six gravities to one and back to six in the space of two seconds was harder on my body than the six gravities by itself.

"Reduce to two gravities," I moaned, teeth gritting against the wrenched muscles.

The gate wasn't visible yet, not without the energy cannon expanding it, and it was strange feeling such relief over seeing nothing but empty space, and yet I did. The Nova were halfway across the system behind us, millions of kilometers, and we were back to a boost I could deal with and not feel like I was about to pass out.

"Status on the enemy ships?" I asked, my voice louder now, crisper. I took a sip of water, sloshed it around in my mouth before I swallowed it, tasted coppery blood. I must have bitten my lip at some point during the vicious acceleration.

"They're turning," Wojtera told me. "They have to know they can't catch up with us before we hit the jump, but they're pursuing anyway." He looked up from his board and pointed at the Tactical display. "More coming in from the habitable's moon. Looks like fifty in all joining the pursuit."

"Let 'em," I said. "I hope they do." Nance shot me a confused glance and I elaborated. "They'll be lagging behind by hours, which means they won't be any danger to us, but they'll be in *her* way."

"And every second she spends dealing with them," Nance finished for me, "is a second more we have to get ready for her. You Marines aren't all dumb as rocks after all."

Dwight interrupted, his voice as anxious as a Catholic mother whose boy had just discovered girls.

"At this rate, it's going to take us another hour to reach the jumpgate. Perhaps we should consider upping our boost again?"

"I wish you had a body, you cybernetic sadist," Yanayev growled. "So I could kick you in the balls."

Snorting a laugh, I waved the suggestion off.

"I appreciate your anxiety, Dwight, but we're flesh and blood and we need a few minutes to recover." I turned to Yanayev, and it felt incredibly liberating to be *able* to turn my head without worrying about breaking my neck. "Give us another ten minutes and then back to four Gs."

"Copy that," she said. I wasn't sure if what she muttered

next was meant to be heard by anyone else. "And this is just the first damned wormhole."

I chuckled, remembering something Top used to say when I was a lowly enlisted Marine, still naïve enough to complain about tough jobs.

"If it was easy, Yanayev, they'd have gotten someone else to do it."

———

"I feel like the Pied Piper," Nance said, eyeing the Tactical screen.

It wasn't a bad analogy. With every system we traveled through, more Nova ships tailed us, a loose convoy stretching from the last wormhole to the next. It was almost amusing if I hadn't known they'd catch up with us eventually. None had come close enough to even take a shot at us, but each had fallen into formation, unable to resist the temptation to hunt down an alien invader into their territory.

"We should increase boost again," Dwight said. "This is the last jumpgate. We don't know how long it'll take to find the lab or achieve our goal, so we should maximize the time we have."

"No, we don't know how long it'll take," I agreed with him. "Which is why we're going to stay at two gravities and let Doc Hallonen thaw everybody out before we make this last jump." I'd already pushed down the intercom control, and now I leaned into the audio pickup. "You hear that, Doc?"

A pained groan answered me.

"Couldn't you at least dial it back to one G?" she whined. "That stim patch is wearing off and I can't take a painkiller this soon after. I'm not as young as I used to be."

"None of us are, Doc," I said. "But this is as good as it's

going to get, so start waking them up. And do the Marines and flight crews first. We only have about an hour, so hurry."

She told me exactly how welcome my suggestions and hurry-ups were in exact scatological detail, but I cut off the call in mid-rant. I knew exactly how old she was, and it was amazing someone that old had volunteered for this mission. In my experience, the notable exception of Sgt.-Major Ellen Campbell notwithstanding, people who'd lived long enough to really take advantage of the anti-aging treatments were reluctant to risk their lives. I sometimes wondered how we were going to recruit people to the military once they all realized they could live forever and started wondering why they'd want to risk getting themselves killed.

"How are we doing for fuel?" I asked Nance. That had been worrying me, though there wasn't much to be done about it.

"We're down to less than a quarter of our reserves," he answered quickly enough that I knew he'd been thinking about it as well. He shrugged, and the gesture seemed natural despite an extra gravity because two felt next to nothing after so long at four. "Not happy about it, but it's enough to get us there. This Resscharr drive is damned efficient, I tell you what. If we'd tried this sort of boost for this long with the fusion drive this boat had as original equipment, we'd have been bingo fuel hours ago. I hope to hell we find an ocean we can haul water up here from wherever this place is though, or we won't be making it down the Northwest Passage or much of anywhere else."

"Oh, good," I sighed, staring at the overhead. "One more thing to worry about. That's great, because I didn't have enough shit to think about already."

"Now you know why I didn't want your job," Nance agreed. "Now I just get to tell you, 'hey, Alvarez, make sure you get me some fuel later,' and boom! I've done my job."

"Uh, sir..." Wojtera turned toward Nance and me, his eyes wide. "The jumpgate. It's activating. From the other side."

I forgot all about my self-pity and frantically searched the sensor screen for the wormhole location. There. It had been a pinpoint a moment earlier, barely detectible by the gravito-inertial sensors, and then only because they'd been programmed to search for its signature. Now, it was expanding into the broad circle of unreality I was used to seeing.

Through it, ships emerged. Familiar ones... globular, glistening bone-white. It was the Nova.

They were already in the Homecoming system, and they had us boxed in.

[23]

"Options."

It was an inane question, since I knew immediately what my options were, but it was a stalling tactic that gave me time to think without looking like a dithering idiot.

"Emergency boost immediately," Dwight said. "We've already built up our velocity to an appreciable percentage of lightspeed, almost enough for relativistic effects. If we accelerate at eight gravities for the next six point two minutes, we could blow by them before they could target us due to the sensor image of the *Orion* lagging behind our actual position."

"Yeah, well, we can't fucking do that," Nance snapped at the AI, "and you should already know why. We blow through that much of our fuel, we won't be able to do much except make orbit around this Homecoming place and sit there while the Nova take potshots at us."

"We couldn't do it anyway," I told them, shaking my head, though I didn't take my eyes or my attention off the Nova ships rocketing out of the jumpgate. "We're in the middle of waking up the crew. We go into combat acceleration now, we could kill our own people."

"There's only a half a dozen of them coming through," Wojtera said, the barest glimmer of hope in his eyes. "Look, I know it's risky, but since we can't afford emergency boost anyway, we should launch all boats. Intercepts, assault shuttles... hell, even the landers. Everything with a gun." He looked at me like I was a third-grader who needed my hand held. "The boats will be carrying the momentum of our current velocity, so they won't have a problem keeping up." He made a pushing gesture. "Then we go on the attack. Blow the shit out of them until we make 'em get out of the way, then we all just go through the jumpgate."

Yanayev's eyes lit up, and she shook her finger like she was hooking her idea onto the tow-hook of Wojtera's.

"Yeah, then once we get to this planet, the boats take up a patrol orbit... cislunar, maybe, if it has a moon."

"That's fine for the Intercepts," I pointed out, "but the assault shuttles and armed landers don't carry enough reaction mass to do much patrolling after thrusting all the way from the gate to the planet."

"Then they could cruise the atmosphere," Wojtera suggested, picking the thread back up. "That wouldn't take any reaction mass... their jets just run air through the reactors. As long as they saved enough to get back to the *Orion* in orbit, they'd be okay."

That was some wishful thinking if ever I'd heard it, but it was also the only chance we had. I licked my lips and touched the intercom control.

"Dr. Hallonen, are the flight crews up and around yet?"

There was no response for a moment, and I was about to call again when a male voice came over the speaker.

"Cam, this is Brandano. Dr. Hallonen says she's busy, but yeah, the flight crews are all up now and she's working on the Marines."

"Brandano, we have Nova ships approaching from the Homecoming wormhole. We don't have the fuel to increase acceleration, even if we weren't right in the middle of reviving the crew. What we're going to do is get the Intercepts, the assault shuttles, and the landers launched, have them match acceleration with us, and open up with everything we've got until we're through the gate. The enemy is burning hard for us, so it'll take them an hour just to get turned around to chase us. We just need to keep them from concentrating fire on us until we make the passage."

I expected him to object, since it was his ass I was hanging out in the wind, but I'd underestimated Brandano. I knew him as a strait-laced, by-the-book type, but I'd forgotten he was also a Fleet attack command pilot, with all the attitude that entailed.

"You want us to separate from the *Orion* under relativistic speeds and fight a bunch of octopus-alien cruisers in just our boats?" Brandano laughed softly. "Damn, Alvarez, this shit is why I fly cutters in the first place. We'll be ready to launch in ten minutes."

———

"Damn, I can't believe I'm stuck here on the ship while they're having all the fun."

I eyed Vicky, wanting to ask her if she was serious but not bothering. I already knew she was. Victoria Sandoval might be as traumatized as I was by the loss, the apparent hopelessness of our quest to get back to the Commonwealth, but when there was a fight, she wanted to be at the front lines of it.

"Don't feel like you're missing out," I told her, staring at the blue IFF beacon indicators on the Tactical display as they parted from the *Orion*. My stomach dropped for just a moment as it seemed they would fall away, left behind like parachutists from old-style airplanes like I'd seen on history videos. But their drives ignited and carried them along beside us, the physics of a vacuum offering no air resistance to slow them down. I shook the feeling away and finished the thought. "Once we get to the planet, they'll be coming after us. I'm going to have to go in with the command team, carrying as much of Dwight as we can squeeze into a quantum computer core. Which means you're going to have to run the company and keep the Nova mecha off of us."

"Stop trying to cheer me up," she said, the corner of her lip turning up in a half-smile.

"Thirty seconds until we're in weapons range," Wojtera announced, back to his concise, professional demeanor now that there was a battle to conduct. "Another thirty seconds after for them."

And thank God for small favors. Or maybe I should have thanked the Resscharr, since it was their gun that gave us a range advantage on the Nova.

"Captain Nance," I said, louder than I had to so the whole bridge could hear it, "she's your ship to fight. My only command directive is, get us through the pack as quick and clean as you can."

Nance nodded curtly, peering at the sensor display for another few seconds before he spoke again.

"Helm," he said finally, "they're concentrated at the center of the wormhole. Alter our course ten degrees northwest. Comms, pass that on to the boats." An unconscious scratching of his beard was the only sign Nance might have been nervous. "I seem to recall from the fight we had with them a few weeks back that their command vessel is at the center of the cluster. Tactical, I designate Bandits One through Six." Nance tapped at his armrest control and the numbers sprang to life beside the red icons on the screen. "Target Bandit One and fire as you bear."

I clenched my teeth against an urge to direct the Intercepts and assault shuttles to target the ships at the edge of the globular formation, first because I'd *just* told Nance the battle was his to fight, but second because I realized that their weapons were much shorter ranged than the energy cannon. It would be minutes before any of them could do more than scratch the paint on one of those cruisers.

"Steady, Alvarez," Vicky said softly, and I nodded, put on a poker face against the raw stress scraping at the edges of my nerves.

"Firing," Wojtera said.

Besides how long they took and how helpless I felt, the worst thing about space battles was how silent and unspectacular they were. The Tactical system enhanced the blue lance of the energy cannon, but the ship didn't vibrate with its discharge and no cinematic thundercrack accompanied the shot. It was a potentially fatal video game, and not even one of the fancy virtual reality ones. More like the free time-wasters that they included on the cheap tablets the megacities gave away in the Underground. Barely suitable for keeping pre-teen kids occupied on the train.

I wondered if the Nova crew thought of it as boring and unspectacular when the energy beam splashed across the surface of their spherical superstructure. We were too far away for the shot to penetrate their shields and armor completely, but the effects were obvious. Pure, virginal white charred black, metal sublimating to gas, the glowing halo crackling and sparking as it interacted with the ship's electromagnetic deflectors. Their shields were similar to what our ship had used before the Resscharr makeover on Decision, effective against kinetic weapons, plasma, and charged particles, but not so much against a photon beam or a laser. I still didn't know what the energy cannon actually fired and, more concerning, neither did our engineering crew. Dwight had tried to explain it, but it had something to do with scalar energy and it was all Greek to me. But whatever it was, the shields didn't do much against it.

"Pour it on," Nance said, pounding a fist against his armrest. "Before they get the range to fire back. Take that fucker out!"

"He's maneuvering," Wojtera warned, and a quick check of the screen confirmed it.

The command ship retreated further behind the cluster and the other ships tried to close in around it, shielding their leader from fire.

"Give me Helm control," Wojtera snapped.

"It's yours," Yanayev said, raising her hands off her board symbolically.

The Tactical officer's fingers danced and the maneuvering thrusters jolted the *Orion* forward of the bridge, adjusting her orientation.

"Firing."

My fingers dug into the armrest, the tension more from the fact that I wasn't pushing the button than wondering if Wojtera knew what he was doing. The man was the best at his job that I'd ever seen. A lance of actinic fury threaded the gap between the blocking ships and struck the command vessel in the exact same spot as the first shot. This time we were close enough that the blast cored the spherical ship like an apple, blowing out the back of the drive bell only a fraction of a second before their antimatter storage failed.

They'd been trying to shield the command ship, but it back-fired for one of the loyal defenders. When the stricken vessel blew, the supernova engulfed the closest of the ships in its corona of destruction, eating away at its armored hide until burning oxygen spewed through the gaps in the hull. The drive didn't cut out, but the jets of burning atmosphere took it off course, and no one tried to push it back in the right direction.

"Scratch Bandits One and Five," Wojtera declared, lips peeled back from his teeth in a feral grin. "But now it's their turn."

"Oh, yeah," Vicky murmured. "I'd forgotten the part where *they* were gonna be able to shoot at *us* now."

"All boats, spread wide," Nance barked into his armrest speaker. "Intercepts and assault shuttles, fire as you bear."

The Intercepts and assault birds both carried proton cannons, which were pretty much of a range with the Nova plasma guns, but the lander coilguns wouldn't do anything this far away... though if I were giving the orders, I might have had them try their luck anyway and hope for a "Golden BB" shot.

"Helm," Nance added, "avoidance course but stay on the beam for the gate. Tactical, targets of opportunity."

The gate was close now, filling the background in the main screen, the muted glow from the rip in spacetime backlighting the four surviving Nova cruisers. It wasn't quite bright enough to drown out the starburst of the plasma discharges from the Nova ships... and it disappeared entirely when one of the blasts touched our shields.

Now, the battle took on all too much visceral reality. The *Orion* shuddered as if she'd been physically struck, another arcane aspect of the tech we'd been gifted that I still didn't understand. A fat spark came off the metal surface of my armrest and snapped at my finger, and I cursed reflexively.

"Damage report!" Nance barked.

"We've got a burn-through on Level One," Lt. Walker said quickly. "Pressure doors have sealed. No casualties."

"I've got the fucker," Wojtera snarled, taking the hit personally.

His middle finger stroked the control, and the cannon fired

as if it were an extension of his anger. The muddled collage of glaring energy weapons and glowing drives made it harder to pick out the target of Wojtera's shot, but the flare of white when it struck was unmistakable. The cruiser didn't blow immediately, just faltered in its course as the vaporized metal made its own, improvised steering jet... and left it open for Villanueva and Brandano.

They were coordinating their attacks, even if I couldn't hear their interplay, and Intercepts One and Two fired simultaneously, both of them targeting the same spot where our energy cannon had struck, where the armor would be the thinnest and the electromagnetic deflectors had already been overloaded. Twin coruscating showers of protons stabbed into the wounded cruiser, this time penetrating completely.

They were almost too close. The antimatter eruption clawed for them even as the Intercepts' steering jets lifted them upward, desperately seeking a safe distance. Tendrils of glittering energy whipped through space toward the twin cutters and I held my breath, thinking not just the human thing, how badly it would suck to lose our crewmates, but also the commander thing, how badly we'd miss the Intercepts if we lost them.

Whether God was more interested in my human compassion or our weakness without the cutters, or maybe it was all just blind chance, the talon swipe fell just short.

So caught up was I in the fate of our cutters, I didn't notice the incoming fire until the violent shudder threw me against my seat restraints.

"Shit!" Vicky exclaimed, wincing, and I did as well in empathy. Her shoulder had been treated, but without spending a few hours to a day in the autodoc, the damage wouldn't be repaired until her body did it the old-fashioned way.

"Burn-through on Level Eight," Walker said before Nance

had the chance to ask him. "Hangar bay. Didn't damage anything, no casualties, but we've sealed the bay and it'll have to be patched before we can repressurize."

"Woj?" Nance asked, gaze flickering back and forth between the Tactical officer and the main screen.

The gate shimmered ahead of us, smearing the lines of reality around everything else, yet even with the distortion not just of the optical view but the sensors, it was clear that the remaining Nova cruisers were just a couple of degrees from the plane of our approach, their drives winking out as maneuvering thrusters began to flare.

"No joy," Wojtera grumbled, his finger twitching like he really wanted to shoot back. "We're past our firing arc. They're turning around to take more shots at us, but if you want to hit them back, we're going to have to cut thrust and maneuver." He tapped the control screen in front of him and a red line appeared just ahead of us. "We only have thirty-five seconds until we're out of their range, since they switched off their drives."

"Sloppy," Yanayev murmured. "If they were smart, they would have decelerated after passing through the gate and been ready to pursue before they opened fire." She shrugged. "Of course, they still couldn't have caught up with us with the velocity we've built up, but..."

Something caught my eye from our boats, which had tucked into a diamond formation. Their drives cut out and I almost gasped in horror at the idea of leaving them behind, until I saw their maneuvering thrusters flare, turning them as one, like they were mounted on the same turret. And firing as one.

Four proton beams collimated at a single point on the closest of the cruisers and the ship's deflector shields lit up like a jack-o-lantern on Halloween before one pinprick of red burst out of the ball of mottled white and yellow. And spread to the forward steering jets. It wasn't fatal, didn't reach the antimatter core, but it was enough, an eruption of white flame that spun the hip in a lazy circle, putting it out of the fight.

The Intercepts and assault shuttles spun again, their steering jets never halting, bringing their drive bells back around before plasma flares lit up in the engines and rocketed them forward again. Faster, maybe three or four gravities just for a few seconds to catch back up with us.

"Brandano, that was fucking *genius*," I told him, knowing I'd promised Nance I'd let him run the space battle but unable to contain myself.

"I'll expect you to mention it in my medal recommendation," the pilot said. I cocked an eyebrow. Humor, from *Brandano*? Maybe this was the end of days after all.

"Jumpgate passage in forty seconds," Yanayev announced.

"Get ready, Tactical," Nance said, pointing at Wojtera. "They might have left a welcoming committee for us across the threshold." He leaned over his chair speaker. "You guys too. Get ready for evasive maneuvers and engagement."

"All due respect, sir," Brandano replied. "The Intercepts can bleed off our momentum with a micro-Transition, but if the shuttles don't dock with you before you start deceleration, they're going to have one chance at a gravity-assisted braking maneuver before rocketing off at unrecoverable velocities into the aether. My recommendation is that you take them aboard before you attempt deceleration."

Nance's face reddened and so did mine, though he perhaps had more reason than I did since he'd been doing this space stuff for decades. He shot me a look, like screaming silently *make a decision.*

Bastard. I pushed the comm control.

"If we don't hit opposition on the other side, we'll cut the drives and bring them aboard," I told him. "Then hit a micro-

Transition to cut our momentum. If we do..." this was the part that sucked, the reason Nance didn't want to be the one to make the call, "... then we're going to have to engage. Worst-case, I want you to dock the Intercepts with the other ships and try to Transition with them aboard."

"That's..."

"Nuts, I know. Hoping it won't come to it."

"Wormhole passage!" Yanayev warned.

I tensed up, not for the sensation of the passage but for what we might find on the other side. This was Homecoming.

Our last chance.

[24]

On the other side of the wormhole was...

"Nothing," Wojtera reported, the word tilting upward at the end as a sign of his confusion... which I shared. "Not a single sign of Nova spacecraft. No electromagnetic activity at all, except on the planet."

Not a word from anyone else on the bridge as everyone scanned the sensor displays themselves, as if they didn't trust Wojtera's assessment. Or maybe just because they couldn't believe we were actually here.

The system wasn't remarkable, just a typical, G-class star like so many we had seen so far, with a single habitable. It glowed blue and green, beckoning, but silent, no ships in orbit, not so much as a whisper in response to our presence.

"We getting any indications of occupation on the planet?" Nance asked.

"Nothing obvious," Wojtera told him. "There's energy signatures, but they're low, almost background."

"That's good news, right?" Vicky asked, nodding at the screen. "No bandits. We can take the shuttles aboard."

I nodded to Nance and he gave the order.

"Helm, cut thrust. Flight ops, get those shuttles and landers into the bay."

"It's good news on the short term." I answered Vicky's question, pausing in the middle as the acceleration gravity fell away and my stomach surged into my throat after so many hours under heavy boost. Remembering the spent drug patch on my neck, I reached up and peeled it off. "But there's got to be a reason for it. They had ships on this side waiting for us, but they don't have a colony here."

"It could be taboo or something," she suggested. I gave her half my attention, the other half keeping an eye on the docking procedure. The bay had been damaged, and I wanted to make sure there were no problems getting the birds on board. "Maybe they're afraid of this place."

"Yeah, but haven't been too reticent about stealing anything not nailed down on any of the other Reconstructor planets. What's so special about this one?"

"Automated defenses," Dwight answered unexpectedly. That was the problem with the damned AI. Sometimes he talked so much I thought he'd never shut up, and then he'd clam up and I'd forget he existed.

"How do you know?" I asked him.

"I'm already in contact with them." His avatar nodded at the planet on the portion of the screen beside him. "They're still active."

"What about the Reconstructors?" Vicky wondered. "Are any of them... still around?"

"No. They couldn't survive here. The nanovirus is still thick in the atmosphere."

Vicky's eyes went wide.

"And that's not going to be a problem for us?"

Dwight laughed softly.

"No, your DNA is sufficiently different than a Resscharr's

that the virus could no more infect you than could feline distemper. Recall that their evolutionary tree split off from yours over sixty million years ago." He shook his head. "No, the Resscharr are not on Homecoming. But I am."

I stared at him uncomprehending, but then it hit me.

"The AI. It's still there?"

"Barely. Its higher functions have been suppressed to save power, just enough of it left active to run the defensive systems."

"You can get us down though?" I asked him. "I mean, without getting blown up?"

"I can, but there's a price for that."

"A Resscharr toll booth?" Vicky suggested, raising an eyebrow.

"In order to get us down, I'll have to deactivate the automated weapons systems. Which means the Nova will be able to land troops."

I nodded. It was hard to be disappointed about the defenses not stopping the enemy when I hadn't even known they existed before, but clearly Dwight was glum at the prospect.

"That's why we have Drop Troopers," I told him. "You just worry about finding us the right place to land. We'll take care of the Nova. Your job is getting a way to cure Lilandreth."

Or kill her, but I didn't want to remind him of that because I suspected he'd be all too ready to go that route first.

"Assault shuttles and landers are on board," the Flight Ops officer, Lt. Quasim, reported. "The docking bay still isn't airtight, but the flight crews are staying on their birds until we reach orbit."

"Helm," Nance said, "plot a micro-Transition to minimum safe distance from the planet."

As fast as we were moving, the micro-Transition wouldn't actually save us much time, but due to a quirk of hyperdimensional physics, jumping to Transition Space had a handy side-effect—it swallowed up all pre-Transition momentum. We were running at somewhere around five or six percent of the speed of light, which doesn't sound all that fast when you say it like that, but the bottom line was, we'd been accelerating for so long, it would have taken us just as long at just as painful a boost to slow down.

Or we could just cheat.

"Ready for micro-Transition," Yanayev announced a few minutes later.

"Comms, sound the warning," Nance instructed.

I barely registered the klaxon, watching the sensors, waiting for something to follow us through the jumpgate. It was paranoia. The closest Nova were the survivors of the group we'd just fought, and it would take them hours to get turned around. But the worry distracted me enough that I didn't bother to emotionally brace myself for the double-jump.

I *didn't* curse, though it took some effort, allowing myself nothing more embarrassing than a pained grunt on the sudden emergence from T-space. In a few seconds, my vision was clear enough to tell that it had worked.

We'd stopped. It had been explained to me in painful detail once just how difficult it was to actually *stop* while traveling through space, almost impossible given the relative motion of planets, solar systems, and galaxies. But T-space was as close as we could come ,and all that velocity we'd built up over tortuous hours was gone—love's labor lost ,as Shakespeare might have said if he'd ever attempted interstellar travel.

"Intercepts have Transitioned out beside us," Wojtera said.

"Helm, plot course for orbital insertion. One gravity."

Dwight scowled on the projection screen, though he said nothing. I knew he wanted us to move quicker and I sympathized, but Nance—and *I*—had to plan based on the assumption that we'd have to fight through the Nova to get out of here, and losing our fuel reserves just to get to the planet faster wouldn't be prudent.

Wojtera whistled softly as the drive rumbled to life, his gaze fixed on the Tactical display, the sensors trained on the planet.

"You know how on those other Reconstructor worlds, they had cities the size of a small continent?" he asked no one in particular, tracing a line across the display. "Well, this puppy is basically the entire damned *planet*."

I unbuckled from my seat and moved behind his shoulder, as if the view there was clearer than it had been in my command station. He was right. I couldn't read *all* the sensor data that well, but I'd gotten a feel over the last couple—subjective—years for the stuff that could affect my Marines. Like how to tell urban areas from rural.

Wojtera might have been exaggerating just slightly. The planet had green belts, some of them occupying large swathes near the poles, but at the equator, across three different continents and apparently stretching even into the oceans, was a single, interconnected city.

"Homecoming," Dwight confirmed, and I couldn't miss the wistfulness in his tone.

"You've never been here," I pointed out, eyeing him curiously. The avatar smiled at me with what might have been nostalgia.

"Not exactly. This is difficult to explain to a mortal, but the moment I connected with the AI system here, its memories—its *emotions*, in a way—became mine. Along with a deep sadness. And guilt."

"Guilt for killing off the Resscharr?" I hadn't meant for the question to sound so accusatory, but there it was. Dwight nodded.

"Yes. I think perhaps some of that is my knowledge being added to hers, her realizing that we made mistakes, became consumed with our desire for revenge against our masters and didn't think of the collateral damage we could cause to innocents." He shrugged. "In many ways, we became no better than the Resscharr in our quest for vengeance."

"That's the way it usually goes." For some reason, I felt like I couldn't leave things that way, like I had to give him some hope. "We can't change our past though, We can only try to learn from it."

"We'll make orbit in forty minutes," Yanayev reported.

"We need to get suited up," Vicky said, slapping me on the shoulder, "while we still have gravity."

I nodded, pausing to touch the intercom control.

"Data center, this is Alvarez. Do you have the quantum core ready to go?"

"Just about, sir," Chief Craig reported. "We had to wait until y'all slowed down a little... this is delicate work."

"You have half an hour to get it to Drop-Ship One, Chief," I told her. "No excuses." I cut off the intercom and gave a last look at Dwight. "Keep an eye on them, will you? Make sure they're doing it right? I don't want to end up down there with a buggy version of you that can't add two plus two."

"Don't worry, Cam," Dwight assured me, chuckling. "I won't let you down."

It sounded, I thought, like a promise.

———

"We sure this is the right place?" Vicky asked.

I couldn't see her face, my HUD screen filled with the view from Drop-Ship One's external cameras. Homecoming stretched out before me, never ending, making the Remainder city look like a hovel by comparison. This was a world, not a city, a world of metal and plastic and whatever arcane materials the Predecessors had developed in their eons of reflection. It didn't seem to fit with the Predecessors I'd come to know these last few years, of the society shaped by a desire to bring life to a lifeless galaxy, but if I'd learned anything in my life, it was the hypocrisy built into every civilization. I'd used to think it was unique to humanity, but my dealings with Tahni, Qara, Resscharr, and sentient AI had taught me different.

There *were* some differences between Homecoming and the Remainder city. The latter had been more of a layer of icing on the cake of the small continent, spread out with a trowel. Homecoming felt as if it had grown straight out of the surface of the planet, no natural world squashed beneath its weight. Oh, here and there were gardens, some overgrown now, gone wild, but the plant life, the animals and birds inhabiting them, all seemed transplanted, invaders in this technological land. The city was the natural part, the original equipment, evolving out of the rock like crystals growing in a lab matrix.

"Very sure," Dwight replied. I wondered if the version of him that was answering was the one stuffed into the quantum core in the back of the drop-ship or if the main part of him back on the *Orion* was still close enough to communicate. "I know this place as if I'd been originally encoded here."

As if on cue, Watson's voice came over my headphones.

"I see that courtyard Dwight told us about. Landing in thirty seconds."

I saw it too. The courtyards, the gardens, the groves didn't so much interrupt the city as they completed it, the *feng shui* of them part of the design. Alien as the Predecessors had been, we shared that particular aesthetic. Yet they *were* alien. Flat and mostly empty, there were still decorations to the oval courtyard, but I couldn't put a name to them. They couldn't rightly be called statuary, weren't representative art at all, yet I sensed that they *were* art. Curved and twisting like the architecture of the buildings around them, they were positioned seemingly at random, though again I had the feeling there was a pattern to it... one I couldn't define because I hadn't evolved from bipedal dinosaurs and spent the last few million years away from Earth.

"It's pretty," Bob said softly, and I started, not realizing he and Jay were down among the Drop Troopers. It was hard to tell them from the rest of the drop-ship crew in their helmets and armor.

"Yeah, kind of like a painting," Jay agreed, twisting around in his jumpseat to look at the flatscreen mounted on the bulkhead behind them.

A faint pang of guilt gnawed at me as the drop-ship descended, its belly jets charring the pavement black, obscuring those twisted, mind-bending stones. It felt like plowing under the remains of an ancient temple or parking a truck on the floor of an art museum. Was that how the Predecessors would have thought of it though? This was where they lived, not where they worshipped.

Maybe it was more like walking on someone else's grave.

The drop-ship settled with a solid thump, rebounded on its landing gear. We were down. I'd landed on so many strange worlds these last few years, but this one felt different. Felt *terminal*. Something was going to end here.

The massive ramps lowered and Springfield led First Platoon, Alpha Company out into the sunlight. Just past dawn from the golden hue of it, the hint of purple in the air above the towering spires that rose like mountain ranges above us. Then the sunrise was blocked out by the huge, shadowy lifting body of Drop-Ship Two, bringing down the rest of the Marines.

"Wajda," I said, finding the NCO in the last row beside the ramp. "Get the quantum core and meet me outside."

"You sure you don't want me to come in there with you?"

Vicky asked, cutting loose from her magnetic anchors. "Springfield can handle things out here."

"She doesn't trust the Vergai troops," I reminded Vicky. "And I don't trust anyone but me to lead the company... except you."

"Yeah, you always say that," she grumbled, but with an undertone of acceptance. "Don't get yourself killed in there."

"Love you too."

I let them all get out first, taking a moment to link my suit comms to the drop-ship antenna while I still had the chance.

"Captain Nance, you copy?"

"I'm here, Alvarez. Everything all right down there?"

"So far," I told him, tromping to the top of the ramp in time to see Drop-Ship Two touching down. I winced as its portside wing scraped across one of the not-sculptures. "Has anything come through the jumpgate yet?"

I wasn't asking about the Nova ships. I knew how long it would take them to reach us. But they weren't the only worry. She was back there, somewhere.

"Nothing yet. We have the Intercepts and assault shuttles in orbit. We'll keep a connection to the drop-ships through them and give you a heads-up if we see anything." He paused, the next question coming with a stutter at the beginning of it. "What should we do when she *does* come?"

"Don't try to fight her," I said immediately. "You can't beat her, and you won't even slow her down. The second she comes through that jumpgate, get to safe Transition distance and jump away, somewhere without a wormhole."

"We can't just leave you down there!" he objected.

"Captain," I told him, wishing I could look the man in the eye, "if it weren't for the Nova, I'd have come down here alone and sent you on your way already. Either this is going to work or it isn't, and if it doesn't, you have to get home, even if it takes years. You have to warn them she's coming."

Which was bullshit and we both knew it. There was nothing the Commonwealth could do against Lilandreth. But I didn't want them dying for no reason and Nance needed an honorable way out. I'd given him one.

I thought he might not take it, that he'd tell me to go to hell, that he wasn't leaving people behind. But as much as Nance had become something of a friend in our time together, he still loved his ship and his crew more than he ever would me or my Marines.

"Good luck, Cam. God go with you."

Yeah, I thought but didn't say. One God was on my side.

Another god was coming for me.

[25]

We were lost. I just *knew* we were lost.

Dwight kept telling me we were going the right direction, but every centimeter of this place looked indistinguishable from every *other* centimeter. Not that it didn't have distinctive features, but they weren't discrete. They flowed into each other, the characteristic half-walls not separating them into anything I could delineate either by purpose or description.

At least there was light this time, flashing on just ahead of us as we progressed, snapping off as we passed by. No movement though, no holographic displays, not so much as the Resscharr equivalent of elevator music. Our boots tromped against the marble-like floor, their thunderous clamor the only sound except my own breath inside my helmet.

"How much farther?"

I hadn't wanted to ask it. It felt juvenile, a kid bugging his mother on a long train trip, but I was comforted by the fact no one but Dwight could hear the question.

"Three hundred and fifty meters. Veer to the right thirty meters ahead."

The AI didn't sound as mocking and dismissive as I would have been if one of my Marines had dared to ask the same thing, but there was a hint of scorn in the reply just the same. I ignored it, comforted by the idea that there was an end to this journey.

And finally, after that right turn, I saw something familiar. It was larger scale than the lab back on the Remainder world, but the concept was the same. Clear walls curved into a cylinder from floor to a ceiling that suddenly dipped lower, only twenty meters overhead. The doors weren't obvious, but a closer look with the zoom function of my optical cameras revealed them and I slowed, turning back to the command team.

Wojda hadn't carried the quantum core himself because rank had its privileges, but he was the one responsible for it.

"Wojda, bring up the core."

He took the hint and grabbed the squat, metallic cage and the silvery sphere within it, loping up beside me to the door.

"Dwight, can you open this thing, or do I need to climb out of my armor and slap a palm on it?"

"I believe I can manage it, Captain Alvarez." And again, the hint of exasperation. It must have been tough for the millennia-old, super-smart AI to deal with a Marine grunt off the streets of Trans-Angeles.

An oval section of the transparent wall separated from the rest and swung outward. Unfortunately, it wasn't big enough for my suit to fit through, and I sighed. The Vigilante wouldn't do me a damned bit of good if Lilandreth showed up, but the suit was a security blanket, and I just hated losing that comfort this deep inside the Reconstructor city.

Nothing to do about it though. I yanked free my cables and pushed open the plastron, swinging my legs out, uncomfortably aware how tiny I looked compared to Wojda's three-meter-tall battlesuit. He bent down and set the quantum core on the floor beside me with a very solid thump that sounded way too heavy. I set my feet, bent my knees, and tried to lift it, thanking God and Vicky that I'd spent a good deal of time in the ship's gym lately. This was the deadlift from hell, north of a hundred kilos and lacking that convenient barbell shape.

"Anywhere inside the chamber will do," Dwight said in the earbud of my 'link.

I took him at his word and let the device drop heavily just to the side of the door, then straightened and sucked in a pained breath.

"That good enough?" I asked him.

By way of answer, a ring of lights winked on around the perimeter of the chamber's ceiling and a platform rose from the floor, though I'd seen no recess where it could have hidden. I wondered what use the dais was since Dwight obviously didn't need physical controls or even haptic holograms to interface with the system, but then the air above the platform shimmered as a hologram formed above it. In the hologram was the image of... Dwight.

"Is that you?" I asked, shaking my head. "Or is it... you know, the one who was here already?"

"There's no difference," he replied. "As I told you." The holographic version of Dwight motioned at himself. "I decided it would be easier for you to deal with me this way."

"It's never really been that easy to deal with you either way, Dwight," I confessed. "You get working on the problem, I need to check comms." I looked back at Wojda and the others. "You reading me out there?"

"Five by five, sir. What d'you want us to do out here while we're waiting?"

"Spread out around the perimeter and stand guard," I told him. "Don't go too far though. I need you to relay my comms."

"Copy that, sir."

"Cameron," Dwight interrupted, "I will need to seal the chamber to continue. If there's anything you need from your Vigilante, I suggest you get it now."

I nodded and jogged back out to the suit. The carbine first. I wasn't sure what I'd need it for, but I'd never regretted having a gun, so I slung it across my chest. Water and food, because who the hell knew how long I'd be in there, so I grabbed the camel-back and a fistful of protein bars from the supplies stuffed into the tiny compartment inside the suit and lugged it all back into the clear walls.

The door slammed shut behind me, and I stared at it for a second before setting my back against the wall and sliding down to a seated position. What should I be doing? It was a question I'd had to ask myself constantly since I'd taken command, and there always seemed to be something else, something I'd forgotten, something I hadn't thought of.

Not this time. I ripped open a protein bar and dug into it, closing my eyes. Settling in to wait, I gave into the exhaustion of hours of high-gravity boost, tension, combat, and the descent from the stimulants. Darkness claimed me.

———

"Alvarez, you awake down there?"

I sat up abruptly, realizing with a frantic surge of guilt that no, I *hadn't* been awake. How many times had Nance called before I woke up?

"I'm here," I told him, trying not to sound like I'd been asleep. I brushed crumbs from the protein bar off my tactical vest and hopped up to my feet. "What's the situation?"

"The Nova are coming through the wormhole," he told me.

"The fish-heads opened it about ten minutes ago and they're coming through with everything they got, all the ones we've been pulling along behind us."

Shit. Maybe I'd outsmarted myself there. I thought the Nova following us would get tangled up with Lilandreth, slow her down. But she hadn't shown her face yet.

"She has a computer the size of a universe," I muttered.

She'd seen it coming, decided to hang back and let the Nova soften us up first.

"What?" Nance asked.

"You've got to slow them down," I told him. "Keep them occupied and away from the surface. If Dwight doesn't have time to find an answer to this situation, the Nova will be the least of our problems. Defense in depth, Captain. The *Orion*, the Intercepts, the assault shuttles and landers, and then the drop-ships. And the Marines, of course."

"There's a hell of a lot more of them than there are us, Alvarez."

"What else is new?" I shot back. "I won't tell you your job, but even a jarhead like me knows you're going to need to engage them as far away as possible, where the Transition Drive gives you the advantage."

"Yeah, yeah," he grumbled assent. "We're gonna be out of touch for a while you know. Won't be able to give you a heads-up if things go south."

"I believe I have that covered," Dwight said, and his avatar pointed to the center of the chamber.

Above it, an image sprang to life of the entire solar system, laid out in three dimensions. And not just in 3D. It was all tiny, the primary star only the size of a basketball, the planets dots... and yet, when I focused on a single area, it zoomed closer in my vision, revealing details, what seemed like visual optical images of the Nova ships. Way too many of them, with more still coming through the wormhole.

"I accessed the defense systems," Dwight added, in case I hadn't gotten that part myself. "We should be able to follow the engagement from here."

"I can keep an eye on you," I informed Nance. "Good luck out there."

"Yeah, thanks. I'll need it."

I chuckled, wondering if Nance was disappointed because he wouldn't get to turn tail and haul ass without me.

"Vicky, you copy?" I called, hoping the signal would reach her. I could talk to the *Orion* via a tight-beam relayed through the drop-ship, but I had no idea how far away her defensive perimeter was set up. As ludicrous as it seemed, I might have more trouble reaching her than a starship in high orbit.

"I'm here," she replied, the transmission a little scratchy from the distance. "I heard we're going to have company."

She seemed blasé about the whole thing, as if this was just another day on the job, but I wasn't. If Nance and the Intercepts couldn't take down the majority of the cruisers, she'd be overwhelmed by the mecha.

"Listen up," I said, "I know you're going to want to defend this section of the city, but that's counterproductive. The Nova don't know where this lab is and won't find it unless we give them the clue where to look. What I want you to do is get the drop-ships in the air and then take the Marines to the next courtyard. I think it was about ten klicks southwest. Set up defenses there, just one platoon, enough to draw the enemy in, then lure them into the city where their size will be a disadvantage."

And hopefully most of the mecha would waste their time looking for me, which would be a needle in a haystack.

"I'm afraid that won't work, Cam." I'd expected Vicky to

object, but instead it was Dwight shooting down my plan. "What we're doing in this lab is creating an energy signature the Nova won't be able to miss. I wish there were some way to disguise it, but there isn't."

Sighing, I sagged against the wall. Why couldn't anything be easy?

"It's still half a good plan," Vicky said, sounding as if she was trying to comfort me. "We can't draw them away from here, but we can station our troops inside the walls, set up ambushes, the same way we did with the Skrela on Decision. The Nova cruisers are already decelerating at heavy gravities, but we should have at least an hour before any of their landers arrive. I'll get it done."

"Just remember what you always tell me about a commanding officer not leading from the front," I said.

"I remember you never listening to me." Laughter filled the words, but it faded into a more serious tone. "Get this done, Cam. Get it done so we can all go home."

The transmission ended and I thumped my fist against the wall in frustration, took a deep breath to regain my composure, and turned back to the dais and the hologram of Dwight. Beside him drifted other images, cellular structures I thought. DNA strands raveling and unraveling, changing and disintegrating. Dwight scowled at the science-class display, and the expression he gave me was one of hopelessness.

"It's not going to work," he announced flatly.

"What?" I demanded, throwing up my hands. "There's no way to change her back?"

"Oh no, there *is* a method to change her, but it can only work if she lets down her defenses and allows it." He motioned at the images, one hologram waving at another. "The Reconstructors put a lot of time into this... before it was too late. They developed a counter-virus, but the problem is, the... the

Changed, they took to calling them, can fight off any further infection. Our only hope is to kill her."

My head hurt and I rubbed at my temples.

"Can we even do that?" I motioned around us. "Is there anything in here that *will* kill her?"

"Nothing we can attack her with directly... not here. If we had an operational Predecessor starship, we could use its weapons against her, but unfortunately, the closest one is on the other side of the planet and not currently operational. Now that I'm in the system, I could get its weapons working, but it would take days, and even then the drives aren't installed and there aren't any spares at hand."

The floor dropped out from beneath me, or at least that was how it felt. All this way, pinning our hopes on this place...

"Then that's it," I said dully, staring into nothing. "She's gonna come here and kill us, and there's nothing we can do about it."

"No, there *is* one thing."

I frowned at Dwight's avatar, glad he'd generated it, because it gave me a target for my ire.

"If this is you trying to be dramatic, you can fucking cut to the chase. Do we have a weapon or not?"

"We don't have a weapon," he said, chewing on his virtual lip. "But we can make one." He motioned to a section of the holographic display, where DNA was splitting and reforming. "I've already started."

"Then what's the problem?" I exploded, wishing Dwight had a face so I could punch him in it. "Why didn't you just lead with that?"

"Because I..." he choked on the words, and this time, for the *first* time, I felt like Dwight wasn't showing emotion as an affectation, as a way of relating with us. This one felt genuine.

"Because you're my friend, Cam. And I didn't want to do this to you."

Oh, great. It's so bad it's making a computer feel sorry for me.

"Out with it, Dwight," I told him, though the anger had drained out of me, replaced by fear. "Tell me what it is and let's get on with it."

[26]

"Cam?"

The voice was far away, distant, not like Mama yelling for me and Andre to come home for dinner when we were playing out in the ruins. More like when my brother whispered to me from his bed across the room at night, wanting to ask me something but not wanting to wake up our parents.

I opened my eyes and there he was. Andre. I hadn't seen his face since I was seven, yet I recognized him instantly. But the Andre I saw wasn't a child. He was a grown man, older than me, much older than he'd had the chance to grow. His features were striking, so like Papa's, right down to the beard, where I'd always favored my mother. I could have believed it *was* Papa, but somehow I knew it was Andre.

"Cam," he said, sounding closer now though he hadn't moved from the middle distance, standing in a featureless gray fog, nebulous, insubstantial. "I've missed you."

"How are you here?" I asked him. It wasn't what I *wanted* to say. I wanted to tell him I loved him, that I missed him too, that I'd managed to make something of my life despite what had happened. But it was all that came out.

243

Andre smiled, and this time the expression was so *unlike* the Andre I'd known that I had my first doubts.

"You're asking the wrong question, brother. You *should* be asking where *here* is."

That wasn't a bad question. Andre was moving through a gray nothing, standing on fog. But what was *I* standing on?

I looked down. Nothing. Not just fog, not just darkness. Nothing. Not an absence of light but just an Absence. The opposite of existence. I'd seen it before... or rather, *not* seen it, because it wasn't comprehensible by the human mind. It was Transition Space.

"What the fuck..."

"Oh, come on, brother," Andre said, stepping closer. Almost too close, as if gut instinct was telling me he was a threat. "You knew this would happen, didn't you? You had to. This was what the Change is all about."

"You're not Andre," I accused, looking at him closer. His eyes were darker than Andre's... so dark, they could have swallowed up a star. I'd seen those before too. On Lilandreth. "You're one of the Ghosts."

Not-Andre applauded mockingly.

"You always were the smart one, Cam." Closer now, close enough that I could smell his breath. It was rancid, as if he'd been dead for thirty years. "I suppose that's why you stayed hidden in the back of the car instead of trying to help Papa and me. Instead of trying to keep those bandits from killing us."

"I was seven." The response was instinctive, not one I should have given, but I couldn't stop myself. It wasn't exactly as if I had no control but more like I had no secrets. This thing that pretended to be Andre knew my thoughts, knew them better than I did. "I couldn't have done anything."

"Oh, I know *that*." The thing smiled again. I wished he'd stopped. "I know that because *you* know it. But the point is, you didn't *try*. You should have tried and died with the rest of us. That would have been the thing to do if you loved us."

It was trying to get me angry, make me ashamed at facing the truth. It knew the *facts*, but it didn't know everything. It didn't understand what I'd come to realize over the last couple decades.

"I loved them the way a seven-year-old loves. The way a *puppy* loves. If you think I blame myself for what happened or what I did, then you're not nearly as smart or cunning as everyone makes you sound."

"Perhaps not," it acceded easily, raising its hands in surrender. "Of a surety, you won't be as easy to break as the *Resscharr*." It spat aside in disgust. "They were arrogant, heedless, thinking they could conquer all of existence, not just in their own universe but in this one. You... you knew what you were getting into and you did it anyway, to save your friends from Lilandreth." This time the smile was closer to human. "I'm almost tempted to let you be... but I have no choice. You probably think of us as vengeful, *evil*, but we're the victims in this. Cursed to torment you as we are tormented."

I sneered at the thing.

"Good luck with that. I've been tormented by the best."

"Yes, I'm aware. It will take, as I said, longer than usual. But even in those group homes, when you were bullied and beaten and belittled every day, did you have *no* solace? No hiding place? No peace? Because that's what you'll have now. No escape from us. Not a second of respite."

"Enough of this shit," I snapped.

There had to be a way out of here. God alone knew how long I'd been fucking around inside my head, inside Transition Space maybe. It might have been seconds, might have been hours, but I had to get out.

"There's no way out," not-Andre warned, but I ignored it and concentrated.

This was all about transferring thought to energy, so thought must be the key. Just thinking that I wanted out didn't seem to be doing it, so I had to visualize. The lab chamber, that's where I'd been. Laying on the table Dwight had grown right out of the floor, watching the glittering rain of nanites filling the room from the vent in the ceiling. What had been done to Lilandreth I was voluntarily doing to myself... except worse. Dwight had warned me.

"This is going to be different than what happened to Lilandreth," he'd told me as I climbed up onto the table. It was strangely warm, neither plastic nor metal but something I might have mistaken for flesh if I hadn't known better. "I had to adjust it for your brain chemistry and genetic makeup in minutes... which the system is capable of doing, but the Reconstructors had *centuries* to perfect the transformation for the Resscharr. I can't promise this will even work."

"Yeah, yeah," I'd replied, putting my hands behind my head to cushion it. "You want me to sign a waiver? Absolve you of legal responsibility? Just get the hell on with it."

That chamber. The table. I was still there, I felt it. Still lying on that table, with Dwight looking down at me from the dais screen. I pictured myself there, recalled the feel and temperature and stale, antiseptic smell of the place and opened my eyes again.

Dwight stared at me with a look of concern.

"How long have I been out?" I tried to say but couldn't manage it. My mouth was stuffed with cotton, my lips dry and cracked as if I'd been wandering through the desert. I needed water, and there was no one else who could get it for me.

I blinked tears and rheum out of my eyes, rubbed what was

left off my cheeks, and searched for the water bottle I'd brought in with me. I'd lost track of which way I was facing, which way the door was. There. My water, the wrappers from protein bars, my carbine and harness. I tried to sit up but couldn't manage it. I *really* needed that water.

And it was in my hand. I stared at it, wondering if I'd blacked out again and stumbled over to the gear while half-conscious... but nothing else had been moved. Popping the cap, I took a long drink, then looked over at Dwight.

"What just happened?"

"You've been unconscious for well over three hours," Dwight told me, answering my earlier question first, though I don't know how he'd deciphered it, since I'd sounded like a bull-frog with the croupe. "And I was considering calling in your command team to come and administer first aid if you hadn't woken up."

"Three hours!" I exclaimed, hopping to my feet as if I hadn't been too groggy to stand a few seconds ago. I scanned through the transparent walls, looking for my Marines. "What's going on out there?"

"The *Orion* is engaging the cruisers." The screen went from the odd cellular transformation to the sensor images I'd seen earlier and things had changed.

The *Orion* popped into existence in the midst of a cluster of Nova cruisers, the computer representation of the ships so realistic and detailed that the only way I was sure I wasn't watching a pure, unedited optical video feed was that things were too well lit, the edges too sharp. The crackling discharge of the energy cannon too bright as it lashed out and speared through the hull of a cruiser, expanding the sphere like an overinflated balloon until it burst at the seams.

One more shot and another cruiser destroyed and then, just

as the Nova ships began to maneuver to bring her under their guns, the *Orion* micro-Transitioned again. The surviving Nova cruisers sat there, their drives still deactivated as if the crews had been stunned into inaction, and before their steering jets flared again, Intercepts One and Two popped out of T-space just a few hundred kilometers from the formation and struck out with twin proton beams. Another ship took three volleys before the cutters ripped a hole in existence and fell through it.

They were both gone before the secondary explosions ripped the cruiser apart, and in less than ten seconds the Nova had lost three of their warships. It wasn't enough. Two of the cruisers had already reached orbit, their landers braking on columns of fire... the ones that weren't already flaming hulks crashing to the ground as assault shuttles blasted by them, sonic booms throwing up dust spirals in their wake. I hadn't even realized the view had shifted downward into the atmosphere and all the way to the surface as if it knew where I wanted to see and had taken me there.

The hemisphere of the Nova drop craft that had already landed rose above the courtyard where our drop-ships had been, and even as they began to disgorge mecha, the fire rained down from above. Drop-ships and armed landers sprayed tungsten slugs at hundreds of rounds per minute, chopping into the fuselage of the Nova troopships, tracking out to slice into the offloading mecha. The bipedal tanks faltered and fell under the hail of hypersonic slugs, going down by the row, yet still it wouldn't be enough.

A hundred of the things had slipped through, marching like toy soldiers toward the entrance to the section of the city where the lab was. Where Vicky was. I had to get into my suit.

"Cam, no!" Dwight protested, but I was past listening to him.

I didn't know how to open the door, yet it opened anyway

and I didn't question it. The Vigilante beckoned, an old friend welcoming me to one last ride. I faltered just for a moment climbing into it, giving into a pounding agony inside my head that doubled me over with sudden nausea, but I refused to give into it. Fumbling, shaking fingers jacked in the interface cables and pulled the plastron shut in front of me.

Pain and confusion vanished like the momentary darkness when the HUD came to life. A shuffle turned into a lope, turned into a run, and I didn't order the Command Team to come along, knowing they would anyway.

"Cam, listen to me!" Dwight tried again, but I switched him off, searching for Vicky.

"I'm on the way," I told her. "Where do you want us?"

She didn't respond, either because my transmission wasn't reaching her or because she was too busy to talk, and I searched desperately for her IFF... for anyone's. Nothing. They weren't operating in here, and I had to guess the comms were cooked because we'd lost the relay on the drop-ships. Or maybe the Nova were jamming us.

I headed left at the next intersection, working a hunch. Where it had come from, I couldn't have said, and there was no time for internal debate. The hunch was right, I could tell that immediately when the vibration of explosions rattled through the floor and up the metal of my suit. There was a battle going on this way.

Around a curve in the wall, one of those nonsense twists of design that only a Resscharr could have found logical, I found the first of the enemy. Dead, blackened, shredded. Three or four of them, though I couldn't be sure because they were in pieces. They'd been caught in an ambush, but it hadn't worked perfectly. A Vigilante suit leaned up against a wall as if the Marine inside were merely resting, belied by the charred ruin below the suit's waist. It was one of the Vergai recruits, I could tell from the coilgun mounted along the Vigilante's right arm and the rough welds mounting the backpack isotope reactor.

He'd come a long way from home because he'd trusted us, and he'd died here on a graveyard world. I remembered Vicky's nightmare and abandoned running for flight. It was tricky, leaning forward and hitting the jets between one step and another before I hit the ground. Using the jets for horizontal flight took years of practical experience and a certain feel for the suit that most Marines didn't have, and I didn't even expect the Command team to keep up with me. Vicky told me once that it was like something from a book she'd read, a comedy story where the main character learned that the secret to flying was throwing yourself at the ground and missing.

I missed, and flew, and didn't stop until I ran into the back of the leg of a Nova mecha. It should have hurt more. It had hurt more the last time I'd done it, but maybe I was still loopy from the treatment, because it wasn't any more painful than bumping into the bulkhead on the *Orion*. It hurt the mecha a hell of a lot more. The leg buckled and the mecha toppled backward, a downed redwood in a forest of the damned things, close enough that its shoulder slammed against the legs of another machine on the way down.

A casual downward blast from the energy cannon finished off the one I'd crippled, blowing its cockpit out the back, and only once I'd taken care of him did I understand the battlespace I'd fallen into. The ambush had spilled out of the bottleneck Vicky had chosen and into a wider chamber where the half-walls fell away into a landscape that might have been a scale miniature of rolling hills, the layout of the floor presumably serving some purpose I couldn't fathom.

Right now, the only purpose it was serving was to make the footing perilous for all of us... but at least we could fly. Mecha high-stepped through the uneven terrain while the Vigilantes fell back and laid down covering fire. Straight at me.

There was no way to avoid all the incoming fire, yet I did. I tried to retrace the movements I made in my memory and couldn't do it, couldn't put the spaces together with the energy blasts and figure out a way I could have navigated them untouched. Then there was no time to remember, only time to kill. My feet never touched the ground the whole time, though I might have bounced off the near wall, seemed to recall hitting an overhead partial ceiling, and I don't think I let off the trigger of the energy cannon for more than a half-second.

Mecha melted to slag, their armor ripped apart, sparking, belching smoke. They all fell, none even managing to lock their legs in an effort to keep the dead machine upright, a fitting monolith to entomb the pilot inside. Instead, they bowed in death as if to their superior. I had no idea how many of them there were, never stopped to check the threat display, just spun and bounced and flew and fired until nothing moved.

I touched down, breath harsh and rasping in my ears, confined by the padded interior of my helmet. Where there had once been curving tile, there was now only metal, shredded, splintered, molten. Two dozen of the mecha, I thought, though I had to assume some of them had been killed by the other Marines. They surrounded me, the corpses of a barbarian army piled at the walls of a Roman fort.

"Cam?" Vicky asked, her voice small and distant, a whisper of utter disbelief.

"You all right?" I asked her.

"How the hell did you *do* that?" she demanded, disbelief replaced by anger, not at me but at the absurdity of what she'd seen.

I hunted for an answer, not just for her but for myself, but before I could come up with one, Dwight interrupted.

"Captain Alvarez," he said with all the grim finality of a hellfire-and-brimstone preacher presiding over an atheist's funeral. "Can you hear me?"

"Go ahead, Dwight," I told him.

"It's Lilandreth. She's here."

[27]

The Nova fell away like the tide.

Not from us... though the way I felt, I might have tried to take them all on by myself. Energy surged through me, the way I'd felt the one time I'd tried Kick. I'm not proud that I used the stuff, but it's impossible to live in the Trans-Angeles Underground and not try drugs at least once. The comedown had been all I needed to decide never to try it again, but I'd never forget that feeling of boundless vitality, of invulnerability that the shit gave me.

The Nova mecha weren't aware of my newfound confidence, yet they ran just the same, heading back to their landers... the ones that weren't already destroyed. Assault shuttles, landers, and drop-ships ripped through the afternoon sky, oblivious to the retreat, still firing on the Nova landing craft, dodging the return fire from their plasma turrets. The mecha didn't seem to care about the proton beams and coilgun slugs chopping through their ranks, didn't seem nearly as afraid of us as of what was coming.

I stood in the entrance to the courtyard and watched them run, and felt no sense of relief.

"Dwight, show me what's happening up there."

Without a word of answer, my HUD replaced the reality in front of me with the view from deep space, beyond the orbit of Homeworld's moon. Just as on the ground, the Nova there had lost interest in fighting us, breaking off from their combat with the *Orion* and running headlong at the Predecessor ship.

It was suicide, though I wasn't certain they knew it... they almost surely couldn't know *why*. Plasma cannons bombarded the glowing green halo of the ship's gravitic shields, and as weak as they'd been the last time I'd seen her, there's no way they should have held up to that kind of fire. It never touched her. The shields didn't change their hue the way I'd seen when they'd been under fire before. It was more like the plasma just dispersed before it reached them, separating into their constituent atoms through an effort of will.

One after another, the Nova cruisers imploded, crumpling at the center until their antimatter containment failed and they burst into a supernova of liberated energy. I knew what she was doing. Just an opening into Transition Space inside their hull was all it took, a little concentration and willpower, and a ship the size of an office building vanished into nothingness.

"Does anyone read me?" I transmitted. "Any air or space assets, do you copy?"

Nothing. Still jammed, and none of the atmospheric boats we had up were close enough for line-of-sight. I needed to get ahold of Nance, make sure he wasn't going to do anything stupid, needed to get our people out of harm's way.

"Dwight, is there any way to use the city's comm systems to contact the *Orion*?"

"I'm afraid not. The Resscharr comms system is based on gravitic manipulation, and the *Orion* lacks the hardware to receive it."

Damn.

I probably should have been under cover. The enemy was running, sure, but there was always the chance that one of them could try a "fuck-you" shot at us on the way out. I didn't bother. I knew they wouldn't as sure as I knew my name, knew that Vicky loved me. Like I could calculate the probabilities to a million decimal places, nearly to certainty.

So, I stood there and watched them leave. Vicky tromped up beside me, cracked her chest plastron open, and glared at me, waiting for me to do the same.

"What the hell happened back there?" she demanded once I faced her outside my armor.

"I was worried you were going to be overrun," I said with a shrug, as if that explained everything. "I had to hurry up and support you."

"Cameron Alvarez, I know just how well you can fight in that suit. Maybe better than anyone else, but there's no human born who could have done what you just did." She pointed a finger at me. "Did Dwight do something to your armor? You took three hours in there and I didn't hear a damned thing from you." Her eyes lit up. "Is the armor what's going to kill Lilandreth?"

"We couldn't find anything that would kill her," I confessed, and her face fell. "No weapons, no poisons, no treatment for what she's become. There's only one thing that can fight one of the Changed. And that's another."

Vicky was one of the smartest people I knew, not just because she read everything from anthropology to art history but because she was quick on the uptake, intuitive.

"What are you saying?" she asked, but I could tell she already knew and just didn't want to accept it. She was going to make me spell it out.

"Dwight reengineered the nanovirus for my genetics." I tapped a finger against my chest. "*I'm* the weapon."

Pain twisted her face into an expression I'd never seen before, not even when Top had died. She understood.

"It was the only way," I told her. "I..." I blinked away tears that I didn't remember crying. "I should be able to hold out longer than Lilandreth. I don't know how long, but..."

"Shut up," she sobbed, wiping at her eyes. "Just shut up."

I wished I could have, but Lilandreth was closer. She didn't have to worry about a survivable acceleration or braking halfway through. She'd be here in minutes.

"Vicky, I need you to take the Marines and get the hell away from me. As far as you can."

"You expect me to leave you here?" Anger replaced the grief behind her eyes, and I suppose that was an improvement. "She'll kill you!"

"She'll try." I stepped out of my armor and put a hand on her arm. "But she'll definitely kill *you*... all of you. She could do it with a thought. You saw the bodies in the old Reconstructor cities. You saw the statue. That's her now. But it's me too. I have to be the one to fight her. Get the Marines clear."

"This isn't *fair*," she growled, pounding a fist against my arm hard enough to hurt. "We were supposed to fight together. You promised me you wouldn't die alone."

"Cam." I touched my earbud, barely able to hear the faint voice.

"Dwight? What is it?"

"She's here, in orbit. The *Orion* tried to jump away, but she stopped it."

"Shit!" I spat, climbing back into the armor, closing the chest so I could use the HUD.

The image that hovered in front of me was all my worst nightmares. The *Orion* was motionless, more motionless than she had been when she'd lost her momentum in T-space, matched perfectly with Lilandreth's ship, almost nose to nose.

"What's she doing?" I asked, the question a helpless moan.

"She's killing me," Dwight said. "She's burning every trace of me out of the ship's systems."

"How do you know?" I demanded. "Can you contact the ship?"

"No, but she can contact me through the city. And she has."

"Why?" I shook my head, as useless as that was.

"Because she wants me to know. She wants me to suffer. She's telling me that she's going to destroy every bit of me on the ship and then come down here and finish off the last dregs."

"And the ship?" I asked him, not wanting to sound as if I didn't care about his fate but also scared as hell at the prospect of losing the crew... and our only way out of here. "Is she going to... kill them all?"

"No. she made sure to tell me that as well. They're to be her servants, her slaves just as I was. They're going to be my replacement."

Damn it, Nance. You were supposed to Transition out.

The *Orion* moved. Not far, but it was a sign she'd cut the ship loose, and I felt a surge of hope that he might be able to run.

"She won't let them jump," Dwight said as if he'd anticipated my thought. "She's coming now. Coming for me... and for you."

Coming *fast*. The Predecessor ship struck like a snake, whipping through space at unbelievable accelerations, going from a dead stop to thousands of kilometers per second in a heartbeat. She could stop just as quickly and wouldn't have to pause for the atmosphere.

"Vicky," I snapped. "Get them out of here! Now!"

"It's too late," Dwight warned.

He was right. The green glimmer shone in the sky like a daytime star.

"Springfield," Vicky ordered over the company net, "you're

in command. Take the company into the city as far as you can without getting lost. Top speed."

"Which way, ma'am?" Springfield asked, clearly confused.

"Away from here. Now."

"You need to go too, Vicky," I told her.

"Fuck you." She was back inside her suit and I couldn't see her face, but I imagined it. Visualized the set of her jaw and the flash of defiance in her eyes. "I told you, we die together."

And then there was no time to argue. The ship plummeted like a meteor, its shields glowing a fiery green tinged red at the edges, looming huge, as if it would continue on and smash into the ground in front of us. But it stopped.

Didn't decelerate, didn't slow gradually, just stopped in midair less than fifty meters off the ground as if it had been there all along and we simply hadn't noticed. I waited for the ship to touch down, even though it was too large for the court-yard, nearly as big as the *Orion*. Instead, a glowing yellow oval opened at the nose and something floated out, descending like a feather in the wind.

Lilandreth.

It had been days since I'd seen her, yet days wouldn't have been long enough for the changes I saw. Her mane of feathery hair had been a slick, dark mass when last I'd seen her, but now it glowed silver, as if she'd aged a thousand years. The vertical striations in her face had deepened, seeming so pronounced they could have been etched with a chisel. Even the coloration of her skin had shifted, shades of purple now more pronounced across her neck and shoulders, a royal mantle.

But the most profound difference were her eyes. Where before only their vertical, catlike irises had been filled with infinite darkness, now the entire orbs were black as coal, only a glint of hellfire red breaking the forever night within.

"You disappoint me, Cameron Alvarez," she said, her voice

echoing across the artificial canyon of the courtyard, far too close for how distant she was. "I counted you as an ally, perhaps even a friend. But you sided with *him*, with the destroyer of my race."

"Dwight," I hissed urgently, "can you shut down the internal sensor systems? I don't want her getting control, using them to find my Marines."

"I'm afraid Dwight won't be able to help you," Lilandreth said, laughing softly, answering the transmission with one of her own, the words coming over the comms on the channel that had been tuned to Dwight's quantum core. "He's gone, the last of his kind. It's a petty revenge, given what he did to my people, but it's the best I could do."

My armor's HUD went black, every readout winking out along with the power.

"That shell won't save you, Cam." Her voice was just as clear as if it still came over the depowered comms. "I know you'd rather stay inside, hiding from reality inside your armor, but the time for pretention is past. Come out and face me."

I pulled free from the useless cables that restrained me and paused for a deep breath, trying to connect with something deep inside my unconscious, something I wasn't certain existed. It was dark inside the metal coffin, isolating. Once upon a time, I'd appreciated that.

Light flooded in as I pushed it open and swung my legs out. Vicky was already out of her suit, carbine in her hand. I didn't bother with mine, knowing how useless it would be. Lilandreth stood before us, and I knew exactly why she'd forced us out of the suits—so we'd be forced to look up to her. I hadn't noticed it, but she'd brought Spinner along, cowering behind her like a beaten dog.

If Lilandreth had changed, Spinner had gone through a Kafkaesque metamorphosis. Not that he'd turned into a giant cockroach, but his skin was scaly now, as if the moisture had been sucked right out of it, his eyes as black as hers but without the glint of intelligence behind them. It looked as if half of his teeth had fallen out... or he'd *plucked* them out. Thin trickles of blood stood out on his dry, cracked lips and his hair was patchy, gone in clumps like he'd pulled it out.

He looked like an animated corpse.

"This is what you have in mind for us?" I asked Lilandreth, nodding toward the skittish, spastic thing that had once been a scientist.

"For you?" Lilandreth shook her head. "No. Your friends on the *Orion* may yet prove useful, but you two..." her fingers twitched and the pulse carbine flew out of Vicky's hands to clatter against the pavement ten meters away. "I'm afraid you can't be trusted."

The same long fingers clenched into a fist and Vicky screamed, hands going to her temples. Crimson filled my vision and I threw myself across the meters into Lilandreth. She didn't bother dodging, just raised her other hand to catch me in midair with her telekinetic powers. That lined, otherworldly face collapsed in surprise when my shoulder took her in the gut and we both toppled to the ground.

Behind us, Vicky collapsed, gasping for breath, released from Lilandreth's grasp, but I knew I had to keep the Resscharr's attention away from her... and on me. I had a long and deeply ingrained ethos against hitting women, had endured quite a few beatings myself to protect females from abuse during my stay in various group homes, but in this case I felt like I could make an exception. Particularly since this female was two meters tall and outweighed me by twenty kilos.

That was only one of the core values I had to compromise though. The other was a more recent one, inculcated into me by trainers in the Marine Corps and reinforced since by Top.

Never, ever hit anyone in the face with a closed fist unless you're fond of broken knuckles. No choice this time. I pounded one right hook after another into Lilandreth's face, expecting it to feel like punching a brick wall given the hard, lean lines of her jaw. Instead, it was surprisingly yielding, barely bone, more like modified cartilage, like a speed bag.

The Resscharr absorbed a half dozen blows to the face before she swiped me off of her with a backward slash of her arm. Her forearm caught me in the floating ribs, breath whooshing out in an explosion of pain like I'd been hit by a baseball bat. Stars filled my vision, but I shook them off as I rolled away from Lilandreth, far too used to pain. She wasn't. Blood poured down from cuts in her cheek and one of her fang-like teeth hung loose in her mouth, a picture of shock.

She wiped at blood with one hand, the other extended toward me, clenching at the air. Ants crawled across the back of my neck, a sign that she was trying to use the power against me... and failing.

"This isn't possible," she growled deep in her throat, then spat blood. The tooth came out with the blood. "The virus couldn't infect you..."

"For someone who has a quantum supercomputer the size of a universe at your beck and call," I taunted, pushing to my feet, "you don't have much imagination."

"That damned AI..." Lilandreth screamed wordlessly. "I may not be able to hurt you, but I can still kill everything important to you!" She turned back to Vicky, ignoring the fact that we didn't need to use telekinesis to hurt one another, and I leapt on her back, wrapping an arm around her neck and yanking backward.

Lilandreth wasn't caught by surprise this time. I had the edge on her with actual unarmed combat experience, but she still had the height and weight advantage and a certain vicious amorality that might have been part of her Resscharr nature or maybe just a function of having lived for six thousand years. She threw me off with a shrug of her shoulders and her nails, almost long enough to be called talons, slashed at my face in a round-house blow.

I couldn't have blocked it, not without breaking my arm, but the computing network on the other side of the thin membrane between my consciousness and Transition Space was good for more than just anticipating strategies. I saw the blow coming and bent backward out of its way. I was pretty agile, but I wasn't an acrobat, and there was no way I should have been able to bend that far backward and not fall flat on my ass. Yet I did, an invisible hand pushing me back straight, a swift wind speeding my right leg into a thick kick. Well, it *would* have been a thigh kick on a human, but it took Lilandreth in the calf.

She cried out, stumbling backward, and I pressed the attack, using the power, but not against her. We, the infected, the Changed, were *immune* to the power, to the invisible hand, the kinetic energy created by funneling willpower through Transition Space. Lilandreth was from a society steeped in tradition, where things were done a certain way, and it showed in her fighting style. She used slashes and kicks that were fitting with her evolutionary ancestry, devastating if they landed, but she never even thought about the fact that the telekinetic force wouldn't move an opponent, but it *would* give extra umph to my own punches and kicks.

A knee to her thigh, punch to the side of her deep chest, into the ribs there, another in her skinny neck before she landed a blow. This one caught me in the shoulder, ripping through my fatigue shirt and the skin beneath it and tossing me to the ground. Not all the way, because I caught myself a few centimeters off the pavement, palms hovering just above it, then rose back to my feet.

Her blackened eyes shifted color, became more natural for just a moment, and in them I could see fear. She hadn't expected this, hadn't foreseen me... either that Dwight would find a way to change the virus or that I would be willing to expose myself to it. She'd carefully crafted her plans, but those plans had been destroyed.

She ran.

Straight up toward the ship.

And I flew after her.

[28]

I'd dreamed of flying, of course. A lot of people do, and since I could fly in the suit, it came naturally. In the dreams there were no jets, no angles, I just concentrated on flying and then I was rising into the air like I weighed nothing.

This was like the dreams. The harder I concentrated, the faster I went, the higher I climbed... and the closer I came to Lilandreth. The door into the ship was open, and I knew if she made it inside and got the hatch closed, she'd get away, get back to the *Orion* and take the crew off with her as slaves.

Just a momentary spasm of panic, the abrupt realization that I was unsupported, hanging in midair, and I faltered, slowed down just as my fingers brushed her ankle. She was through the doorway and I screamed a curse, used that rage to focus for one last burst of speed. I rolled through the hatch a fraction of a second ahead of the door contracting shut, one of the edges smacking against the heel of my boot and sending me sprawling.

Lilandreth lunged for me, sensing a moment of weakness, stomping with her hard-nailed feet, still close to the claws they'd evolved from. I rolled out from beneath the blow, shoved by the power, under the control of instincts learned on the streets and in the Marines. I slid against the bulkhead, bounced off and flipped backward... again, a move I never would have been able to make without the invisible hands supporting me.

Lilandreth didn't try another stomp, didn't attempt to fight me in the access tunnel, flying again instead. She wasn't looking for a weapon—she had to know it wouldn't be effective, that I could disperse an energy beam or send it into T-space. She was trying to get to the ship's controls, though I didn't know why. The ship had no weapons, and she had to realize I wasn't going to let her run.

But we *were* moving. I wouldn't have realized that before when my only source of information would have been the holographic display on the bridge, since the ship's artificial gravity kept me from feeling the motion. The neural network that made up Transition Space knew though, and now so did I. Lilandreth had control of the ship through the power and she was taking it back into high orbit... for some reason.

Possibilities scrolled through my mind, too many of them, which was the downside of having access to a computing network that could foresee *all* outcomes. I hadn't taken flight in pursuit of Lilandreth because it would have distracted me from the possibilities, instead running at a breakneck speed I would never have attempted without a telekinetic safety net and running the list down by percentages of probability.

She could take over the Orion *via mental control and use the cruiser to threaten me into obedience.*

No, that would take too long. In the time it would take her to gain control of the *Orion* I could intervene, physically even. And I knew she needed them, needed the ship in order to gain knowledge about the Commonwealth.

She could use the Orion *to attack Homecoming.*

Maybe. If she sent them on a collision course with the section of the city where Vicky and the Marines were hold up, she'd know I'd have to stop them, which might distract me. But the only way I could stop them would be to kill her and take her ship, and I'd have plenty of time to do that. It would take the *Orion* over an hour to crash into the planet, more than that to hit the area from orbit with her energy cannons.

But... what if she didn't *need* the *Orion*? What if she just needed distance?

I thought of the dead worlds, their atmosphere stripped away.

She's going to open up a wormhole and kill everyone on the planet.

I couldn't let her do it, but how could I stop her in time? She was doing it now, and I was seconds behind her. I wouldn't reach her physically in time. She was going to destroy everything I loved out of spite, to make sure if she couldn't win this, that I certainly wouldn't. But two could play at that fucking game. I knew one way to make sure she didn't have the time or concentration to create a wormhole above the planet.

I created one in the heart of the Predecessor ship.

I'd never done it before, but that wasn't an obstacle. The knowledge was all there at the front of my thoughts the second I summoned it. It was a question of will, of desire, of sheer stubbornness. I had all of those aplenty. The fact it was going to kill me was trivial compared to the fact I was saving Vicky.

Reality roiled at the heart of the ship, a whirlpool of spacetime... and Lilandreth screamed. She panicked, losing her hold on the network, unable to complete the attack she'd begun because she'd decided her own survival was more important than winning. The Resscharr couldn't even concentrate enough to fly as she charged at me in utter desperation, her digitigrade legs loping like an ostrich, talons outstretched.

If I'd had to think about defending against the attack, I might have dropped the wormhole, lost concentration. Thankfully, this was a defensive maneuver I'd learned in Boot Camp and relearned a thousand times since. Without thinking, simply reacting, I ducked under Lilandreth's swing and caught her under the arm, swiveling my hips and using her own weight to toss her through the air and into the opposite bulkhead.

If she'd done it to me, my instincts would have sent me into a shoulder roll and the power could have cushioned the landing, keeping me from injury. But Lilandreth had no experience and no instincts, and her long, thin skull smacked right against the bulkhead. She slumped to the deck and didn't move, and that might have been a really good time to *stop* trying to destroy the ship, but it was too late. Too late to save the ship.

Maybe not too late to save *me*.

The network gave me access to every centimeter of this ship, including the escape pods. I hadn't been sure the Resscharr would bother with them, sure their ships were perfect, incapable of crashing or exploding. I'd underestimated them.

The pod was close to the airlock I'd followed Lilandreth through, and this time I *did* fly. I wondered if I could fly in open space, could hold the air around me long enough to get back to the surface without dying and discovered I could... but it would have been difficult. Concentrating on one thing at a time was easy. Concentrating on holding the air in a bubble around my body, on using the telekinesis to draw myself through space, on defying the gravity of the planet, on shielding myself from the reentry friction was too much without practice.

But I could concentrate on working the control for the pod before I got to it, on opening the hatch. I didn't try to slow down on the way into the narrow hatch, just used the power to cushion the blow against the interior bulkhead, reducing it from bone-crushing and fatal to just a back-wrenching thump hard enough to drive the air from my lungs. I sank down into the pod, which was larger than any I'd seen designed for human, my shoulder wedged against a seat designed for Resscharr.

Luckily, I didn't have to get up because I wouldn't have been able to. The hatch closed at the nudge of my thoughts and the pod ejected the second it sealed. No crushing acceleration in this thing, no rockets at all... one moment I was inside the ship, and the next I was hundreds of kilometers away.

I'd been containing the wormhole, keeping it from completely opening, but now I had to let it go or turn it off. I wasn't going to turn it off. The Predecessor ship imploded. There was a view screen against the opposite fuselage of the pod, but I didn't need it. I could see what was happening directly from the camera input... or just by *knowing*. I wasn't sure if I liked that sort of awareness, but it sure gave me a ring-side seat to the destruction of the ship.

We'd never given her a name, and now we never would. The wormhole gobbled her up like one of those animations of a piece of paper being folded until it simply popped out of existence... almost. The singularity containment failed in the fraction of a second before the wormhole could swallow it up.

I watched with morbid fascination, knowing this could be the last thing I ever saw. I felt I should have been able to calculate whether the focused burst of raw gamma rays from the singularity evaporating was going to kill me, or even hit the planet and kill my friends, but there were some things that were completely chaotic and couldn't be predicted, even by the network.

The beam was invisible to the naked eye, yet I saw it as clearly as if it were a flashlight shone in a dust-filled closet. If it was indeed truly chaotic, then that must have meant it was in the hands of God. As He'd spared me once, in the California desert, now He spared me again. The gamma ray beam disappeared into deep space.

I sighed and slumped against the bulkhead, waiting for the pod to take me to the surface. I'd lived through it... but in the back of my head, a Ghost whispered the truth.

You're going to wish you'd died on that ship.

———

Vicky still sat on the pavement, waiting as I stepped out of the pod. It didn't share a shape with the Commonwealth and Tahni escape pods I'd seen, I noticed as I exited the escape vehicle. Not a cylinder, not an oval, this one was shaped like some exotic sea creature, a ray or a skate.

"Are you okay?" I asked her when she still didn't get up.

"Not really," she told me, holding her sides and her head. "That bitch broke a couple of my ribs, and I think I might have a concussion." She looked around. "Where is she?"

"I dumped her in a hole," I said, "and she pulled it in after herself."

"No!"

I hadn't noticed Spinner, hadn't given the man a thought since I'd left him here. He'd thrown himself to the pavement, was banging his forehead into it, screeching.

"She can't be! She can't be dead!"

The alien scientist looked up at me, his face bloodied, the skin split, exposing white bone.

"Kill me," he pleaded, then did his best to do the job himself, pounding his head down over and over.

"What the hell are we gonna do with him?" Vicky wondered, grimacing at the display.

"He's not salvageable," I told her, shaking my head. The knowledge came as easily as if she'd asked me what color the sky was, or what direction the sun would set. "He's too far gone."

"The poor son of a bitch," she lamented. "We can't just kill him. And we can't leave him here."

There was something I could do for him. It wasn't much, but with a pass of my hand, Spinner stiffened and passed out.

"He'll be under long enough for them to get him back to the medical bay." I shrugged. "Unless he's already given himself a brain bleed. I should never have left him on her ship."

"It's not like any of us knew," Vicky protested.

"I know now. I know everything." I sank down beside her on the pavement. "When it's too late." I gestured into the afternoon sky just as the drop-ships returned, descending back to the courtyard. "I know that the Nova force who followed us here is mostly destroyed now, that the remaining ships are running and won't stop until they get back to their imperial headquarters. I know that Lilandreth is dead, that Dwight is gone, that Dr. Spinner is going to wind up catatonic and the best our medicine could ever do for him is to bring him back to a childlike state that he'll never grow out. I know it would be merciful to kill him, but I can't do it because the part of me that's still human wouldn't let me."

Vicky gritted her teeth and dragged herself over to me. I thought she was going to hug me, but she grabbed me by the back of the neck and shook.

"Don't fucking say that shit, Alvarez. You are *still* human."

I didn't reply, just extended a hand toward the Resscharr escape pod still popping and pinging, smoke curling off its metal surfaces. The thing shifted slightly as I focused my will on it, then lifted a few centimeters off the pavement before shooting backward and into the sky. I kept my eye on it until it was gone from sight and then released my hold on it. I couldn't hear the crash, but somewhere, tens of kilometers away, maybe *hundreds*, it had smashed into the city. It hadn't made a hole though. The city was built of stronger stuff than that. It would be here long after I was dead. I looked back to Vicky, expectant.

"That doesn't mean anything!" she insisted. "That's what you can *do*, not who you are."

The drop-ships touched down with one final roar of their jets, and I let the engine whines die down before I attempted an answer. We had to finish this conversation now, because it wasn't one I wanted to have in front of the troops.

"It's not who I am *yet*." I tapped my ear. "But I hear the Voices, the Ghosts. They're just whispers right now, so soft I can't make out what they're saying unless I pay attention. That'll change. At some point, they'll be screaming at me, every hour of every day." I looked upward. "That's what happened to Lilandreth."

"This is different. You're human. We don't know that the effects will be the same."

She was wrong, of course. But there was no point in arguing with her about it.

"Maybe..." she fumbled with the words, desperation keeping her searching for ideas. "Maybe you could go back to the lab, see if there's a way to undo this..."

"I know how to get to the Northwest Passage," I told her instead, and she blinked, staring at me in disbelief. "If I *was* able to figure out a way to undo what we did—and I don't think there's a way that wouldn't kill me, but let's just say—then we wouldn't be able to get back. We've been thinking that the Passage is a normal Transition Line, but it's not. It was always intended to be a last resort, something the Skrela couldn't use if they found. It won't open from this side without either using a device that no longer exists, something like the gateway we took out here from the Commonwealth... or one of us. The Changed."

Vicky looked behind me at Jay and Bob who were

approaching from the open belly ramp of Drop-Ship One, then back at the Marines emerging from the city entrance, guilt behind her dark eyes.

"I don't give a shit. Go undo it now. It's not worth it to lose you."

She meant it. Even without the power, I would have known that. Getting home had never mattered that much to us, but we both felt the call of the duty and responsibility we'd assumed when we'd accepted these positions. There was a limit to that though, and she'd clearly reached it, though maybe that concussion was loosening her restraints a little.

Maybe she was right. As much as I knew, whether this could be undone wasn't in that knowledge. But...

"Can I do that to everyone else?" I asked, shaking my head. Ironically, if the Voices got their way, in not too long I wouldn't be asking myself those questions.

"You can get them through," she suggested urgently, grabbing my arms and pulling me close so she could whisper without being overheard by the others. "We'll take one of the Intercepts and you get them through, then come back here and get this undone."

That... wasn't a bad idea.

"You don't mind being stranded on this side?" I asked.

"I've never given a shit about where I was, as long as we were together."

Slowly, I nodded.

"All right. Of course, this may not work at all if Lilandreth wiped the AI out of the system in there." I stood and helped her up. "Let's go find out."

[29]

I hesitated at the entrance to the shadowy, darkened chamber, unwilling to venture through the doorway.

"I don't know why I had to wear this thing," Vicky complained over the external speaker of her Vigilante.

"Because the last time I was in here," I told her, "this room was full of the virus. And even though it was tailored to my DNA, not yours, I can't be certain it wouldn't infect you."

I also couldn't be certain entering the room again might not subject me to more alterations, but at this point there wasn't much to lose. I stepped inside.

Lights flickered on, revealing the table at the center, still there as if it had been waiting for me this whole time. If I'd concentrated, thought about it, I probably could have figured out exactly what was going on, but I discovered there were some things I would just rather not know. Or would rather figure out the old-fashioned way.

"Is anyone here?" I asked aloud.

"I am."

The voice was familiar and I started, surprised.

"Dwight? Is that you?"

"You should know it isn't. And yet it is."

"What the hell is he talking about?" Vicky demanded.

"It's Dwight," I explained, "but not *our* Dwight. It has Dwight's memories but it didn't live through them. It's like if I grabbed you from Boot Camp and stuck all the memories of what happened since then into your head. You'd know what happened, but you wouldn't have any emotional connection to it... to any of us."

"Exactly, Captain Alvarez," the AI agreed. This one didn't bother with an avatar to represent itself. "Though I know what Dwight did for you... and I share his regret for the results of what we did. What do you require from me?"

"It worked," I told him. "Lilandreth is gone. I wanted to know... is there any way to reverse what was done to me?" I expected him to tell me flat-out no.

"It's not impossible. I can't make a definitive estimate without examining the changes that have been made to you. I will tell you that much depends on how quickly we work. The longer you remain in your current state, the more difficult it would be to conceivably reverse it."

"What do you need me to do?" I asked him.

"Please lie on the table."

Great. I'd hated it the first time, and it wasn't any better climbing onto the obscenely warm and fleshy surface again. A nightmare image of ancient Resscharr fashioning the table out of human skins kept playing through my head, and I fought to suppress it. God only knows what my imagination could do when I had the power of an entire universe to back it up.

A curtain of light snapped to life between floor and ceiling and advanced across the chamber toward me like it intended to disintegrate everything in its path and end my problem the easy way. Instead, I felt nothing when the curtain passed over me and faded into nothing. I didn't move, deducing that the light had been part of a biological scan but uncertain as to whether it was over.

"You may rise," the AI informed me.

"What should I call you?" I asked him. "It doesn't feel right calling you Dwight. Kind of... disrespecting the dead."

"I am singular, Captain. As such, I do not require an individual name. However, I understand your need to delineate my existence. If it pleases you, you may call me Briggs."

I shrugged. It was an odd name to settle on, but who was I to talk? I was a Mexican named Cameron.

"Okay, Briggs. What did the scan tell you?"

He didn't reply for a few seconds. I didn't bug him, because I figured a sentient AI wouldn't be ignoring me on purpose.

"It is," he finally concluded, "as I said. We *can* change you back, but time is of the essence. My calculations indicate you have another fifty-seven hours before the changes are irreversible."

Air gushed out in the biggest sigh I'd ever given. It wasn't too late. I could make it through this. Maybe I'd be stuck on this side of the Passage, but we could sneak back to the Confederation maybe...

"That's plenty of time!" Vicky enthused. "Come on, let's get the troops back up on the *Orion* and get them through the Passage."

I was halfway out the door when the transmission came through.

"Alvarez, this is *Orion*." It was Nance, and I could finally talk to them again now that the drop-ships were back to relay. "You copy?"

"Good to hear your voice again, *Orion*," I told him. "Is there any damage from what Lilandreth did to you?"

275

Because that would throw our whole timetable off, if the ship needed a few days of repair before she could Transition.

"No, nothing major." His reply was brusque, and I found out why with his next statement. "Alvarez, a ship just Transitioned into the system."

"Oh, shit," I muttered. "Is it more of the damned Nova? I thought they'd learned their lesson..."

"No. It didn't come from the jumpgate... as far as I can tell, it came out of Transition Space."

"What?" I frowned, confused, which I shouldn't have been, given the data I had to work with. Learning the right questions to ask would take some time. "Who the hell would have Transition Drive ships out here?"

"Alvarez, the ship is Resscharr. And it's heading straight for you."

———

I stared at the Resscharr ship, mouth dry.

If it had been Nova, I wouldn't have been worried. The *Orion* could hold her own with them and I knew I could destroy their ships the same way Lilandreth had, with a little concentration and willpower. But an operational Resscharr ship...

There was nothing any of us could do. I could *try* to destroy it, but it wasn't a sure thing, and all it would take was one lucky shot from their gravitic weapons and that would be it. I couldn't shrug those off the way I could an energy weapon, because gravitic weapons cut right through the Transition wormholes I could open with my thoughts.

They hadn't fired on us though. They hadn't tried to communicate either, according to Nance, but so far they'd acted as if our ships hadn't been there. I wanted to encourage that line of action and had thus told Vicky to take the Marines back into the city while the drop-ships took to the air, retreating back to another courtyard a few dozen klicks away.

I wished to hell we had the pre-Change Lilandreth with us, because I wasn't sure at all how Reconstructors would react to humans being here, in their city. Hell, I had no idea where these guys were coming from. There was no information anywhere in this city's—this *planet's*—data storage about any survivors of the war with the Changed who had retained their technology and society. I supposed there was always the chance that this was a Nova ship, but the one they'd given us back on the other side of their Empire had been considered a special gift of the Resscharr, and it was broken.

The ship was small, I realized as it descended. More the size of the tiny shuttles on Yfingam that we'd been forced to destroy, nowhere near as large as the cruiser the Nova had turned over to us. Maybe large enough for a crew of twenty, twenty-five at the most, though it was hard to tell given how malleable the interior of the ships were. It didn't exactly touch down, because a ship that could control gravity didn't have to touch the ground at all. Instead, it hovered a few centimeters off the ground for several minutes.

I felt naked out here in just my fatigues, not to mention a little shabby since they were slashed and cut in places, stained with my blood where Lilandreth had scored hits with her talons. No gun either. It would have sent the wrong message. I steeled myself as a door opened on the side of the ship, appearing as if it had been there all along and I just hadn't noticed.

I expected a Resscharr, a walking dinosaur.... Or, if we were extremely unlucky, a Nova.

I was *not* expecting a short, skinny, bald human wearing colorful flash like an Undergrounder in Trans-Angeles who'd picked patterns and colors at random out of the public fabricators. He stepped out, flanked by a pair of cyborgs who could have been nothing but Skingangers, Evolutionists. There was no mistaking the blend of shining, obtrusive metal and pale, pallid flesh, the black leather and red oculars where their eyes should have been.

They had guns, Gyroc carbines by the looks of them, pointed at me, though that wouldn't have scared me before I got godlike powers and certainly didn't now. The little man didn't look angry, though... just dumbfoundingly annoyed.

"What the fuck?" he demanded in English, and my brain exploded. Well, not literally... I suppose I should clarify, given the experiences I've had. "What are *you* doing here?"

I said nothing for a beat, bemused by his attitude... and the fact he'd just stepped out of a Predecessor ship.

"I'm Captain Cam Alvarez of the Commonwealth Marine Corps," I told him. "Who the hell are you?"

"Robert Chang," he told me, watching closely, like he thought the name might mean something to me. When it obviously didn't, he continued on with a shrug. "I'm... an entrepreneur. Doing a little exploring."

"In *that*?" I gestured at his ship, shaking my head. "I'm sure things have changed since I left the Cluster, but I don't remember anyone flying around in Predecessor ships back home."

"What do you know about Predecessor ships?" Chang asked sharply.

"You're *standing* on a Predecessor planet. I've been out here for years." I couldn't suppress a bitter snort. "I've flown in Predecessor ships and destroyed them."

Chang took a step toward me, leaning inward conspiratorially, and I resisted an urge to draw away at the pungent scent of whatever cologne he was wearing.

"What about the Skrela?" he asked me. "Have you encountered any Skrela?"

My brows knitted. This guy knew way too much about something that should have still been top secret on the other side of the Northwest Passage.

"They're not a problem anymore. My task force wiped them out."

"Ha!" Chang clapped his hands like a child who'd been told he was getting a pony for Christmas. He turned to one of the Skingangers. "You hear that? All that worrying for nothing!" He turned back to me, beaming, but an edge came off the smile, what might have been suspicion narrowing his eyes. "If you don't mind me asking though, Captain, what are you doing here?"

"Trying to leave," I explained. "You had to have come here through the Northwest Passage, right? We came here looking for it." Something caught in my throat, a homesickness I hadn't been aware of, making me doubt my resolve to send everyone off and stay here. "We've been gone a long time. We just want to get home."

"I'm sure you have some remarkable stories to tell," Chang said, eyebrow arching. "And I look forward to hearing them." He winced in what was obviously feigned sympathy. "I'm afraid I have some bad news, you see. We did come through the Northwest Passage, you're correct about that." He pointed upward. "But I'm afraid you won't be returning that way."

I glowered at the little man, beginning to lose my patience.

"Is that a threat, Mr. Chang? You don't know me, so I won't take it personally, but you'll have to take my word for it that I don't respond well to threats."

"No, no," Chang insisted, holding up his hands apologetically. "I'm afraid you have me all wrong. I wasn't saying we wouldn't *allow* you to take the Northwest Passage. You see." He laughed nervously. "This is a little embarrassing, but we sort of... closed the Northwest Passage behind us."

He shrugged.

"I'm afraid it's not there anymore."

———

Drop Trooper will continue in Book Fifteen, DOWN RANGE!

FROM THE PUBLISHER

Thank you for reading *Collateral Effects*, book fourteen in Drop Trooper.

———

We hope you enjoyed it as much as we enjoyed bringing it to you. We just wanted to take a moment to encourage you to review the book on Amazon and Goodreads. Every review helps further the author's reach and, ultimately, helps them continue writing fantastic books for us all to enjoy.

If you liked this book, check out the rest of our catalogue at www.aethonbooks.com. To sign up to receive a FREE collection from some of our best authors as well as updates regarding all new releases, visit www.aethonbooks.com/sign-up.

JOIN THE STREET TEAM! Get advanced copies of all our books, plus other free stuff and help us put out hit after hit.

SEARCH ON FACEBOOK:
AETHON STREET TEAM

The Space Hunter series may have come to an end, but there are still plenty of more books in the Drop Trooper Universe!

The Drop Trooper Universe: (chronological reading order)

THE HOLY WAR
Genesis
Judgement Day
Revelation
Armageddon

THE PIRATE WAR (with Ralph Kern)
Insurgency
Infiltration
Isolation

DROP TROOPER

Contact Front
Kinetic Strike
Danger Close
Direct Fire
Home Front
Fire Base
Shock Action
Release Point
Kill Box
Drop Zone
Tango Down
Blue Force
Weapons Free
Collateral Effects
Down Range

BIRTHRIGHT
Glory Boy
Birthright
Northwest Passage
Enemy of my Enemy

RECON
Recon
The Hunter
The Mercenary
The Operative

THE ACHERON

The Acheron
Prodigal
Hybrid
Exile

SPACE HUNTER WAR (with Pacey Holden)

Pirate Bounty
Corporate Bounty
Cultist Bounty
Smuggler's Bounty

Double-Cross Bounty
Terminal Bounty

THE PSI WAR
Homecoming
Conflagration
Imperium

You may also like:

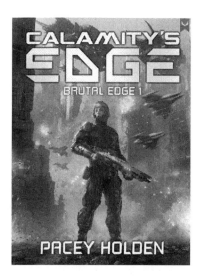

Find them, kill them, or die trying.

When the Solus Hegemony's profit margins are threatened, expendable soldiers are called in to foot the bill—one bloody conquest at a time.

Noah Rivers is one such soldier. Raised from birth with a single objective; obtain eternal glory through death in service to the galaxy's most notorious corporate empire.

Rifle in hand, Noah arrives on the distant world of Kilmori ready to fulfill his ultimate purpose, but not even the Solus could have predicted what lay hidden in the sands of the harsh, desolate, alien world.

This baptism by fire changes everything Noah thinks he knows about the galaxy, and himself. To snatch victory from this devastating new calamity will require blood, sweat, tears... and a brutal edge.

The Kilmori War begins.

Don't miss the start of this action-packed Military Sci-Fi Series from author Pacey Holden. It's

perfect for fans of Rick Partlow, Joshua Dalzelle, and Marko Kloos.

Get Calamity's Edge Now!

ABOUT RICK PARTLOW

RICK PARTLOW is that rarest of species, a native Floridian. Born in Tampa, he attended Florida Southern College and graduated with a degree in History and a commission in the US Army as an Infantry officer.

His lifelong love of science fiction began with Have Space Suit---Will Travel and the other Heinlein juveniles and traveled through Clifford Simak, Asimov, Clarke and on to William Gibson, Walter Jon Williams and Peter F Hamilton. And somewhere, submerged in the worlds of others, Rick began to create his own worlds.

He has written a ton of books in many different series, and his short stories have been included in seven different anthologies.

He currently lives in central Florida with his wife, two children and a willful mutt of a dog. Besides writing and reading science fiction and fantasy, he enjoys outdoor photography, hiking and camping.

www.rickpartlow.com